"MAY WE COME IN?"

My body began to shake. It didn't take a rocket scientist to know what was coming.

"No," I said.

Luna took my arm and moved me inside. The man came in behind us. She sat me down on the sofa and took the place next to me. The man sat in the armchair across from us.

I didn't look at him. He carried something in a bag. I didn't look at that either.

Luna took my hand and held it in hers. "No," I said again.

"E. J., this is Patrick Salazar, an investigator with the Travis County Medical Examiner's office."

"No." It was the only word I could get my mouth around. I kept my eyes riveted on Luna. If I didn't, I'd have to look at the man, and the man was death.

Other E. J. Pugh Mysteries by
Susan Rogers Cooper
from Avon Books

ONE, TWO, WHAT DID DADDY DO?
HICKORY DICKORY STALK
THERE WAS A LITTLE GIRL

HOME AGAIN, HOME AGAIN

SUSAN ROGERS COOPER

AVON BOOKS NEW YORK

This is a work of fiction. Names, characters, places, and incidents either are the product of the author's imagination or are used fictitiously. Any resemblance to actual events, locales, organizations, or persons, living or dead, is entirely coincidental and beyond the intent of either the author or the publisher.

AVON BOOKS, INC.
1350 Avenue of the Americas
New York, New York 10019

Published by arrangement with the author
Visit our website at **http://www.AvonBooks.com**
Library of Congress Catalog Card Number: 96-95162
ISBN: 0-380-78156-5

First Avon Books Printing: June 1997

Printed in the U.S.A.

WCD 10 9 8 7 6 5 4 3 2

This book is for
my own personal Willis,
Don Cooper

Acknowledgments

I have a lot of people to thank for sharing their expertise. Any mistakes in this book are due to my inability to interpret, not the information so graciously given.

I would like to thank my brother, Greg Rogers, rock climber extraordinaire; Anna Lujan and Ricardo Barrientes, Texas Hill Country natives; Minnie Mynar; Travis County Assistant Medical Examiner Kelly Burns; Travis County ME Investigator Jesse Solis; Ira Kennedy, editor and publisher of *Enchanted Rock Magazine*; the rangers and personnel at Enchanted Rock State Natural Area; and the personnel of Whole Earth Provisions Company.

I would also like to thank Jeff Abbott, Megan Bladen-Blinkoff, and Don Cooper for their early and endless editorial assistance. And a special thanks to my agent, Vicky Bijur, and my editor, Tom Colgan.

Author's Note

Although the towns usually used in this series, Codderville and Black Cat Ridge, are figments of the author's imagination, the towns of Dripping Springs, Johnson City, and Fredericksburg are not. They are real towns in the very real and very beautiful Texas Hill Country. Also very real and very majestic is Enchanted Rock and the Enchanted Rock State Natural Area. I hope the wonderful people of that area will forgive me for plopping down the very unreal truck stop in the middle of all that pristine beauty. Scoggins Truck Stop & Turkey Farm is a figment of the author's imagination and should not be confused with any existing truck stop and turkey farm if, for some reason, there really is such a thing.

HOME AGAIN, HOME AGAIN

Part I

E.J.'s Story

One

Sunday

"Mommy, how come Mr. Badger can talk to Toad when they're not even the same feces—"

"Species—"

"And Bert and Ernie are both cats and they can't talk to each other at all?" Bessie asked. She sat cross-legged on top of her covers, not the least bit sleepy from tonight's chapter reading of *The Wind & the Willows*. I'd brushed her straight, almost waist-length dark brown hair until it shone. Tiny six-year-old toes peeked out from the hem of her rosebud nightgown.

"Because it's a book, huh, Mommy?" Megan chimed in, stretching out luxuriantly on her twin bed. Her hair, brushed as furiously as Bessie's had been only half an hour before, was back to a jangled, curly mess of strawberry blond locks. "Mommy writes books so she knows these things," Megan added.

Bessie rolled her eyes at her sister. "I know that, stupid."

"You're stupider," Megan said.

"You're the stupidest in the whole world."

"You're stupider than anybody in outer space."

"Megan's right," I said, tucking both girls into their beds. "All sorts of magic happens in books. Badgers talk to toads, nannies fly with their umbrellas, and lost boys live in Neverland. But, then again, who's to say Bert and Ernie don't talk to each other while we're asleep?" I kissed both girls and headed to the door. "Go to sleep, girls. Tomorrow's a school day. First-graders have to be sharp, you know. This isn't kindergarten anymore."

I turned off the light, pulling the door almost shut, leaving just a crack so the hall light could shine in. Bessie wasn't good with the dark.

I crossed the hall and knocked sharply on my son Graham's door. After a grudging "What?" I opened the door and peeked my head in. "Put the comic book down and turn off your light. Tomorrow's a school day."

"Dad home yet?" he asked.

I shook my head. "He'll be here soon," I said, forcing a smile.

"Tell him to come in here when he gets home, okay?"

I nodded my head. "Sure. Good night, honey. Lights off for real, understand?"

Graham grunted and reached out a pajama-clad arm to turn off his light. If I knew my son, the light would be back on the minute my feet hit the stairs.

I went downstairs and into the kitchen, making a pass through to see that all was well. A weak "meow" came from the door to the utility room. Bert, one of our trio of cats, sat guard on the countertop closest to the door of the utility room. He looked at me and grinned. I grinned back. Bert had had a bad time a while back with a nervous disorder. We finally discovered a lot of it had to do with the fact that Axl Rose, Graham's giant one-eyed mountain lion, who only pretended to be a domesticated cat, had been harassing Bert every chance he got, especially while the rest of us slept. Bert had seizures, lost hair, and generally was in pretty pitiful shape. Since we started locking Axl Rose in the utility room at night, Bert's condition had improved considerably. Bert, however, still spent every night standing guard over the utility-room door, lest Axl Rose eat his way through the wood.

I scratched Bert's ears, made sure his and Ernie's bowls were full, checked that the back door was locked and bolted, and that the alarm system was turned on. With nothing left to do, I wandered into the living room and turned on the TV. I only sat for a minute watching. There was nothing on to hold my interest. I walked to the window and looked out into the still night.

It was a lovely night—stars bright in the heavens, a light, southerly breeze tinkling the wind chimes on the front porch and rattling the leaves in the pecan tree in the front yard.

John, the neighbor directly across the street, was winding up his hose, the light from his open garage door spilling out onto his driveway and touching the street. I watched him walk into the garage, hang the rolled-up hose on a hook on the wall, then walk to the back of the garage to the door that led into his kitchen. His hand reached for the switch by the door and the garage door began to slowly descend. By the time it reached the ground, the light in the garage had gone off, leaving the street and yards in darkness, punctuated only by the faint glow of the streetlight on the corner and the distant light of the stars.

I continued staring out the window. Waiting. Waiting for headlights to turn from Morning Glory Lane onto Sagebrush Trail.

I'm not sure how long I stood there, I only know that the vague sounds of car chases on the TV had turned to the slick sounds of the news team from the station in Austin.

Headlights lit up the corner of the street. My heart beat faster as the car slowed, turning onto Sagebrush Trail. The streetlight at the corner illuminated the car as it turned, so I wasn't surprised that it didn't turn into our driveway. It hadn't been Willis's car.

When he left the morning before, he said he'd be back no later than five on Sunday. It was now after ten. Where was he? This wasn't a man who would stop off for a quick one on the way home and lose track of time. If anything, Willis was usually early. He had an immense dislike of people who kept him waiting when he was habitually on time. One of his few real engineer's anal-retentive traits, one I'd always admired, except when I kept him waiting and had to hear about it endlessly.

So, where was he? At what point did I call the police, the highway patrol, whomever it was that would start the search?

He'd gone camping with his partner, Doug Kingsley. I could call Doug—see if he was home yet. Then I remembered the reason they'd taken two cars was that Doug was going straight on to San Antonio for a Monday-morning meeting with a company he and Willis were bidding a job with.

Would their secretary know where Doug was staying in San Antonio? I moved toward the phone, thinking about calling Miss Alice, but stopped myself. Miss Alice was one of my mother-in-law's best friends. The minute she knew I had no idea where Willis was, she'd be on the phone to Vera. Vera had lost one son in a car wreck. I wasn't about to have her start worrying ahead of time about losing another.

I shook myself like a dog shaking off water. Stop it. He hasn't been in a wreck. I'd have heard by now. To get home by five, he would have had to leave Enchanted Rock no later than two, probably one-thirty. If he'd been in a wreck, I would have been called.

But what if it hadn't been a car wreck? He and Doug had gone to Enchanted Rock to try rock climbing. Willis had never climbed in his life and tended to get nose bleeds on stepladders. Doug, although experienced, hadn't done any rock climbing since his college days, sometime in the midseventies. What if they'd both fallen? The buddy system was great in theory, unless the buddy was down, too. But Enchanted Rock was in the middle of a crowded state park. There were rangers and other climbers all over the place. I would have been called. I would have been notified by now if something like that had happened.

I sat down on the couch, using the remote control to silence the TV. I had to think. Did he tell me he'd be home no later than five o'clock? Yes. He'd definitely said that. Doug had a date with some bimbo in San Antonio tonight. He wanted to leave fairly early to get to his hotel and take a shower and get ready to dazzle his lady. They'd be breaking up camp early in the afternoon. Home no later than five.

I walked back to the window and looked out again at the darkness that surrounded me. Where was he?

One month earlier

"Whose idea was this anyway?" Willis asked, staring bleary-eyed out the window of our bedroom to our driveway below. On the driveway resided the station wagon, already top-heavy with camping gear.

"We promised the kids we'd take them camping this summer," I said. "*You* promised. School starts next week. This is it, babe. The last weekend of summer. We take the kids camping or live with the guilt."

Willis crawled back into bed. "I can live with the guilt," he said, pulling the covers over his shoulders.

The door to our room burst open. "Hey, Dad!" Graham yelled. "Can we take the baseball stuff? And the Frisbee! Where's the Frisbee? Dad, get up! We're gonna be late! Mom, where are my hiking boots? Do I have any hiking boots? Luis says we need hiking boots . . ."

"Take those shoes you never wear with the rubber soles," I suggested, "unless you want to take the time to go shopping—"

"No, that's cool. Dad, get up! Where's the Frisbee? Mom, do you have the sun screen? Megan burns, you know. Oh, I forgot to pack my Swiss Army knife!" He ran out of the room.

Willis pushed himself up by an elbow and looked at me. "What's wrong with our son?" he asked.

"He's excited," I said.

Willis turned slowly and looked at the door. "He's . . . E.J., it's like he's . . . human."

I grinned. "I know. Weird, huh? And you want to break his little heart?"

Willis pulled himself out of bed. "You are a mean-spirited woman, E. J. Pugh."

He walked into the bathroom and slammed the door.

I'm sure it took longer to pack and load for that two-day camping trip than it did to plan the invasion of Normandy, and I'm sure it was even more traumatic for some members of our invading force.

"What do you mean I can't take Ernie?" Bessie said, clutching her cat to her chest, the stubborn look I'd seen so often on her birth-mother's face firmly in place.

"Cats don't go camping well, honey," Willis explained. "If we had a dog—"

"Are we getting a dog?" Megan exclaimed, jumping up and down in excitement.

"No, Megan, we're not getting a dog—"

"But, Daddy, you said we were getting a dog!" Megan started, tears already bubbling up in her blue-gray eyes.

"I wanna take Ernie!" Bessie screamed, drawing the wanted attention back to herself.

I squatted down next to her, holding my hands out for Ernie. "Honey, Ernie would get lost. Give him to me. He needs to go back inside the house so Eduardo can earn his five dollars feeding him."

Bessie held the cat away from me. Ernie, the most docile of the three cats, oozed bonelessly over Bessie's shoulder, his eyes closed, his purr motor engaged. "No," Bessie said. "Ernie's not going, I'm not going."

My friend Elena Luna, a detective with the Codderville Police Department and my next-door neighbor, stood on the driveway watching the debate. She walked up to Bessie and rubbed her silky hair. "That's great, *mi hijita,*" she said. "You can stay here with me while the others go camping. And you can help Eduardo take care of the animals, okay?"

She smiled at me. I nodded my head. "Great, Luna. We really appreciate that." I kissed Bessie on the cheek. "We'll miss you, honey, but we understand." I stood and headed for the already packed car.

Out of the corner of my eye I saw Bessie thrust Ernie into Luna's hands. She was in the backseat of the wagon before I even got in the front. "Okay," she said, her arms crossing her chest. "You win."

Luis, Luna's youngest son, came barreling out of the house and jumped in the car with his backpack, ready to go. Although he was twelve and my son, Graham, barely nine, they'd become buddies, after a fashion, since Luna and her sons had moved into the house next door. Luis's ability to get along with Graham improved considerably when he was invited along to Enchanted Rock. There was an outside chance after this, Graham figured, Luis might even let him hang out with him when his way-cool real friends were over.

Since all the camping supplies had been tied to the roof of the station wagon, there was plenty of room for the boys to ride in the cargo area, while the girls shared the second seat.

Willis got in and started the car. "Seat belts?" he asked. All applicable heads nodded (the boys would be on their own in the cargo area. Another mother-guilt thing to help ruin my weekend). "Everybody set?"

"Daddy, when are we getting the dog?" Megan asked.

It was over a three-hour drive from Black Cat Ridge to Enchanted Rock. We caught Highway 71 outside of La-Grange and took that through the south side of Austin, to where Highway 71 and 290 merge, then took 290 west into the Hill Country. We stopped for lunch in Dripping Springs, and forty-five minutes later we were in Johnson City, birthplace of Lyndon B. Johnson. Most of the black-topped roads in all of the Hill Country had L.B.J. to thank for them. We pulled the car off to the side of the road by the L.B.J. Ranch to let the kids stand by the fence and stare at the buffalo roaming the grounds.

The girls pressed their noses up against the chain-link fence, their fingers entwined in the metal, staring awe-struck at the beautiful animals. Graham and Luis looked in their general direction, then took out their Game Boys and ignored nature. After about two and a half minutes, Graham said, "Are we gonna stand here all day staring at those smelly buffalo or are we going CAMPING?"

With the last word, he and Luis both jumped in the air and did a high-five. They call it an "airborne five." We gave the girls a few more minutes to stare in wonder, then Willis and I pried their fingers off the chain-link fence and herded all back into the car. Next stop: Fredericksburg.

I doubt if there is anywhere in the world quite like the Texas Hill Country—or maybe my Texas chauvinism is just showing. The land of rolling hills with abrupt out-croppings of tall, jutting rock, covered in cedar and pin oak, was breathtakingly beautiful, even with the sun-browned grasses and sunbaked earth of late August. The road would go gently upward for miles, then open up for some of the most beautiful views in the world.

Flocks of Angora goats roamed pastures, their bodies skinny from summer shearing. We passed vineyard after vineyard, home of the fast-growing Texas wine industry. The closer we got to Fredericksburg the more peach groves we saw, laden with the last of the summer's crop. Grove after grove after grove, with a pasture or two in between studded with prickly pear and deep with sheep or Angora goats.

We finally pulled into Fredericksburg, the second-to-last lap of the journey. Although it was early afternoon on a weekday, Friday, the tourists were already out in full force in the town of Fredericksburg. Like so many hill country towns, small towns with little industry and no way of making money, Fredericksburg had turned to its one asset to become rich—its charm and beauty.

The new tourism industry, which ran to antique shops and boutiques, couldn't hide the true charm of old Fredericksburg—the Sunday houses, tiny one- and two-story structures built in the late 1800s by ranchers and farmers as a place to stay for Saturday shopping and Sunday church services; the beautiful wrought-iron galleries on the second floors of buildings that now housed expensive German restaurants or tourist-trap Mexican food; the spires of churches built back when church building was an art form. We passed the Admiral Nimitz Museum (the one famous native-born son), three and a half stories, built of rock, wood, and stucco in the style of a ship.

It was slow going through Fredericksburg, but we finally made it to Ranch Road 965 and turned east toward Enchanted Rock.

Once outside of town, the traffic lessened.

"Wait till you see it," I told Willis. "I can't believe you spent your whole life three hours away from this and you never came out here."

"Hey, we had better things to do when I was a teenager

than go stare at rocks. There was beer to be drunk, girls to lay—''

I slapped him on the leg and said, ''Shhh—''

''And my daddy never took us camping. He always said—''

''He had to sleep in the open for two years during the Big One, and he wasn't about to go do that for fun,'' I finished for him.

''Have I mentioned that before?'' Willis asked.

''I believe so,'' I answered.

We took twisting Ranch Road 965 up a steep hill, through turns and twists, up and down. On the high grounds, the vistas laid out before us were spellbinding—at least to Willis and me. The girls seemed to be much more interested in seeing how Barbie looked with burnt sienna-colored hair from their new sixty-four pack Crayola box, while the boys appeared totally engrossed in something wickedly funny Luis was saying.

The car bumped over a cattle guard in the middle of the road, passed a sign instructing us to beware of wandering farm animals, made a slight turn—and there it was. Willis let his foot off the accelerator.

''Jesus!'' he said, staring ahead of him.

''That's it!'' Graham yelled from the backseat. ''Look at that mother!''

The girls were out of their seat belts, leaning over the front seat to see. ''Mommy, is that it?''

''That's it,'' I answered.

Looming before us was what resembled, more than anything, the very, very large dome of a bald man's head. We were still miles away from the rock itself, but the billion-year-old slab of granite, the geologic center of Texas, looked close enough to touch and was more than large enough to intimidate. Willis put his foot back on the accelerator and we moved forward, crossing the other cattle guard.

Three minutes later we were pulling up to the ranger

station and paying our seven bucks for camping privileges. The kids were out of the car, running through the ranger station, staring at the small museum of rocks and horticulture, some specimens of which were known only to this one spot in all the world. We herded everyone back into the car and made our way to campsite twenty-two.

Although it was August, the last week of summer, the grounds were strangely empty. I got out of the car and herded the children toward the campsite, wondering if the ungodly heat might have something to do with the fact that ours was the only tent in sight being pitched—which may have also been the reason we had one of the best campsites in the place.

Campsite twenty-two was on the rock side, by the road, with good access to the car park and the bathrooms, as opposed to all the others, which were either across the park road, in a big empty field away from the rock, or a climb up the rock face itself. We had to go over roots stretching out like stair steps down to the campsite, which was covered with big, sheltering trees. There was a picnic table, an upright barbecue pit, and a fire ring—a metal ring about three feet in diameter with a grill covering part of it and a pit in the ground. And there was a flattened and marked-off area just big enough for the tent.

We had passed Enchanted Rock getting to the campsite and were now at the base of Little Rock, which was connected to Enchanted Rock by a saddle of granite. Below the fire ring was a dry creek bed, which the girls had already found. The graveled bottom was better than any sandbox at home. The boys were already scrambling up the big slabs of granite on the other side of the creek bed, their feet slipping on the pale green lichen.

"Stay away from the prickly pear!" I yelled at anyone who might be listening.

Willis was standing by the car. He hadn't moved. I walked up the root-steps. "Hey, baby," I said, smiling at him. "What do you think?"

He didn't answer me, he just stared straight ahead at the rocks surrounding us. I touched his arm. "Yo, earth to Willis!" I said.

He turned to me, his face looking like he'd just come back from another galaxy. "What?"

I frowned at my big hulk of a husband. "What's with you, kiddo?" I asked.

He shook himself. "Better start getting this stuff unloaded. Boys!" he yelled. "Get your butts back and help unload."

The tent was a major chore. As we'd never been camping before in our married life—except for excursions in Mexico while we lived there, and that had been in the back of our VW van—we'd had to borrow the tents: one for Willis, the girls, and me; and a pup tent for the boys. The pup tent belonged to Luis and his brother, Eduardo; the larger tent we'd borrowed from another neighbor. It took Willis, the engineer, and me most of the afternoon and a lot of money into the cussing jar before it was erected, and even then it was listing slightly to the left.

Willis was quiet—except for the occasional swear word. At first I didn't notice because the kids were making such an unholy racket—all that open air and freedom. But once we'd gotten the tent as erect as it was going to get, I found him standing in the dry creek bed, staring off at Enchanted Rock.

I went up and put my arms around his waist. "Penny for your thoughts," I said.

He didn't answer for a minute, and when he did, it wasn't the answer I'd expected.

"I have to climb it," he said. "I have to."

Two

Monday

I awoke with a start. I'd heard a car. I ran to the back door, barely remembering to turn off the alarm system, and ran to the gate that led to the driveway. There was no car in the drive. I ran inside the backyard to the side door of the garage. It was locked. Looking through the small window in the door, I could see there was still only my car on the far side of the garage. Willis's car wasn't there. And neither was Willis.

I went inside the house, closing the door behind me and leaning against it. I hadn't prayed. Seemed like a good time to do it. I looked at the clock. It was five A.M. Twelve hours since he should have been home.

I went back in the living room and lay down on the couch, covering my eyes with my arm. I spent a few minutes making deals with God: bring him back and I won't cuss in front of the kids. I promise. Bring him back and I'll go to church every Sunday. What a deal, huh? Bring him back and I'll be eternally grateful. Forever and ever, amen.

I closed my eyes, willing myself to sleep. Best way in the world to pass the time, to make time speed up. Ernie crawled onto my lap. I stroked his fur, listening to him purr.

What was I going to tell the kids? They'd ask the minute they got up. ''Where's Daddy?'' How could I tell them I didn't know?

There were only two answers: One, he was lying on the side of a road somewhere between here and Enchanted Rock, either dead or dying.

Or two, he'd left me.

Next Saturday, less than a week away, was Willis's birthday. He'd be forty years old. He'd acted so strangely on our camping trip to Enchanted Rock. Then going back this weekend, climbing the rock. This wasn't Willis-behavior. Forty is an age where a lot of men go through the midlife crazies. I could handle going in debt for a sports car. I couldn't handle him leaving me. Not without a word, a note. Just not coming home. Could he do that? Was Willis capable of doing that? Yes, probably anybody was. Man or woman. Humans have a strange way of being able to justify their own behavior. If he had done this, then he'd call in a couple of days. Wouldn't he know, though, how frantic I'd be? How awful the waiting would be?

But if he could do this, would he care?

I pushed Ernie off my lap and sat up, cupping my face in my hands. Not now, I thought. Don't break down now. The kids will be up in a couple of hours. Keep cool. With any luck he's lying in a ditch somewhere. I laughed at myself, catching the laugh and pulling it back in before it turned to hysteria.

I walked to the window and looked out at the still-dark

night. A touch of pale gray to the east told me day was coming. Would it be an overcast day? A bright, hot, sunny day? A rainy day?

Or just the day my husband never came home?

"So when's he coming home?" Graham asked. I set the bowl of oatmeal in front of him and he made a face. "Eat it," I said.

I'd opted for a lie. How do you tell children the truth when you don't know it yourself? I'd told them Daddy had called in the night and he'd gone to San Antonio with Doug on the new project.

"He'll be back soon," I answered vaguely.

"But Daddy never goes anywhere," Megan said. "He's a couch vegetable."

"Potato," I said. "Couch potato."

"That's what I said. A potato's a vegetable, right?"

"But why did Daddy go?" Bessie asked. "Does Daddy like Doug better than us?"

My stomach contracted and I could feel bile at the back of my throat. No, not Doug. But did Daddy like somebody else better than us?

"No, honey," I said, forcing a smile and rubbing her dark hair. "It's just business. You know Daddy and business."

Bessie started to cry. I knelt down next to the chair. "Honey, what's wrong?" I asked.

She sobbed in a breath. "I broke my shoelace and Daddy's the only one who knows how to fix it and now he's not here and I can't go to school because I don't have any other shoes to wear that still fit—'cept my Sunday shoes and my shoelace's broke!"

I pulled the offending shoe off her foot. "Well, Daddy's not the only one who knows how to fix a shoelace, honey. I know how to do it, too. I just let Daddy do it so he'll feel useful."

I heard myself say that. Would I have said that in front

of Willis? I have said that, or its cousin, in front of Willis on many an occasion. It's just a joke, I told myself. The way he and I communicate. We're always slinging little barbs at each other. We both know they're just jokes.

I went to the kitchen junk drawer and found some new shoelaces and changed both shoes, then gave them back to Bessie to put on her feet. Luna honked the horn in the driveway and I hustled the kids out to her car.

Leaning in Luna's window, I said, "Call me as soon as you get to the office, okay?"

She raised one eyebrow and asked, "What's up?"

I smiled. "Nothing. Just call me." I slapped the side of the car and watched as they backed out of the driveway and headed for school.

We had a good arrangement, Luna and I. She drove the kids to school in the morning, I picked them up in the afternoon and kept an eye on her house and children until she got home around five-thirty or six. If she was on a case and couldn't get home on time, I brought her boys over to our house and they ate supper with us.

Was that it? I wondered as I went back inside the house. Was that the proverbial straw that broke Willis's proverbial back?

First I gave him our two little accidents (not that he was totally innocent in their conception), then, after Bessie's birth family died, I'd brought her into our home and we'd legally adopted her. Was it now having these two extra mouths to feed two to three times a week that had totally thrown him? Then why hadn't he said something? Or had he? Had he made one of those comments I only half hear and had I ignored and forgotten it? Had I gotten so wrapped up in home and hearth that I'd let the excitement leave our marriage?

When had we made love last? I couldn't remember. Oh, God, I couldn't remember! Had I rejected him at some point, not even consciously doing it? Or had he stopped wanting it? A week? Two weeks? More?

I picked up the phone and called Willis's office. Miss Alice answered on the first ring.

"Pugh Consulting?" she said, a question in her voice.

"Hi, Miss Alice, it's me, E.J."

"Well, hello there, E.J. I bet that man of yours drank too much on his camping trip and he's a slug-a-bed this morning, am I right?"

That answered one question. Willis wasn't at his office. I forced a laugh. "Something like that. Look, when do you expect Doug back from San Antonio?"

"Oh, goodness, probably not till tomorrow. He'll probably check in, though. Does Willis want him to call?"

"Yes. Have him call the house just as soon as you hear from him, okay?"

"Sure, honey. Is everything okay?"

I put a smile on my face, hoping it would translate over the phone. "Everything's just fine, Miss Alice."

I hung up and started frantically cleaning the kitchen. Something in my head told me I was doing exactly what my mother did in times of crisis. Clean. My father in the hospital for bypass surgery—Mother in the kitchen scrubbing the floor. My father yelling at my teenaged sister who just told them she was pregnant—Mother in the kitchen scouring the oven. My father waiting silently by the phone to see if he got the loan that would save his business—Mother in the kitchen defrosting the refrigerator.

I threw Graham's half-eaten bowl of oatmeal across the kitchen. The bowl shattered against the wall in the breakfast room, brownish gray gobs of milk and oatmeal sliming the wall.

"If he's not dead I'll kill him!" I said aloud, then sat down abruptly on the floor and burst into tears.

The phone rang. My heart stopped. So did my tears. I jerked myself up and ran to the phone that hung on the wall of the kitchen. I picked it up.

"Hello?" I said, my voice barely above a whisper.

"You wanted me to call. You got a cold?" It was Luna.

I leaned against the wall, taking in lungfuls of air. It was, I told myself, best to breathe occasionally. "Luna, Willis isn't home," I said.

"Where is he?" she asked.

"I don't know. He was supposed to be home from his camping trip at five o'clock yesterday. I haven't heard from or seen him since he left on Saturday."

"Doug was with him, right?"

"Yeah, but he went to San Antonio straight from the camp. I left a message with Miss Alice to have him call when he checks in with her."

"Okay. That's good. I'll check with DPS. What's Willis's license number?"

"Just a minute." I went to my purse where it hung on a hook by the back door and found my book with telephone numbers. I kept both license-plate numbers listed on the front page. I read off the number to Luna.

"You okay?" she asked me.

"No. Would you be?"

"Honey, I've been there. And no, I wasn't either."

She hung up. I knew nothing about Luna's husband. She'd never mentioned him and neither had the kids. Was he dead? Was that what she was saying? Or had he gone out for a pack of cigarettes and never come back? Was that what Willis had done? And he didn't even smoke.

I cleaned off the wall and finished the breakfast dishes. I couldn't work. I knew I wouldn't be able to concentrate on the problems of orphaned Bethany Albright and her on again/off again romance with McKinney West, captain of the sailing ship taking her from her sedate London home to the wilds of Australia in my latest bodice ripper, *Storm Surge*.

I went into the living room and flicked a dust rag over the furniture, straightened cushions on the couch, and stared out the window.

The phone rang. I turned and looked at it. Would this

be it? Would this be the news that I was a widow? That my life as I knew it was over? I walked to the phone and lifted it to my ear.

"Hello?"

"E.J.? Hey, it's Doug. Willis wanted to talk with me?"

"He's not here, Doug—"

"Well, hey, give him this number and tell him to call—"

"He never came home."

There was a silence. Then he said, "What?"

"He never came home from the camping trip. Did he say he had to go somewhere else? Did he say anything, Doug?"

"Honey, geez, no. He was going straight home. God, have you called the highway patrol, or whatever?"

"Luna's checking that for me."

"E.J., God . . ."

I cleared my throat. I had to ask. "Doug, did he say anything about—about . . . leaving?"

"Yeah, he said he was taking off right after me. He was stowing his gear in his car—"

"No! Not . . . I mean, what I mean to say, Doug, about . . . leaving me?"

"What?" Doug laughed. "Good God, Eeej, have you lost your mind?" He was quiet for a second, then said, "Honey, no way. Don't even think that. He's probably had a flat tire, couldn't get to a phone—"

"It's been almost sixteen hours. He could have walked home by now."

"Look, I'm in the middle of this meeting now, but if I left right this minute—"

"No, Doug, don't. Finish the meeting." The practical part of me was thinking, "Groceries, mortgage, shoes . . ."

"I'll be finishing up here in another half hour—hour at the most," Doug said. "It'll take me two hours to get to your house. Maybe a little more, but you know me and the Miata—we can really move. By the time I get there, you and Willis will be laughing at me rushing back to check on him. You know that, right?"

"Doug, right now I don't know anything."

"I'll be there as fast as I can."

"Be careful. Okay? Just be careful."

"Yeah. Okay."

One month earlier

"Climb it?" I said, laughing. "Willis, you can't climb a stepladder."

He didn't laugh back; instead he began walking down the dry creek bed, heading toward Enchanted Rock.

I stared after him, then called over my shoulder, "Luis! Watch the kids!"

"I ain't no baby-sitter!" he yelled back.

"Do it or I'll tell your mother," I said, scrambling over the gravel bed in an attempt to follow my husband.

There was no back talk from Luis. Strangely enough, threatening to tell their mother on them worked with both Luna's boys. I'd have to ask her her secret.

Willis had left the dry creek bed and started climbing up the granite boulders toward the saddle between Little Rock and Enchanted Rock. Some of the boulders were the size of fifties-vintage automobiles, some as large as tract homes. I scrambled up the ones I could, walking around those I couldn't, going higher and higher. The heat was excruciating. The sun beat down relentlessly on the uncovered rock, frying it and anything on it. My body oozed liquid at a steady rate. I yelled Willis's name several times, but he either didn't hear me or ignored me. I made it to the top of the saddle, worried that my dripping wet clothes were beginning to dry. Was it from the dry breeze that blew at this height or was it merely the fact that my body was totally dehydrated and I was on the brink of death?

I looked around me. The views were wonderful. The

only problem was that they didn't include Willis. I croaked out my husband's name. From below me I heard a muttered, ''Here.''

I worked my way down the back side of the saddle. Trails led off in different directions. Cliff faces loomed over me. The front of the rock was rounded, smooth, dotted with clumps of trees. That was the walking side. The back was cliff faces—the climbing side. Willis stood at the bottom of one cliff, talking to a man in climbing gear with a rope in his hand, which he was winding into a small circle.

''Naw, man, you go up now, you fry your brain,'' the climber was saying. ''Here, touch the rock.''

Willis put his hand on the sun-exposed rock, pulling it back immediately. The climber laughed. ''Like touching a lit stove top, am I right?''

Willis nodded. I scrambled down to stand next to my husband.

''Me, I climb at night or like four or five A.M. Not many people out here in August 'cause of the heat, am I right?''

Willis nodded again.

''Come back in a month, man. September's good climbing weather, less of course it's raining or you got your tornadoes or hail, understand?''

Willis nodded. The climber looked at me, smiled, nodded his head, and jumped flat-footed up to a four-foot-high granite slab leading to the saddle, and was gone.

I touched Willis's arm. ''Honey? Are you all right?''

He leaned his head back, looking up at the shear cliff face. ''I have to climb it.''

''Okay,'' I said, trying to sound reasonable. ''Like the guy said, come back in September. Okay?''

He reached out a hand, touching the rock again, and again pulled his hand sharply away.

''September,'' he said softly.

Monday

Luna filled the tea kettle at the sink and put it on a burner to heat.

"Willis isn't the type," she said.

"Then you're saying he's dead," I answered, sitting at the breakfast-room table, my hands clasped primly in front of me.

"No. I am definitely not saying that."

"I'm not that great a wife," I said, staring at the floral-patterned wallpaper.

"What exactly is a great wife?" Luna asked, pulling out the chair next to mine and sitting down.

"I haven't mopped the floor in two weeks," I admitted.

"I could have you arrested for that."

"Sometimes I don't cook dinner because I'm busy with my writing."

"I've noticed how your children are starving."

I could feel the tears behind my eyes. "We haven't made love in a while."

I felt Luna's hand on my arm. "If he's left you, I'll track him down and kill him."

I turned to face her and smiled. "You'd do that for me?"

She grinned. "In a New York minute."

The kettle began to whistle. I pushed away from the table and went into the kitchen, Earl Gray for Luna, Swiss Miss with a dollop of Amaretto for me.

"DPS is on the lookout for Willis's car. We'll find it and him and everything's going to be fine."

I brought her cup to the table. Turning, I looked at the kitchen clock. It was two-thirty. My husband had been missing for twenty-one and a half hours.

The blast of a car horn was heard from the driveway. I beat Luna out the door.

Three

It was Doug's red Miata in the driveway, not Willis's aging Karman Ghia. Doug got out of the Miata and stretched. He grinned. "I was right, huh? He's in the house and I rushed back here for *nada.*"

I leaned against the fence, my face telling Doug what he probably didn't want to hear. "Shit," he said.

I turned and walked back into the house, Luna and Doug following me.

Luna said, "Tell us what happened."

Doug flopped into the gray armchair by the window, stretching his chino-clad legs out in front of him. Doug had been Willis's partner for less than six months, and one of the few things I really liked about Doug Kingsley was the fact that he definitely was not a strain on the eyes. At about my height, five-eleven, he was slender with dark wavy hair, always worn just a touch too long, and a finely chiseled face. He had a smile that did uncomfortable things to the female anatomy. Other than that, he was totally self-centered, self-absorbed, and self-involved—the perfect poster boy for Narcissism. But he was good for Willis. Willis needed a friend and he needed a partner. And Doug did have his moments.

He rubbed his face with his hand. "Damn, I don't even know where to begin," Doug said. "Willis's been acting . . strange, I guess that's the only word for it. Ever since y'all got back from that camping trip."

I nodded. He'd get no argument from me on that point.

"He couldn't stop talking about that damn rock," Doug said. "It was like he was obsessed with it. And the whole time we were camping, he was acting weird. Just staring at that blasted thing. But nothing out of the ordinary happened, E.J. I had to take off early because I had a date in San Antonio, and Willis was packing up his gear when I left."

"That was the last you saw of him?" Luna asked.

I stood up from the couch, walking to the window. "Where *is* he?"

Doug came up behind me and put his arms around me. "I don't know, I swear to you. Nothing was said—I mean nothing!"

I turned to Doug, pushing him slightly away. "Tell me the truth, Doug. Is there another woman?"

He shook his head. "I swear to you he's never, ever mentioned another woman."

I walked away from Doug. "Then he's dead," I said.

"No! We would have heard something by now if he'd been in a car wreck—" Doug started.

"Then where the hell is he!" I screamed.

Luna and Doug exchanged looks. This wasn't totally lost on me—I was acting like someone unhinged. But I wasn't sure of the proper etiquette for a woman in my particular situation.

"Look," Doug said, sitting down next to Luna on the

couch, "I'll start making some phone calls. I can call our clients . . ."

I shook my head. "What are you going to say? 'My partner's missing—have you seen him?' How many clients will you lose?"

Doug rubbed his face with his hands. "Yeah. Dumb idea. But I feel like I should *do* something!"

"Join the club," I said.

"DPS is on the lookout for him,' Luna said. "Unfortunately, that's all we can do right now. The rest is just waiting."

"I'll stay here with you and the kids . . ." Doug started.

I shook my head. "Thanks, Doug, but no. The kids think Willis is with you. If you were here . . . well . . ."

"Yeah," he said. "That makes sense."

I walked Doug to the door. "Just don't tell Miss Alice that Willis is missing, okay? I don't want Vera finding out until I have a chance to talk with her."

"No problem. Where does she think he is?" he asked.

"Here. At home. Sick."

Doug put his arms around me and kissed my forehead. "Call me," he said, and headed for the Miata.

I sank down on the couch. "When will we hear from DPS?" I asked.

"When they find something."

Luna left to go back to the station. I had several hours before I needed to pick up the kids. The thought of sitting in my house, waiting, was more than I could bear. That thought was worse than the horrible duty of notifying Willis's mother. It had to be done.

I drove the twelve miles to Codderville, pulling the wagon into my mother-in-law's driveway.

I rapped on the screen door of Vera's home. We'd had central air-conditioning installed for her shortly after moving to Codderville, but I've never known her to use it except possibly in August. I could see her walking toward the door from the kitchen, wiping her hands on a terry-cloth kitchen towel.

"Well, E.J., honey, what brings you here?" she called. "Door's open, come on in."

Vera's a small woman, but feisty. I'd called her Mrs. Pugh for the first fifteen years of our marriage. It wasn't until after Bessie's family had died that we'd gotten on a totally first-name basis. Her steel gray hair was tightly permed, as always. Short and wiry, close to her head. She wore steel-framed glasses that were perpetually loose and that she had to keep pushing up to the bridge of her nose. She was wearing her at-home uniform—thirty-year-old polyester bell-bottom trousers and a floral tunic-style top, her feet clad in brand-new Reeboks.

"Vera, we have to talk," I said, coming in and following her to the kitchen.

You only sat in the living room with the preacher or to watch TV. And since it was daytime, and Vera didn't believe in daytime TV (as if it were a religion she thought slightly heathenish), to the kitchen we went.

I sat at the table and she poured us both cups of coffee from the ever-present coffeepot. She handed me two packets of Equal and sat down opposite me.

"What's on your mind, girl?"

So I told her, finishing with, "I'm sorry I didn't call you sooner, but I didn't want you to worry—"

"No, now worrying's just for you, right?" She reached out and touched my hand.

She didn't hate me. I burst into tears.

Vera put her arms around me, patting me stiffly on the back. "Just get it out, child. Go ahead and cry, then we gotta start making some plans."

I got up and grabbed a Kleenex from the counter. Sitting back down, I asked, "What plans?" hoping my ever-practical mother-in-law didn't want me to pick out the suit to bury my husband in.

"Well, I think since the DPS and your friend Luna

certainly aren't doing diddly-squat about finding my boy, maybe you and me best do something.''

''Like what?''

Vera sighed. ''Well, Lord, E.J., you solved two murder cases in two years, the least you can do is find your own husband, for pity's sake!''

''Vera, I didn't exactly solve—''

''Hogwash. Okay, think. Where could he be?''

I stared at her. ''I have no idea,'' I finally said.

''Okay. Willis don't know nobody in those little towns around there, right?''

''Not to my knowledge.''

''How 'bout San Antonio and Austin?''

''Fred's still in Austin.''

Vera nodded. ''He'd surely go to Fred's if he was having trouble he couldn't tell me or you about. Let's call him.''

Fred had been Willis's roommate in college—before me. To my knowledge, they hadn't seen or spoken to each other since our wedding. ''Vera, I'm not even sure really if Fred's still in Austin, and we haven't seen him in years . . .''

She handed me her phone. ''Call information. 'Member how to spell Fred's last name?''

''W-y-e-m-a-n, right?''

''Think so,'' she said.

I called information for Austin and got a listing for Fred Wyeman on Colgate Court. I dialed the number. After four rings I got an answering machine.

''Hi, this is Fred and I'm not available to answer the phone right now, but if you'll leave a message I'll get back to you—fast if you're cute.'' So, Fred was still single. Or married with a very pissed off wife.

''Hi, Fred. This is E. J. Pugh. Willis Pugh's wife? Ah, I need you to call me. I know this is really off the wall, but have you seen Willis? It's very important, Fred, so please call back.'' I left both my number and Vera's number.

''Okay, we've taken care of Fred. Always liked that boy. Made me laugh,'' Vera said. ''Now, how about San Antonio?''

I shook my head. ''I have a friend there from high school. We send each other Christmas cards, but Willis's never even met her. She was out of the country during our wedding.''

''Anybody else?''

I racked my brain. Everybody we knew was either here—in Codderville or Black Cat Ridge—or back in Houston. We had friends in Mexico, but we hadn't kept in close contact with them—a Christmas card every year or so, but that was all. Could he have gone to Mexico? Why? Why would he go to Mexico?

''Do you think he's in trouble?'' I asked.

Vera frowned. ''You mean like he did something and he's on the lam?''

''Yeah.''

''What could he have done? And if that's the case, honey, he woulda called.''

I took in a deep breath. ''Vera, there's a very good chance he's left me.''

Vera laughed. Actually laughed. ''E.J., I wish that were all it was. Not that I would approve of him leaving you—for any reason. Way I look at it, you make your bed—you lie in it. But I know my boy—if he'd left you he'd more than likely be hiding out in my back room. And he's not. You wanna look?''

I shook my head. Vera stood up. ''What have you told the kids?''

''They think he's in San Antonio with Doug Kingsley.''

''Good. Way you usually act, I'm surprised you ain't already told 'em. In my day we didn't tell children every little thing that's going on in our private lives, but this ain't my day and it's not for me to say how you should handle your own children. Much as I might like to."

"Vera—"

"I know, I know. I'm *di*-gressing." She shook her head. "He ain't dead," she said. "I'd know it if he was dead. I knew when Rusty was dead. God came to me and told me to have strength. Twenty minutes later I get the phone call. When Earl was dying, God came to me and told me to have strength. Half hour later, Earl was dead. So I'd know if Willis was dead. And he ain't."

I shivered. It was time to pick the kids up from school. I kissed Vera goodbye, promising to call with any news, and headed back to Black Cat Ridge.

Graham had soccer practice tonight. Willis was the assistant coach. I better call the head coach and let him know Willis was out of town. Life must go on. Even when you didn't really give a damn.

The girls were fed and in bed, the new chapter of *The Wind & the Willows* read and digested, lights off, door partially open. I knocked on Graham's door and called "lights out," then headed down the stairs for another night of uncertainty.

I didn't know what to do. When the commode backs up, you call a plumber. When the lights go out, you call an electrician. When someone's breaking in your windows, you call the police. When a Molotov cocktail explodes in your backyard, you call the fire department.

Okay, so I have some givens that are a little different than other people's givens. But who do you call when your husband just doesn't come home?

Under certain circumstances you call friends, relatives, somewhere he might have gone for some reason. The only place Willis would have gone—could have gone—was his mother's. I now knew he wasn't there.

I remembered her phone call to me on Sunday, when

Willis was only a few hours late, and my ordeal was just beginning.

''Willis still think he's supposed to clean my gutters on Saturday?'' she'd asked.

''Far as I know,'' I'd evaded.

''Good. This is going to be a wonderful surprise party. You're going to make those tortilla rolls I like, right?''

''Yes, ma'am.''

''Well, you just make sure he doesn't find out about the party.''

''Yes, ma'am,'' I'd said.

Now I wondered about the party. If he'd left me, would he show up without me? Was this what it was all about—that goddamn fortieth birthday?

Knowing Willis wasn't at his mother's, I was left with the thought that there was no one to call. No service that could clean this up. No agency that could put this in a computer and make it all come out right. My husband had driven off and never come back. It was as simple as that.

I avoided shows like ''America's Most Wanted'' and ''Unsolved Mysteries,'' but I knew that cases like this showed up on them all the time. Vera, my mother-in-law, was an avid viewer and would give me details of missing persons cases. This would be one that would generally fascinate her—if it hadn't been her son who was missing.

''Mom?''

I turned from where I'd been standing at the window. I wasn't sure how I'd gotten there, but it seemed to be my post now. Visions of Miss Havisham waiting for forty years in her wedding dress sprang to mind, but I pushed them away.

''Hi, honey,'' I said to Graham who stood in the foyer by the living room door. ''You're supposed to be in bed.''

''Where's Dad?''

''I told you he's in San Antonio with Doug—''

''I just called Mr. Kingsley, Mom. He answered his phone.''

"Did you talk to him?"

"No," Graham said, coming into the room and curling up on the couch, holding his knees with his hands. "Should I have?"

"Honey—"

"Tell me, Mom. Just tell me. I can understand not telling the girls, they're little. But I'm old enough. Do I need to tell you what I've handled already?"

He didn't need to tell me. Sometimes I stay up late at night, enumerating the things my children had seen in their young lives. Bessie had lost her entire birth family to a maniac. But that loss wasn't hers alone; Graham had lost his best friend, Bessie's brother, and Megan had lost her baby-sitter, Bessie's big sister, and her beloved Aunt Terry and Uncle Roy. Last year Megan had been given chocolate laced with glass, and all three had watched as firemen set about destroying our home—so much for such little kids.

"Where's Daddy?" Graham repeated.

I sank down on the couch next to him. "I don't know," I said.

"Are y'all getting a divorce?" Graham asked, his voice tight.

"Not that I know of," I answered truthfully. "I just don't know where your father is."

Graham jumped up from the couch. "Well, for God's sake, Mother! He could have had an accident!"

I took Graham's hand. "I know that, honey. Luna's checking into that. So far, nothing's come up. DPS is on the lookout for his car. There's been no record of any unidentified accident victim in the area."

"What did you do?" Graham asked, pulling his hand away from my grasp.

I just stared at him. I had no answer for that question.

"What did you do?" he shouted. "My dad wouldn't just leave me unless you did something to make him really mad!"

"Graham . . ." I reached for him again but he moved away.

"You're always harping on him! Well, I don't blame him for leaving! If I could, I'd leave you, too!" He screamed this last and ran for the stairs.

I just sat there—numb. He was right. Whatever Willis's reason for leaving me, it had to be my fault. My entire life was falling apart and I had no way to stop it.

Four

"**When's Daddy coming** home?" Bessie asked.

"Ha," Graham said, getting up from the breakfast table and going upstairs.

"Graham, where are you going?" I called after him. "Luna's going to be ready in less than five minutes. Graham!"

There was no response. "When's Daddy coming home?" Bessie repeated.

"Yeah," Megan said. "Where is Daddy?"

"He's away on business and I don't know when he's coming home—now, get ready for school both of you." I left the girls at the table and went quickly to the bottom of the staircase. "Graham! Get down here now!"

"I'm not going to school!"

"Oh, yes you are!"

"No I'm not!"

"Graham! Don't make me come up there!"

"You're the only one around here that makes anybody do anything!" he yelled back at me. "And I'm not going to school, so you can just forget it!"

His bedroom door slammed—hard.

I got the girls ready. "What's wrong with idiot boy?" Megan asked.

"Get ready for school. Get your shoes. Where are they?" I looked under the breakfast-room table, finding them.

"How come he doesn't have to go to school and me and Bessie do?"

"Bessie, you have your lunch?" I asked.

"Mommy, where's Daddy?" Bessie asked.

"I don't know!" I screamed it. At the top of my lungs.

Both girls looked at me, their eyes big. Luna chose that moment to open the back door. "Hey, girls, you ready?" she asked.

The girls just kept staring at me. I turned my back on them, resting my head against the cool of the refrigerator door.

Then I heard Graham's voice. "You heard Mom. Daddy's on a business trip. And if we don't get to school, he's really gonna be pissed when he finds out, huh, Mom?"

I turned around. "When you're right, you're right," I said, forcing a smile.

Graham herded his sisters out the door. Luna stayed behind. "You okay?"

"No," I said.

She nodded and followed the children to her car.

The doorbell woke me. I was unsure where I was, then realized I'd fallen asleep on the couch. I had that feeling in my stomach again, the one I'd had the day after Bessie's birth family had been killed. That feeling that said something was terribly wrong; I just wasn't sure what it was.

It was nine o'clock in the morning. I never slept during

the day. I gave up my morning naps when I was two years old. But somehow, now, sleep was the only escape. I rubbed crud from my eyes and stood. The kids were already at school. I knew that much. Then reality hit me.

The doorbell rang a second time.

I walked to the door and opened it. Luna was standing on the porch with a man.

"May we come in?" she asked.

My body began to shake. It didn't take a rocket scientist to know what was coming.

"No," I said.

Luna took my arm and moved me inside. The man came in behind us. She sat me down on the sofa and took the place next to me. The man sat in the armchair across from us.

I didn't look at him. He carried something in a bag. I didn't look at that either.

Luna took my hand and held it in hers. "No," I said again.

"E.J., this is Patrick Salazar, an investigator with the Travis County medical examiner's office."

"No." It was the only word I could get my mouth around. I kept my eyes riveted on Luna. If I didn't, I'd have to look at the man, and the man was death.

Luna nodded her head at the man.

"Mrs. Pugh," the man said.

"E.J., please," Luna said. "Look at Mr. Salazar."

I turned my head. Inside me, it sounded like the creaking of a great gate on rusty hinges.

The man put his hand inside the bag and brought out a boot.

"Mrs. Pugh, can you identify this as belonging to your husband?"

It was one of Willis's brand-new climbing boots. He and Doug had bought identical boots while they were at Whole Earth Provisions. Because there was only a half-size difference, I'd written Willis's name and address inside in heavy black marker, just like I was sending him off to camp. To camp. Not death.

My hand shook as I held it out to take the boot. Inside was the black marker—my husband's name, address, and phone number.

''Yes,'' I said. ''That's my husband's boot.''

The man put his hand inside the bag again and brought out another boot. He handed it to me. ''And this?'' he asked.

The left boot. The first had been the right. This was the left. Inside was the black marker.

''Yes,'' I said. ''This is my husband's boot.''

''Ma'am, the description you gave of your husband—six foot, four inches tall, approximately two-hundred and fifty pounds, blond hair, green eyes. Is this an accurate description, Mrs. Pugh?''

''Yes,'' I said.

The man sighed. ''Ma'am, we have a body now at the Travis County morgue that had been involved in a hit and run accident. We have now, with your help, identified the remains as those of your husband, Willis Pugh.''

I shook my head. Luna squeezed my hand.

''I have to go to Austin and identify him?'' I asked.

The man shook his head. ''No, ma'am, that won't be necessary. You can view the body at the funeral home of your choice. The identification of the boots is enough.''

I stood up, stunned. ''No it's not!'' I said. ''Did you find ID on him? His wallet?''

''No, ma'am, I'm afraid the body'd been picked clean, by transients probably.''

''Then it's not Willis!''

The man bowed his head, then looked up at me. ''Ma'am, the physical description fits, and we have the boots as identifier—''

''I want to see him!''

''Ma'am, generally we don't do that. We're not set up for family viewing at the morgue, ma'am . . .''

I was slipping on my shoes and grabbing my purse as he spoke. "I don't care what you're set up for, I'm going to see him!"

"Pat," Luna said, "let me drive her down there."

The man shrugged. "Y'all can follow me. Mrs. Pugh, we don't really like to put family members through this kind of ordeal—"

I slammed the door in both their faces on my way out. They followed anyway.

Luna and I drove in silence the hour and a half to the Travis County morgue.

Once in Austin, my mind screamed as we waited at red lights in a long line of cars, stopped for no reason in the middle of a block, or got cut off by someone thinking they could make their destination a lot quicker if they were just one car-length ahead.

How dare these people get in my way like this? Didn't they know? Didn't they know we weren't heading to a mundane job, or taking the kiddies to school? This was different. They had no right to be in our way.

Luna reached over and squeezed my hand. I squeezed back, holding her hand as tight as I could.

"Just hold on," she said.

We followed the man to the city's Brackenridge Hospital, taking a side street that went behind the hospital and between hospital-owned buildings. He parked on the street in front of a dilapidated redbrick building with broken and boarded-up windows. We got out of the car and followed him down a steep driveway between the redbrick building and the hospital's maintenance building. At the back of the maintenance building was a double-wide door, beyond that four multicolored plastic chairs.

"Ma'am, if you'll just sit here a minute," the man said, and went in the door marked MORGUE.

We sat. Directly in front of me were two doors and a drinking fountain. Each door had a picture—one of a man and one of a woman, yet they both said PRIVATE. I decided to wonder at length why the bathrooms were locked and private.

The man opened the swinging door. "Mrs. Pugh?"

I followed him in. It was a very tiny room, crowded with shelves filled with boxes. Four refrigerator drawers were against one wall. It didn't look at all like what reruns of "Quincy" had led me to believe.

I looked around the room because if I didn't I'd have to look at what was on the gurney in the middle of the small room. The body lying there was long, its feet draping over the end of the gurney. Just like Willis's feet did in any regulation-size bed. That's why we had a king-sized bed.

It was covered with a white sheet, all but the face. A hole was cut in the sheet exposing the face. The face that had never belonged to Willis Pugh.

I was giddy as we left the morgue. It wasn't Willis. Thank God Almighty, it wasn't Willis. I tried to pray for whoever would eventually have to identify the man I'd seen, but I couldn't. All I could do was thank God it wasn't *my* man.

Luna used her car phone to call DPS. After a brief conversation, she said, "DPS found Willis's car."

I used the car phone to call Black Cat Ridge and made arrangements with another mother to take the kids all home with her and keep them until Luna and I returned. This mother owed me—I'd supplied forty-seven cupcakes for her kid's birthday party at school because she was out of town on business.

We headed west toward the rock. They'd found Willis's car. They had not found Willis. I wasn't sure why we were going to look at his car—but I knew I had to. I'd somehow be closer to him; I'd be able to feel him, know if he was dead or alive. Maybe. Maybe not. I only knew I had to go.

Luna drove. We were quiet as we pulled through Austin,

heading west toward Dripping Springs. Once through the traffic, I asked her, "Where's your husband?"

Luna turned and looked at me, then quickly looked back at the road. She sighed. "Wondered if you'd ever ask. I also wondered what I'd tell you if you did."

"The truth?"

"Hum. Interesting concept." She thought about it for a moment. "Okay," she said.

"Is he dead?" I asked.

"No."

"Are you divorced?"

"No."

I didn't ask any more. I didn't know what question was left. Was it the same question I had left of my own marriage: Where is he?

Luna seemed to make a decision. Her body, which had been rigid beside me, relaxed; her hands unclasped from the steering wheel, and she rested one hand lightly atop it.

"I told you I'd been in the marines, right?"

I'd known she'd been in the service, but which branch I hadn't known. I nodded my head in encouragement.

"I graduated high school Saturday night, left for boot Monday morning. My daddy was alive then and he had a shit-fit, you better believe. His little girl joining the jar-heads." She grinned at me. "He'd been a sailor during the Korean War."

Luna passed a slow-moving farm vehicle and pulled expertly back into our lane. "I'd been in almost eighteen months when I met Eddie Luna." She smiled. "God Almighty, he was something to see. You ever take a good look at Eduardo?"

"He's a doll," I said.

"Gonna look like his daddy. Best-looking *guapo* I ever saw. We were both from Texas, both Mexican. Not a lot of either of that in Camp Lejeune, North Carolina, I can tell you that. I fell in love like you never did see. One, two, bump, down for the count.'' She laughed. ''Remember that old song, 'Book of Love'?''

I nodded.

''He wrote it,'' Luna said.

I frowned. ''The song?''

She laughed. ''No, *amiga,* the book! We got married in Maryland where you can do it quick. Like to broke my mother's heart, but Eduardo was on the way, so we just did it. I mustered out 'cause I was pregnant, thought being a marine wife would suit me just fine. But Eddie was always getting in trouble. He'd get a stripe, do something stupid, and lose it. Been in the corps five years and never made it past buck private for more than a week. But it didn't matter. I got a job as a secretary on the base and brought home more money than he did. Everything was just fine. Then one night, when I was six months along with Luis and we were stationed at Pendleton, Eddie was at a bar off base, having a few drinks with some buddies, and this guy starts ragging on him. Eddie had a temper—that's what kept him down his whole time in the Corps. His buddies all said the guy swung on him first, but that didn't matter much. Eddie hits the guy back, he falls down, cracks his skull and he's dead, like boom.''

''Oh, God, Luna, I'm sorry—''

''The bitch was that the guy was an officer. Out of uniform. They took Eddie and his buddies in that night. I spent three days like what you've been going through. Not knowing. Then I found out. Eddie's been in Leavenworth now for twelve years.''

I touched her lightly on the arm, and she patted my hand. ''Catfish Watkins is the only one in town knows. I told him when I applied with the P.D. That was something the police chief needed to know about one of his officers.'' She smiled. ''He said didn't make him no never mind. He had to have a woman on the job to meet some quota. So I got it.''

''Do you ever see him? Eddie?''

"Once a year the boys and I take my two-week vacation and drive to Kansas. We stay with a family up there who boards rooms at a reasonable rate. We go every day of those two weeks and see Eddie. All three of us."

"Relatives in Kansas," I said under my breath.

"Huh?"

I laughed. "Last summer I asked where y'all were off to and you said, 'visiting relatives in Kansas.' "

"Did I lie?"

"No, I guess you didn't."

"He's gonna get out in six more years. The boys will be all grown up by then, but at least he's been able to see them once a year. Watch them grow."

"How long did he get?" I asked.

"Twenty years. No parole on federal charges. He'll do the whole twenty."

"You still love him?"

Luna laughed. "That man's hand touches mine through the grill once a year, and it's better than nightly sex with any other guy in the world."

"Aren't you worried about . . . you know . . ."

"A guy tried messing with him Eddie's first week in the joint. The guy's been singing soprano ever since." She shrugged. "It gained him respect. You gotta have respect in the joint. You also gotta keep your old lady's occupation a secret when she's a cop."

"It must be really hard on your boys," I said, absently staring out the window.

"Why?" she asked.

I looked at her. "Because their dad's, you know . . ."

"Because their dad's a jailbird? A con?" Her voice was getting hot.

"No, that's not what I meant . . ."

Luna let out a mirthless laugh. "You liberal gringos kill me, you know that? You give all this lip service to the great salad bowl of America, but when it comes right down to it, all us ethnics better tow the line when it comes to politically correct, or you just shake your heads and go tisk, tisk.''

''What are you talking about?'' I demanded.

''Eddie's their father, and it doesn't matter whether he's sitting in the living room watching TV or sitting in a cell in Leavenworth, Kansas. He's the head of our family. The kids know what he did was wrong; Eddie and me have seen to that. We talk to 'em about it every year, but that don't mean he doesn't deserve respect. He's their father. Period. And a father deserves his sons' respect. You people with all your intellectualizing and getting to 'the root of the problem' get yourselves lost sometimes. In true Mexican tradition, a son doesn't go farther in life than his father; that would show disrespect. But me and Eddie want the boys to do better than us. I guess that's what we get hanging around with you gringos. But Eddie's their father, and he's a good man who got caught up in a bad situation, and there's no shame in that.''

''Then why is it such a big secret?'' I asked.

She looked at me hard. ''Because people like you would think less of him and less of the boys because of it.''

''Luna, I don't—''

She gave me a hard look. ''Really?''

This was one of those things that would take some soul-searching, some late-night-when-I-couldn't-sleep thoughts. But my late nights were occupied right now. This would have to come later.

''Thanks for telling me.''

Luna laughed; her voice sounding a little embarrassed. ''You're welcome.''

A thought struck me. ''Did you check—''

''Yeah, I checked. Willis's not in jail anywhere in the state of Texas.''

The Ghia was on the shoulder about a mile before the cutoff from Highway 290 to Junction 180, which led to Johnson City. It was on the other side of the road from us, heading in the direction of home. He *had* been heading home. At least for a while. A DPS trooper car pulled up behind the Ghia as we did an illegal U-turn and pulled up in front of Willis's car.

Luna got out and met the trooper by the Ghia. They shook hands. I got slowly out of the car and walked up to them.

"This is the wife," Luna said, pointing at me. "My next-door neighbor."

The trooper touched the brim of his Stetson. "Ma'am," he said.

"Anything?" I asked.

"Car's locked up nice and tight, but one window's smashed. You got the keys?"

I pulled my key chain out of my purse and found the one for the Ghia. I walked toward the driver's side door, but the trooper stopped me. "I'll do that, ma'am."

He took the key from my hand and opened the driver's door, the one without the busted window, sticking his head inside the car. "Hot," he said, pulling his head out, taking his Stetson off and wiping his brow with his sleeve. "Been shut up awhile. Even with the busted window, it's hot in there."

"He's been missing since Sunday," I said.

"We just got through viewing a body at the Travis County morgue that had been wearing Mr. Pugh's boots," Luna said. "You think that's who busted the window?"

"More'n likely," the trooper agreed. Turning to me, he said, "Well, ma'am, just preliminary, but I don't see no blood stains, nothing like that. I'd say those boots were stolen after your husband left the car. I've got the mobile crime lab on the way. They'll check it out."

"Can we check the trunk—see if his gear's still in there?" I asked.

The trooper nodded and walked to the back of the Ghia. "In front," I said. "This is a Volkswagen. Engine in the back."

"Ha! Shoulda known that," he said, smiling.

He walked to the front and opened the trunk. It was empty. Since none of the camping gear was found with the John Doe we'd seen at the morgue, chances were that wherever Willis had gone, he was prepared.

We waited with the trooper, whose name was Bob, for twenty minutes for the mobile crime lab to arrive. It took them an hour to go over the car, but their report was the same as Trooper Bob's had been: the Ghia was clean. Oh, there was sand on the floorboard, grass on the passenger seat, a candy wrapper on the floor of the backseat, but there was no blood, no evidence of foul play.

When they had finished, Bob got behind the wheel and tried to turn over the engine, using my key. Nothing happened. We traded places—after all, the car belonged to my family; it was an old car, maybe I knew how to start it. I didn't have the heart to tell Bob I hadn't been behind the wheel of the Ghia more than once or twice in the past fifteen years. I attempted to start the car—to no avail. Trooper Bob sighed and went to his car to call in for a tow truck.

Walking back to Luna and me, he said, "Well, we can see now why your husband left the car," he said. "Tow truck should be here shortly. Coming from Johnson City. Where do you want them to take it?"

"Where's my husband?" I asked.

"Well, ma'am, that I don't know. But what I'm piecing together here is that the car broke down, he stopped and locked it up, and then, well—"

"Carrying all his camping gear on his back, walked off into the unknown," I said, the sarcasm not lost on the trooper.

"It would be more likely, ma'am, that somebody picked him up."

Charles Manson. Jeffrey Daumer. Henry Lee Lucas. Or any one of hundreds (thousands?) of lesser knowns using my husband to make themselves famous.

"Look, Bob," Luna said, taking the trooper and leading him away from the Ghia toward his car. I followed, although it was obvious even to me that I wasn't supposed to. "Willis Pugh's been missing now for coming on forty-eight hours. We need to get an all-points out on him, okay? This is a good family man. A business owner. I know this guy—he's not the type to just walk off into the boonies and never come back."

"Yeah, well, Elena, I've heard that one before, I gotta tell ya. We seen all sorts . . ."

He turned his head slightly, catching me out of the corner of his eye. "Ma'am," he said, turning to me. "We're gonna do everything we can to find your husband."

"Yeah, right," I said. I knew the anger building up in me had little to do with Trooper Bob and a hell of a lot more to do with my own inadequacies. But Trooper Bob was there. "I can really tell this is going to get priority with you. You think he's left me, well, let me tell you something, bub . . ."

Luna grabbed my arm and pulled me away, overriding my tirade. "I'm going to get Mrs. Pugh back to Codderville, Bob. Just have them tow the car to the nearest mechanic who works on VWs, okay?"

"Sure thing, Elena. Y'all go ahead and take off."

The relief was evident in his eyes. I turned in Luna's grasp, pointing my finger at Trooper Bob. "And another thing, Bozo . . ."

"You know how when you call a public utility and they put you on hold for a week and a half?" I asked Luna as we drove east toward home.

"Yeah?"

"That's how I feel. My entire life is on hold. I can't breathe." I rolled the window down, sticking my head out, gasping for air.

Luna pulled over to the side of the road. "You're hyperventilating,'' she said. She grabbed a McDonald's sack off the backseat and thrust it in front of my face. ''Breathe slowly.''

I pushed at the bag but she held it firm. ''Come on,'' she said, her voice surprisingly gentle. ''Breathe slow. One thousand and one, one thousand and two, one thousand and three . . . Good.''

She removed the bag. ''How do you feel?''

I leaned my head back on the car's headrest. ''Like punching somebody.''

''You wanna get out and kick my car? Another dent won't mean much.''

I shook my head. ''Thanks. Maybe later?''

She looked in her side mirrors as she pulled back on the road. ''Anytime.''

Five

Luna dropped me off in Codderville at Willis's office, heading back to the station. She promised to pick me up in plenty of time to get the kids from school.

I took the elevator up to the second floor, too tired to think about the stairs. Miss Alice sat in front of the computer at the desk in the outer office, staring at the machine like it was an alien creature. She'd had a little trouble adjusting to the new job—her last one had been working a manual typewriter for the Army Air Corps.

She turned when I walked in. She was a peer of my mother-in-law's, but the exact opposite in both looks and temperament. She was almost twice the size of Vera, in height and weight, and she was everyone's stereotypical idea of a doting grandma-type. Unfortunately Miss Alice had never married and, thus, was unable to conjure up any grandchildren. Therefore any child would do. My kids adored her.

"E.J., darlin', how are you? How's that man of yours? Still feeling poorly?"

I forced a smile. "Doug around?"

"He's on the phone in Willis's office, talking to Branson over in San Antonio. We got the job, you hear?"

I smiled. "No, I hadn't heard. That's great." Part of me was seething that Doug was in Willis's office using the phone. What right did he have to be in there?

Now that I'd told Vera the truth, I knew I had to tell Miss Alice. And I had to swear her to secrecy. Miss Alice loved to talk, and really good gossip was worth its weight in gold. But she still had to know. I told her, leaving out my suspicions that Willis might have left me.

I figured any rational adult could come up with that image all by themselves—after all, my nine-year-old had had no problem reaching that conclusion.

"My, Lord! Eloise, this is just plumb awful! Honey, I'm so sorry!"

She got up from her desk and wrapped her arms around me. She may have been a couple of heads taller than Vera, but I still had her beat by several inches. I've always found it awkward being mothered by women smaller than me. I outgrew my own mother when I was twelve.

Doug came out of Willis's office and Miss Alice unfolded me. "Doug, did you hear?"

"They found him?" he asked, coming quickly up to me.

"No—" I started.

"Well, goodness, this is just the first I'd heard he's lost!" Miss Alice said. She sighed. "Always the last to know anything." She went back to her desk to stare at the computer.

"Come in the office, E.J.," Doug said, graciously extending his arm to my husband's office, a place I had more right to be in than he did.

"Congratulations on the Branson contract," I said.

"We're gonna make a hefty profit off this—if Willis

gets back. I can schmooze the customers all day long, but I need Willis to crunch the numbers, E.J."

"Doug, you're an engineer—"

"I know, I know. It's just that we all have our specialities, E.J., and crunching numbers isn't mine."

"Call in one of the drafters to help out."

"Ricky'll be here by the end of the week."

I nodded my head. "Any word about anything?" he asked.

"They found his car."

I told him what little I knew, leaving out my trip to the Travis County morgue. There were some things best not shared.

"Doug, have you looked around here in the office? To see if there's anything—I don't know what, just anything—that might shed some light on this?"

He shook his head. "No, didn't think about it. Ya wanna?"

We both let our eyes stray over Willis's private domain. I had a real aversion to breaching the sanctity of his privacy. Willis had none at home.

I had my little office under the stairs that was verboten for anyone to disturb without permission. But Willis didn't even have his dresser drawers.

Our kids have come up with the strange concept that anything in that house is theirs and they can do with it what they will. The privacy factor really reared its ugly head before Willis had his vasectomy, when we would try to find places to hide condoms. No matter where we put them, we'd find condom balloons somewhere in the house.

Now his desk stared at me. These were unusual circumstances. I had to look. But not with Doug.

"Let me do it," I said. "No need for both of us to get in trouble when he finds out."

"Well, I've got some phone calls to make anyway," Doug said, getting up from Willis's desk chair. "I'll do it at my desk."

After he'd closed the door behind him, I started with the lap drawer. Pens, pencils, Exacto knives, a credit card-sized calculator, rubber bands. The usual lap-drawer paraphernalia. I moved on to the right-hand drawer. A neat file of business correspondence. Glancing through them, I found nothing out of the ordinary. Nothing that could tell me where my husband was. The bottom drawer on the right-hand side was the deepest and was chock full of drawings, some unfinished.

In the top drawer on the left-hand side I hit pay dirt. His appointment calendar. I thumbed through, quickly getting to August and September. Meetings with clients, lunch with Doug, lunch with our preacher, Keith Reynolds.

Funny, he hadn't told me about that.

Then an early-afternoon appointment with Anne Comstock, our family therapist. We'd used her extensively right after Bessie's birth family had been killed, and gone back during the stressful adoption proceedings when Bessie became a bonafide member of our family. But we hadn't been seeing her lately.

But right there, in royal blue and white, through August and September, one meeting a week with Anne.

I picked up the phone and dialed the therapist's number. When her receptionist answered, I asked if there was any way Anne could squeeze me in for an emergency session sometime that day. "I don't need more than fifteen minutes," I'd pleaded. She'd found me the time. I walked the four blocks to Anne's office. Strangely enough, in a small town like Codderville, where everything was within walking distance, no one over the age of sixteen walked. I made it to Anne's office with a minute to spare. She still kept me waiting for ten. I took that time to call Luna at the station and let her know where to pick me up.

Finally the door opened and Anne Comstock stuck her head out, smiling. "Hi, E.J. Wanna come back?"

I got up and followed her into her inner sanctum, past the play-therapy rooms with their anatomically correct dolls, and into her private office. She shut the door behind us.

"What can I do for you?" she asked.

"Willis is missing."

Quickly I told her everything that had transpired from Sunday night on.

"I didn't want to do it, Anne, but I decided I had to see if there was anything in his desk at work that could tell me what's going on. That's when I found his appointment calendar and saw the sessions with you. He hadn't told me about them."

Anne was silent.

"Anne, please. If you know anything—"

"I have no earthly idea where he is and had no idea in advance that something like this would happen. That's all I can tell you, E.J."

I gulped in air. "Did he leave me?" I asked.

"I don't know," she answered.

It wasn't the answer I wanted to hear. What I wanted to hear was complete and total denial that such a thing could even be dreamed of.

"Would there be reason for him to leave me?" I asked.

Anne shook her head. "E.J., I can't do this." She got up and walked to the door, opening it. "I am so sorry, E.J. But I can't answer any questions. All I can tell you is what I've already said: He gave me no indication that he was thinking about leaving, and I have no idea where he is." She touched my shoulder lightly. "I hope everything works out."

I left the building, getting into Luna's waiting car and heading to the school to pick up the kids, feeling one thing very strongly in the pit of my stomach: Something was wrong with my marriage.

The phone was ringing when the kids and I came in the door. "Make it quick," Eduardo said, "I'm expecting a call."

I shot him a look as I picked up the phone.

"Well, I am!" he said, going to the refrigerator, my two daughters in his wake. Graham and Luis had already headed for the stairs.

"Hello?" I said into the phone.

"Is this the most perfect redhead God ever made?" a male voice said.

I smiled in spite of everything. "Fred?"

"In the mostly perfect flesh. What's going on, E.J.?"

I looked around. Both girls were still in the kitchen, taking entirely too many food items from Eduardo, who appeared to be handing over everything in the refrigerator.

"Give me your number," I told Fred. "I'll call you right back." He gave me a number in Austin and I hung up.

"Don't eat too much or you'll ruin your dinner," I said to all three, and headed for the stairs.

Once in my bedroom, I closed the door and sat on the bed, picking up the phone and dialing Fred.

"So what's going on?" he asked again. "Sorry I didn't get back to you yesterday, but I had a sleep-over at somebody else's house." He giggled.

I told him in gory detail what had transpired since Sunday at five P.M. "Have you seen him?" I asked.

"No," he answered. "Baby, I wish I had and you gotta know that I'd tell you if I did. I always liked you better than him anyway."

"With reason," I said, grinning only the way Fred had been able to make me grin.

"Yeah, you were always softer to hug," he said. "Look, have you called anybody else?"

"No, I can't think who to call—"

"Okay, I'll call Billy—he's still in town. And Paul's back from Africa—"

"When'd Paul go to Africa?"

"Been gone about three years. Doing missionary work—"

"Missionary!"

Fred laughed. "Yeah. He's a preacher now. Church of What's Happening Now, or something off the wall like that."

I wanted to tell Willis. What a kick Willis would get out of that. Paul Monroe, the biggest pot dealer on U.T. campus back in 1972. Well, he did hallucinate one time about seeing shadows turning into nuns, but—

"Thanks, Fred," I said. "Anything you hear—"

"He's gonna be okay, E.J. I know he's okay. You believe that?"

"Yeah, sure," I said. I hung up.

I wanted to tell Willis how great Fred sounded and that Billy was still in Austin and that Paul was a preacher and a missionary—I couldn't tell Willis because Willis wasn't there and I had no idea where he was.

I went downstairs to fix dinner for the kids. No need to wait until six o'clock. Willis wouldn't be coming home at six o'clock today. Or maybe ever.

Trooper Bob called late that afternoon. I handed Graham the phone in the kitchen to hang up as I went upstairs to talk privately. I didn't hear a click when I picked up the phone.

"I've got it, Graham, hang up." Still no click. "Graham, hang up."

Finally I heard the click. "Sorry, Bob. Anything?"

"No ma'am, not yet. But I just wanted to let you know that a volunteer search-and-rescue team here in the area will be going out in the morning—going through the woods and fields around where the car was found."

"What time? I'll be there."

"Now, Miz Pugh, no reason for you to—"

"What time?"

Trooper Bob sighed. "They'll be starting about dawn."

I thanked him and hung up, dialing my mother-in-law's number. I told her about the search-and-rescue starting at dawn. ''Could I bring the kids over tonight so I can leave early?''

''Bring 'em over now. I'll just put some extra fish sticks in the microwave.''

Yum, yum, Grandma's home cooking. ''Thanks, Vera,'' I said. ''You're a lifesaver.''

''Always saw myself as cherry flavored. Now you go find my boy.''

I called Luna and told her what was going on. ''Are you on your way home or do you want me to drop the boys off at Vera's?''

''Think she'd keep 'em the night? That way we can leave early.''

''You don't have to go with me, Luna,'' I said.

''If I don't want to read headlines about Trooper Bob's demise, I think it might be best.''

We rang off and I checked back with Vera. She's always been a big believer in the more the merrier.

I bundled the kids up and herded them toward the station wagon. Graham pulled me aside.

''I'm going with you,'' he said.

''You were supposed to hang up that phone!''

''Okay, fine, but I didn't. You want to shoot me?'' He held his arms away from his body in an act of surrender.

''Graham—''

''Mom, he's my dad.''

Where in the hell was the manual, and what did it say about a situation like this? Did I let my nine-year-old son go on the search for his father? Or did I leave him at his grandmother's to worry? Vera would not approve. Vera wasn't his mother.

''Okay. But you do exactly what the troopers tell you to do, do you understand me?''

Solemnly Graham nodded his head. ''Thanks, Mom.''

He jumped in the car with the other kids, and I took my load to Codderville.

* * *

The phone rang a little after ten. I'd made Graham hit the rack early, knowing how early we'd have to get up in the morning. I picked up the phone, trying to tell myself it was a wrong number, my mother-in-law, Luna, Doug, even Fred. I knew it couldn't be Willis. Don't get your hopes up, it's not Willis.

"Hello?" I said.

"Hey, good-looking." Fred.

I could feel the hope seep out of my body like perspiration on Enchanted Rock. "Hi, Fred."

"I know you were hoping for another voice, Sug. Sorry."

"Anything?" I asked.

"Talked to Billy. He hasn't seen or heard from Willis in longer than me. Paul hasn't either."

"I thought it was a long shot."

"Look, you're back in Codderville, right?"

"A suburb," I said. "Black Cat Ridge."

Fred laughed. "Codderville's got a suburb?" He stopped. "Sorry, Babe. Look, I can be there first thing in the morning—"

"No, Fred. I appreciate the offer, but I won't even be here in the morning. Some state troopers and a volunteer search-and-rescue team are going to search the area where his car was found. I'll be there."

"Tell me exactly where."

I told him the location where Willis's car had been found. "I'll see you in the morning," he said.

"Fred, you don't have to—"

"Are you kidding? If that numb nuts is out there, I'll find him. You realize he still owes me twenty bucks from the seventy-two Longhorn-Aggie game?"

"Thanks," I said and hung up.

The phone rang again immediately. I didn't give myself time to wonder if it could be Willis. "Hello?"

"E.J., it's Keith Reynolds. Your mother-in-law just called me."

''Oh, Keith,'' I said, ''thanks for calling.''

Keith, our minister at the Black Cat Ridge First Methodist, said, ''I'm praying, that goes without saying, but what else can I do?''

''I wish I knew, Keith, I really do—''

''Mrs. Pugh said something about a search-and-rescue mission . . .''

I sighed. I told him when and where. ''Thanks,'' I said, meaning it.

I hung up and sat on the couch in the living room, staring at the front door, knowing that even if Willis came home, he'd use the back door. But there was something significant about that front door. The way it steadfastly remained shut.

Six

I lay in bed counting my evils. *Willis, do you think you could possibly pick up those socks sometime in the next millennium? Willis, how about trying to get it inside the toilet bowl instead of just the general direction? Willis, how do you expect me to buy groceries for this entire family when there's never any money in the account? Willis, not tonight, okay?*

I turned over on my right side, staring at the spill of light on the carpet coming from the partially opened curtains and the high moon outside. Did I still love Willis? I rolled over on my back, looking at the ceiling tiles. Yes. Oh, yes. Would I be able to live with the fact that he was dead?

I rolled over on my left side, staring at the door to Willis's closet. Who would I give his clothes to? Did I know anybody who was big enough to wear them? Maybe save something for Graham. Willis's watch—except he's wearing it, I thought. If they didn't find his body, I'd never get the watch for Graham. Tears began to fall quietly on the pillow. I'd get the Ghia back and have it fixed. Save it for when Graham was old enough to drive. It would really be worth something then. He'd have that of his father's.

I pulled Willis's pillow to me, burying my face in it. I could smell him. His scent was still on the pillow. How long would it last? If I never washed the pillowcase again, how long would the scent remain? I rolled over on my back, cradling Willis's pillow in my arms.

And if he'd left me? What then? The kids would still have him, I hoped. I'd try to be reasonable about child visitation. I'd have to get a job. A real one. I couldn't support myself and three kids on my book revenues.

If he was dead I'd still have to get a job. One of the things we'd learned to live without when Willis had opened his own company was life insurance. It's easy to live without it when it isn't an issue.

I sat up on the side of the bed, resting Willis's pillow on my knees. I was tired of the tears in my ears.

Hey, Funny Face, give us a kiss. Willis with grape jelly smeared all over his mouth, chasing me around the little apartment in Mexico City.

Jesus, I've never seen anything like him. Willis looking at Graham in his arms, minutes after his birth.

Boy, you're gonna get it now! Willis chasing me buck naked out of the bathroom after I'd poured cold water on him in the shower. Catching me by the bed and throwing me down. Megan coming in. "Daddy, you're naked nude!"

All the snapshots we never took, playing like a movie in my mind.

I got up and walked to the window, looking down at the driveway below. No reason to look for the Ghia now. I knew where it was—at a mechanic's shop in Johnson City.

What would life be like without him? If the past two days were any example—not very damn good.

I wandered downstairs, checking the doors and the windows and the security system. All systems A-OK.

I'd always thought I was a fairly liberated woman, but I was beginning to realize I was one of those women who couldn't live without a man.

A very particular man.

Wednesday

It was still dark when we pulled out of the connecting driveways in Luna's car. She kept glancing at Graham in the backseat; she appeared to approve of my mothering methods about as much as Vera had. Which is to say not at all.

We began the long trek back to where Willis's car had been parked. The rains started in Austin and followed us through Dripping Springs, which it literally was at six o'clock that morning. The thunder and lightning started ten miles outside of Dripping Springs, and I was beginning to feel our trip was for naught. No way the search-and-rescue team could do anything in this downpour. But the rains stopped abruptly five miles from where Willis's car had been.

We pulled over to the shoulder at the end of a long line of cars. The sun was just touching the horizon as we walked up to Trooper Bob's car.

"Morning, ma'am," he said, doffing his Stetson. He looked at Graham, holding out his hand to shake. "And you are . . ."

"Graham Pugh, sir. My dad's the one you're looking for."

"Mighty glad you could join us, Mr. Pugh. Need all the help we can get. Ma'am," he said, turning to me, "could I talk with you for just a moment?"

I walked off with Trooper Bob, out of earshot of Luna and Graham. ''Miz Pugh, I hope you understand you and your boy can't be in on the search.''

''Why the hell not?'' I said, arms akimbo, temper not quite in check.

''Miz Pugh.'' He sighed. ''When we do a search like this the 'rescue' part's not really apt, if you know what I mean. If we find your husband, ma'am, chances are gonna be damned good, excuse my French . . . anyway, ma'am, we're gonna be more than likely looking for a body, ma'am.''

I stared at Trooper Bob. He seemed a nice enough guy. Big, like Willis, although skinnier. Short brown hair under his Stetson, long legs, a craggy face with a good smile. Why did I hate him so?

I wasn't sure what I had thought this exercise was all about. I guess somewhere in the Neverland of my brain I had visions of Willis walking aimlessly in the woods, saying, ''Who am I?'' Amnesia is such a good plot device. I'd used it in *In Tune with Each Other*, one of my better books.

But Trooper Bob wasn't looking for my amnesia-ridden husband. He was looking for his dead body.

I looked around me. Four cars down, three women had set up a kitchen in the back of a pickup truck. I walked back to Graham. ''We'll be helping with the coffee and lunches,'' I said to him.

''No way! I'm looking for my dad!''

I put a hand on both shoulders and leaned down to look into his eyes. ''No, Graham. We're needed here. These people know what they're doing. We have to do what they tell us to do.''

Graham pulled away from me and ran up to Trooper Bob. ''Sir,'' he said, ''I can go on the search for my dad, can't I?''

Trooper Bob looked at me. ''No, son, I'm sorry but you

can't. State law. You gotta be eighteen years or older to go on a search-and-rescue mission."

I no longer hated Trooper Bob. He hadn't blamed me—he hadn't taken the blame on himself. He'd figured out a way to blame it on the State. Not bad. I wondered how often I could use that?

It was a long day. Fred showed up around eight o'clock with Paul and Billy in tow. It was like old-home week, except one very key ingredient was missing.

Following closely on their heels were Keith Reynolds and his wife, Robin, and ten men from the church—some I barely knew, but among them was Doug, who didn't even go to our church. It was one of those times when the meaning of community came home to me in a very real way.

We had intermittent showers, one good thunderstorm, and several occasions when the sun came out so strongly everything turned into a sauna.

Graham and I ran back and forth between the search site and Johnson City, picking up supplies. More soft drinks, some hot-dog buns, somebody forgot the relish. Later in the afternoon we made a run for more soda, chips, Twinkies, anything to eat as people staggered back in from the woods and fields.

There was no news, good or bad. There was no sign of my husband.

We picked the kids up in Codderville around eight that night and headed home. The girls were abuzz with talk of Grandma's dogs and their silly pranks, and what Grandma said to miz somebody who called on the phone, and what Grandma fixed them for dinner. I was glad they had so much to talk about—that way they didn't ask where we'd been and what we were doing.

And they didn't ask the big question: Where's Daddy? How long could I put them off? At what point did I tell two little six-year-olds that their daddy was gone? Was high-school graduation too long to wait?

I got the girls bathed and in bed and brought out *The Wind & the Willows* for our nightly read. Megan grabbed her blue jeans before I took them to the hamper and pulled something out of her pocket. She held it out for my inspection.

''What's this?'' I asked.

''Forty-two cents,'' Megan said proudly. ''Me and Bessie cleaned the poop in Grandma's backyard for a quarter and we had some pennies here, so all together we got forty-two cents.''

I smiled. ''That's great, honey—''

''It's for Daddy's birthday present.''

I felt my stomach muscles contract. ''That's great, sweetie, now let's read—''

''Grandma took us to Wal-Mart and we found just what we wanna buy Daddy, huh, Bessie?''

''Yeah,'' Bessie said, excitedly sitting up on her knees in bed. ''A watch.''

''For forty-two cents?'' I asked.

The girls looked at each other. ''Well, maybe you could help us?''

''Daddy already has a watch—''

''Not like this one!'' Megan said, jumping out of bed. ''Mommy, it's grand! Really grand!''

''Really!'' Bessie echoed.

''Well—''

''It's a pocket watch, Grandma called it. And it's got the face of the Lion King right on it! You know how Daddy loves the Lion King!''

''Let's read—''

''Can we go get it tomorrow?'' Megan said. ''Can we?''

''Can we, Mommy?'' Bessie said.

''Okay,'' I said. ''We'll get the watch tomorrow.''

Screams and shouts were in order, and it took some calming down before they were back in bed and ready for story time. I read that night's chapter, then turned off the light.

"Good night, girls. Love you."

"Night, Mommy," came a sleepy voice. "It's really grand."

Sleep was a long time in coming. I'd gone over the checkbook before coming upstairs. There was only a couple of hundred in the account. We had barely a thousand in savings at the moment. Along with no life insurance, we also wisely carried no health insurance. Willis's upper–GI tract infection two months ago had nearly wiped out our always small savings.

There was a great deal of money in Bessie's savings, her legacy from her birth parents, but I couldn't touch that by law, morality, and good taste. It was for her future. A small monthly stipend came our way for Bessie's daily needs, but there was no way I could touch the principal. If I sold Doug Willis's share of the company . . . But Doug had had to borrow to come in as a partner as it was. He probably couldn't come up with Willis's share, and how long could the business last without Willis? How long would I be able to keep the house?

Maybe the best thing would be to move back to Houston and live with my parents for a while, until I could find a job, get on my feet—

No! This is not happening! I sat up in bed, throwing my feet to the floor, willing the knot in my stomach to go away. How could I be thinking of money when I didn't know if Willis was dead or alive?

Because the mortgage was due on Monday, along with the utility bills, the credit-card bills . . .

I got up and walked to the window. Think about something nice, I willed myself. Puppy dogs and butterflies and . . . chocolate.

I went downstairs and raided my above-the-refrigerator stash of contraband chocolate. There wasn't much left. I'd raided it a week ago when things hadn't been going well in chapter seven of *Storm Surge.* I poured a glass of milk to go with my bag of M&Ms and the one Hershey bar left.

I think of chocolate as brain food. As well as comfort food, and just general, all-around sustenance. Think, I told myself. Where is he? Call Jim and Sally in Taxco, see if they've seen him? I looked at the clock, trying to figure out what time it was in Mexico.

I finished the chocolate and went back to bed, remembering that Mexico was in the same time zone as Texas, unless it was daylight savings time, which it was, and it probably wasn't a good idea to call people I hadn't seen in over twelve years at two o'clock in the morning.

I hadn't been asleep long, less than an hour, when the phone rang. I picked it up, still groggy.

"Hello?"

"E.J.! Baby, listen—"

I sat up in bed. "Willis!"

"Honey—"

"Oh, my God! Willis! Where are you?"

"That's what I'm trying to tell you if you'd just shut up—"

"What the hell's going on—"

"Baby, shut up! Listen to me—"

There was a ruckus on the other end of the line and the phone went dead. I sat there staring at the receiver.

He was alive. Thank God Almighty, he was alive! Now I was gonna kill him.

Part II

Willis's Story

Seven

Saturday

It wasn't just the numbers. Forty. I'm an engineer, I deal in numbers twenty-four hours a day. It was the hair coming out in my comb—more of it every day. It was the spare tire around my middle that used to be muscle. It was the wife bitching thirty-six hours a day, the kids yelling, the cats under my feet. It was the fact that we needed a new roof and I didn't have the money to pay for it, and we hadn't had a good hail storm in months. It was the Ghia acting up and the wagon needing new tires and the Magic-Markered wall in the utility room that needed repainting and the lawn needing mowing and the garage needing cleaning and the cat stains on the carpet and the Kool-Aid stain on the couch.

It was the fact that the last time I'd tried to make love to my wife, I hadn't been able to do it.

And then we'd gone to the rock.

It's hard to explain what happened. I'm not a New Age–crystal gazing kinda guy, so I can't tell you exactly what happened. All I can say is that as we pulled out of the ranger station that late August weekend, heading toward campsite twenty-two, I began to feel it.

It was like a pressure inside my head, pushing in and pushing out simultaneously, creating a tension—not at my temples, like a headache, but above my ears, moving to the back of my head. My head felt like it was swelling, but something was holding it closed. My ears were ringing—like I'd been hit in the head or knocked down playing football—kind of tingling. It wasn't a pleasant feeling—but it wasn't unpleasant either.

It just was.

It was akin to a feeling of anticipation. Like something was going to happen—good or bad, but I was waiting for it.

Have you ever stood next to a big piece of machinery, a locomotive or electric power generator or the big oil field pumps—some huge machine? Not the noisy kind, but the kind that just run quietly and yet you know they're really turning over—the feeling of being in the midst of barely leashed power?

That was the rock.

I'm not nuts—I wasn't hearing voices or seeing visions. My last vision was in Taxco, Mexico, behind some really grounded mescaline back in '74, and it was just Janis Joplin offering me a hit off her bottle of Southern Comfort. Nothing like that was going on at the rock. I hadn't even had a beer.

E.J. had been all over me—"What's the matter?" "Penny for your thoughts." What thoughts? The thought that maybe I was going nuts? The definite knowledge that I was getting damned old and didn't like it a bit? That wasn't something I could share with her. That I wanted to share with her. She has her own version of who I am—

what I am. It doesn't always include my real-life flesh and bones.

I couldn't keep my eyes off the rock. It pulled me. The closer I got to it, the stronger the feelings were. I'm not sure exactly when it was that I knew I had to climb it, but the thought came to my mind and wouldn't let go.

I had to conquer the rock. I had to subdue it. The only way to do that was on the rock's own terms—I had to climb it. I had to stick my fingers into its life and pull myself up and stand on top of it like Edmund Hillary at Mount Everest.

Okay, so everybody and their brother climbed Enchanted Rock something like three hundred and sixty-five days a year. But it was calling to *me*. It was only me that felt its strength. I had to climb it.

Then there was the other part of that equation, the part the engineer in me wanted to know: Why? Why was the rock calling to me? What was happening to me? Was I going to end up doing a bad imitation of Richard Dreyfuss making mountains out of my mashed potatoes? I wanted answers to those questions. Which is all to explain why I ended up that Saturday in September, stuck a hundred miles from home with Doug "Duh" Kingsley.

I'm an idiot. Doug said he'd climbed the rock. My mind was in such a state for the whole month after coming back from the camping trip that all I could think of was the rock. I wanted to go back—to see if the feeling would still be there. And Doug was giving me an excuse. Doug said he'd climbed the rock and could help me.

Okay, so Doug said he'd had dinner with Michelle Pfeiffer and it turned out he'd been on the same plane with her once when all passengers were served the evening meal together. Then there was the time he said he'd been in the protesting throng at the 1968 Democratic Convention in Chicago. When I pointed out he could only have been about ten at the time, he said he'd gone with his parents. Later I found out they were lifelong Republicans.

His father, however, had been in Chicago in 1968, a month before the convention, and had stayed at the same hotel where Gene McCarthy would later stay.

Basically, what I'm trying to say is I should have known better. If it hadn't been for my strange obsession with the rock, I might have figured out that Doug's rock-climbing expertise left a little to be desired.

When he and I went into Austin to Whole Earth Provisions to buy our rope and supplies, I found some magazines there that told me a hell of a lot more about rock climbing than Doug had ever known, I soon found out.

That Saturday I'd left home a little before eight to get to the rock by eleven, the time Doug and I had agreed upon. I should have known by the start of the weekend what I was in store for. Although we were supposed to meet at the rock at eleven, Doug didn't even get out of town until ten-thirty, making him three hours late.

By that time, of course, he was hungry.

"Got anything to eat?" he asked, moving toward my ice chest.

"We were both supposed to bring our own food," I pointed out.

"Oh, shit, really?" he said. "Damn, I guess I forgot. Can I borrow something?"

"I'd like to get to the rock before it erodes," I said. I learned sarcasm at the knee of the likes of E. J. Pugh.

He glanced up from where he was browsing through my groceries, an indignant look on his face. "Hey, I was already late. Like I was going to stop for lunch?"

So I sat at the picnic table, alternately watching him eat and staring at the rock. I had a mission and Doug Kingsley was well on his way to screwing it up. Finally he finished, after telling me in detail how he met the woman he was seeing that night (on-line at the office when I, silly me, thought he was actually working), and how she sounded really hot.

"Okay, can we go now?" I asked.

"I have to change clothes before we go up the rock—"

"Change clothes?" I asked, trying not to hit him.

"Yeah, change clothes! It's not like I drove in the clothes I'll need for the climb, right? Besides, I found these really cool climber shorts when we were at Whole Earth—"

"Just do it," I said, sinking back down on the picnic table where I'd laid out our equipment.

We finally started up the saddle around three in the afternoon. Doug complained about the heat, complained about his backpack rubbing against his skin because of the tank top he was wearing that went so well with the new shorts. And he had on these new hiking boots, and they were rubbing a blister. So he stops, leaning against a boulder.

"My feet are killing me," Doug said.

I grabbed his pack, slung it on my shoulder, and kept going. Finally we get over the saddle between Little Rock and Enchanted Rock, down to the back where Doug remembered the trail that led to the place he'd climbed before. It was called "Easier than it looks."

We're heading down this trail and Doug says, "Hey, you hear that?"

"What?" By this time I was so tense from the rock and from Doug, I was ready to start running in circles and screaming.

"I hear music," Doug said.

"I don't hear shit. Come on," I said.

We rounded a boulder, and there was a girl sitting on top of another boulder, playing a pan flute. Of course, that's the last I see of Doug for a while.

It takes two people for a safe climb. I wasn't sure what I was going to do without Doug, but I had no intention of hanging around with the chick and her pan flute. That wasn't why I'd come to the rock. Doug was screwing with my mission, and I was not pleased. I kept going on the trail, finally finding the route we'd talked about taking.

I was laying out the equipment, trying to figure out how to do it by myself, when Doug finally showed up.

We put on our magic boots—special rock-climbing boots that have a slick sole and very tacky rubber on the bottoms to get, according to the books, ''maximum adhesion to the rock's surface.''

We picked out the piece of protection we thought we'd need—protection comes in different sizes, and all the ones we had were made of high-tech aluminum composite or aluminum alloy.

The way to climb a rock is two climbers start off at the bottom, one's the lead climber. That had to be Doug. You're supposed to climb the route you set up and place protection behind you as you go. We were planning on climbing a ''crack,'' which is just that: a vertical crack in a piece of rock.

Ideally the crack is tapered, and almost always you can find a spot where it's narrower at the bottom than it is at the top, slide the piece of protection into the crack, and then it won't slide down any further. Then you move up. The guy on the bottom—the belayer—holds the rope taut.

Once the first piece of protection is placed by the lead climber, the maximum distance that the lead climber can fall is twice the distance between him and the last piece of protection. From the start, where the two climbers are together, the lead climber goes up, places a piece of protection at, say, fifteen feet above the beginning. He then climbs another five feet. If he were to fall off the rock—off-climb, as they say in the mags—he would fall the five feet he is above the protection and then five feet below that, and at that point, the piece of protection will catch and his belayer would stop him there.

The lead climber continues to go up. The lead climber—Doug—gets up to the top—say, a hundred feet—and signals the following climber—me—that he's stopping and he wants the following climber to climb up.

At that point, the former lead climber establishes a belay position from above, not from below. He anchors himself securely on his own, generally by tying himself to pieces of protection that he placed independent from the route.

At this point, the following climber will clean the route; that is, pick up the pieces of protection left behind by the lead climber. Then he too gets to the top.

That's how it's *supposed* to work.

Except Doug slid before he got his first piece of protection in and fell from about ten feet up, landing on his ass. He claimed it was very difficult to walk after that, let alone climb.

By that time I didn't care if Doug had *broken* his ass. I left him leaning against the cliff face and complaining, while I headed down the trail to find a way up the rock.

In spite of Doug, I made it that day. When I found Duncan's crew, one of the guys had lost his partner, who turned out to be the pan flute–playing girl we'd encountered earlier, and they said I could join them. They were doing a three-pitch climb. We had to go up to one section, then take the rope and change it, and then up another pitch, then another; and I was scared spitless. But about two-thirds of the way up I stopped, right there on the last pitch, on the change-over of the rope to the last pitch, and below I saw the buzzards soaring—below me. I was on the face of the rock and the buzzards weren't looking at me, they were looking down—and I was looking down on them. I was tied in, safe, but I wasn't in a hurry to go anywhere. It was one of the most glorious sights I'd ever encountered.

Climbing the rock made the pressure stronger. I hadn't answered any of my questions—why the rock was calling to me, what the pressure was. But coming down I found it hadn't gone away. But it was more pleasant now—something I could live with. Something I wanted to live with.

Sunday

There was one thing about Doug—he's good at his job. Okay, there's only one thing good about Doug—but that's why I keep him around. Maybe I was an idiot to think just because we're partners we have to be friends. But I feel sorta sorry for the guy. He's almost as old as me and hasn't got a pot to piss in. Never been married, no kids, rents his condo. He's got the Miata. And a lot of clothes.

Okay, so my life hadn't been going so well lately either. But did I want Doug's? No. Whose life did I want? My father's? Definitely not. Although sometimes lately it felt like I was married to my mother. Don't get me wrong, E.J.'s a hell of a woman. Always has been.

I can still remember the first time I saw her, flat on her butt on the stairs of the chem building at U.T. 1972. Wild red hair, freckles big as dimes, and blue eyes a guy could drown in. Tall and skinny. Not so skinny now. Little bit of gray in the red, freckles beginning to fade.

But you could still drown in those blue eyes.

I guess the difference is that back then she was crazy about me. I could do no wrong.

Now I'm an afterthought.

With E.J. it's always the kids first. Always. I love my kids. And I'm not jealous of them. Not much, anyway. And I guess a parent should always think of the children first, but the difference between us is I can see a time when the kids will be gone. I don't think E.J. can see that. Sometimes I feel that if I just kept sending my paycheck home, E.J. wouldn't know I wasn't there.

Okay, so a little self-pity never hurt anybody. But I'm turning forty next week, and I guess it's time to do a little reflection on my life. Where I've come from, how I'm doing, where I'm going. I've got a wife who ignores me, a son who thinks of me only as Mr. Deep Pockets, one little girl who adores me, and another who isn't exactly sure who I am and how I fit into her life.

I'm glad we took Bessie. It was the only answer to a terrible situation. But we're not close. She doesn't see me as her father, the way she sees E.J. as her mother. Sometimes I feel ill at ease around her, wondering if she's comparing me in her little head to Roy, her real father. I'd come up lacking if that were the case. He was a hell of a guy.

Maybe that's what pisses me off so much about Doug. He's not Roy.

What else did I have in my life? My business. They say it takes five years for a small business to get off the ground. I'm on my sixth year. Any time now, God, any time. I'm tired of worrying—about money, about Bessie, about whether or not Graham's totally normal. And I'm tired of worrying that my wife thinks I'm less of a man than I used to be.

She didn't say anything about that night—that night that nothing happened. But she hasn't initiated sex since. She's not very aggressive in that department, but she's had her moments. Just none of them have come up lately.

There's less money now that Doug's a partner. I'd known that would happen, but I expected more business to come our way. That part hasn't happened. Maybe the Branson account in San Antonio would come through. If Doug didn't bid it too high.

Of course, if he bids it too low then there's no profit. Profit means the mortgage, the kids' college funds, food on the table, new shoes on slightly larger feet.

Sometimes I'm not sure if we're gonna make it. E.J.'s books help some, but not much. If she could write six books a year, we'd be okay. But she can't. Says she can't. Maybe if we put the kids in day care—then the day-care costs would just eat up whatever extra she was able to produce with the extra time.

I got all the camping gear loaded into the trunk of the Ghia, secured the campsite, and started to take off, then realized I still had my magic boots on. I found some old running shoes on the floor of the backseat, traded them for the boots, and put the boots on the floor where I'd found the running shoes.

The pressure was still there. It had taken longer this trip

for it to come—but it did. I knew it would be gone a mile away from the rock. I drove out of the park, feeling the rock's presence slowly recede. I missed it. The pressure was like an announcement to me that I was still alive. Still kicking.

I drove through Fredericksburg and headed toward Johnson City. The Ghia didn't have a/c, so I had the windows rolled down. I wondered how many hairs the wind was blowing off my head.

Doug would make the bid in the morning. He was good with people—E.J. called him personable, when she wasn't calling him names. He was a charmer. He'd get the contract. I just hoped I could live with the bid. We'd come up with a ballpark figure together, but the actual bid would be Doug's decision—after he'd felt out the territory, schmoozed the clients, saw which way the wind was blowing.

Next weekend—had to go to Mama's and clean the gutters. Better tell E.J. about that fast before she decides I've ruined her weekend. But she and Mama seem to be getting along better now. It had been pretty rough when we first moved here from Houston, but I gotta say, I'm not sure E.J. ever really gave my mother a chance.

Losing the Lesters, Bessie's birth parents, changed E.J. in a lot of ways—a few of them good. I think losing Terry Lester made her turn to my mother. That was good. But she's not as funny as she was. Not as carefree. Guess I'm not either, come to think of it.

Sometimes I wish Luna hadn't moved next door. I mean, don't get me wrong, I like her. She's a neat lady. Sexy. But it's those boys—especially Eduardo. I can take Luis—he's a lot like Graham. But Eduardo's . . . slick. I mean, he's an okay kid, but—do they really have to eat with us every night of the goddamn week? What kind of mother is Luna that she's never home? Maybe I'm getting conservative in my old age, but . . .

The car started acting funny. The engine was coughing. I pulled over to the side of the road.

In the middle of nowhere. Maybe a quarter of a mile from the Johnson City junction, but Johnson City was, like, ten miles back. Dripping Springs was twenty miles ahead. I pulled over on the shoulder and turned the car off.

I got out and went to the back, lifting the hood to take a look. I smelled gas. Getting down on my hands and knees, I stuck my head under the car. Gas was leaking from the fuel pump.

Again. Chronic VW problem. The one thing I knew after having driven this car for the past fifteen years was that driving it now meant catching fire. Since I'd done that twice before, I opted not to try it again.

Especially since the fire extinguisher I usually carried in the Ghia had been used over the Fourth of July when Graham had started a grass fire in the front yard. And I, of course, had forgotten to replace it.

A car passed me going toward Dripping Springs. I waved, they waved and kept going. I kept the hood up. Then, thinking a lot of people would think that was the trunk, I went and opened the trunk, too. The Ghia sat there on the side of the road looking for all the world like a bug in flight. But still no one stopped.

I must have been standing there, leaning against the car, for twenty minutes before someone finally pulled up behind me.

Eight

It was a truck, a big one—and a noisy one. I walked up to the driver's side, wondering what all the commotion was coming from it. Once at the driver's door, I could see the load in back—cages and cages of very pissed-off turkeys.

"Hey, son, you got some trouble?" the driver asked.

"Yeah, my car broke down. You headed for Dripping Springs?" I asked.

"Headed for Houston, truth be known. How far you need to go?"

"If you can get me to LaGrange, I can get my wife to pick me up there. We live in Codderville."

"Ah, hell, I know that town. You know an old boy name a Bill Hooper? Mechanic?"

I grinned. "Yeah. He's the reason I'm stuck out here. He supposedly put a new fuel pump in the Ghia less than a month ago. Hard to tell by the way it's leaking gas everywhere."

"Ha! Well, hop on in."

"Okay if I get my gear out of the trunk? The lock's not good, and I'd lose it if I left it. The tent's borrowed."

"Sure," the trucker said, climbing down out of the cab. "You been camping out on the rock, betja."

"You'd be betting right."

The trucker grabbed the camping gear out of the Ghia's trunk and stowed it in the large space behind the cab before I had a chance to even help. I started to climb up to the passenger side of the truck but stopped in my tracks when I heard a low, deadly sounding growl. I looked up into the anything-but-benign face of a black-and-brown rottweiler. I took my foot gingerly off the running board and stepped back onto the shoulder of the road.

"Hush now, Dumplin'," the trucker said. He leaned over from his seat to call to me out the passenger-side door. "She won't hurt you none—less I tell her to." He laughed and spit a wad of tobacco in a brown-stained cup on the dashboard of the cab. "Give her your hand."

I wondered if he meant that literally. I slowly held my hand toward the massive female. She sniffed it, looked up at me, and smiled, her tongue lolling out of the side of her mouth.

"See now? What I tell you?" the trucker said. "Hop on in, son. Gotta hit the road."

I climbed in. Dumplin' was in the space behind the seats, on a mattress I imagined the trucker used for long hauls. She sat upright, her chin resting on the trucker's shoulder, looking out the window ahead of her.

He put the truck in gear and we slowly inched our way back onto the highway. "Beautiful animal," I said.

"Yeah, she's a beaut. Thought about showing her, but seems kinda sissified, know what I mean?"

I grunted in response. "Hope you won't get in trouble taking on a passenger," I said.

"Naw. I own my own rig. Nobody to get me in trouble but my own self." He stuck out his right hand. "Tater Bascomb's the name."

I shook. "Willis Pugh. Really appreciate this, Tater."

"Ah, hell, I been stuck on side the road many a day in my time. I figured you looked safe enough."

"My mama's always said I have an honest face."

He was a small man—a cocky, bantam-rooster type; bow-legged in cowboy boots and faded blue jeans, wearing a country music station T-shirt and a feed-store gimme cap. I would put him in his fifties, maybe older, but the lines in the face may have had more to do with the sunburnt skin than age. I had a feeling that standing next to each other, Dumplin' may have had the height. She certainly had the weight.

"So what you do in Codderville?" he asked.

"I'm an engineer. Got my own consulting firm."

"No shit? Well, that's real nice. Engineering's a real honest trade. Just glad you ain't a lawyer. Wouldn't wanna be picking up no lawyer." He laughed.

"Where'd you get a name like Tater?" I asked.

He laughed again. The man was an easy laugh. You had to like that in just about anybody. "Christian name's Henry, but when I was just a little fella, my mama caught me out in the garden digging up potatoes and just eatin' 'em. Started calling me Tater right then. When she was feeling kindly toward me, she used to call me her Sweet Potato Pie."

I laughed. "That's nice," I said. "Those your turkeys?"

"Naw. Just haulin' 'em. You know Scoggins Truck, east of the rock, going toward Llano?" he asked.

I shook my head.

"Big ol' place. Got a turkey farm in the back. I been hauling Scoggins' turkeys for twenty years—when I ain't got nothing better to do."

"So you basically rent out the truck?"

"Well, wouldn't call it that. I got the cab here, and I'll

haul just about anything legal anybody's got needs hauling. Though, if I had my druthers, wouldn't never be turkeys."

"They make an awful racket," I agreed.

"Stupidest animals God ever made," Tater said. "You watch 'em sometime in a rain storm. Dumb sons'll just stand there staring straight up and drown."

I laughed. "Ah, come on—"

"God's truth. You don't get 'em inside quicklike, you gonna loose least half your flock. Stupidest animals God ever made. But the turkey bidness been going up steady since all this low-fat crap," Tater said. "Beats the hell out of me why somebody wanna eat turkey when they could get a chicken-fried steak, know what I mean?"

I agreed in spirit if not in actuality.

There was a squeak from the CB radio on Tater's dash. Dumplin's head came off his shoulder, and she cocked her head at the CB. Tater picked up the mike. I could hear a female voice saying, "Tater! Come back!"

"Well, shit," Tater said to me. "She knows better than that. Supposed to use my handle when she's on the radio." Into the mike he said, "Hey, Bouncin' Bundle, you got me, come back."

"Tater, help me! Oh, God, Tater, he's gonna kill me for sure!"

"Rogene!" Tater yelled. "Rogene, come back!"

There was no response from the CB. "Well, goddamn and shit fire, pardon my French." He pulled the big rig over to the side of the road. "Son, I gotta go back to Scoggins. I'm really sorry, but there's nothing I can do."

He began making a wide U-turn on the two-lane highway, down-shifting, reversing, working that truck like the pro that he was. "Well, look," I said, "maybe you can just let me off—"

"Just sit tight, son. Gotta take care a some bidness, then I'll take you right to your door in Codderville. Just hold tight."

I held tight.

Tater got the rig up to about eighty as we passed out of Johnson City, heading back toward the rock.

"Son-of-a-bitch," Tater mumbled under his breath. Dumplin' whined her agreement from the back of the cab.

"Anything I can do to help?" I asked.

Tater looked at me, sizing me up. "You're a big ol' boy. Might could use you if it comes to that."

"What's going on?" I asked.

Tater sighed. "Rogene Scoggins. Well, Rogene Hardy now. That was her on the CB. Married Calvin Hardy twenty years ago, stupidest dumb thing the girl ever did."

"Is that who she said was—"

"Killing her. Yeah. But he don't never kill her. Just beats her up. Sometimes bad, sometimes not so bad."

"Why—"

"Doesn't she leave his sorry ass?" Tater shook his head. "Now ain't that the $64,000 question?"

I really knew better than to ask that question. E.J. had worked off and on with battered women since moving to Codderville, and she gave me all the psychological reasons why women didn't leave in situations like that. But I guess that's something my testosterone level won't let me fully grasp.

When something's wrong, you do something about it. But E.J. always said that's just the male in me—the fixer. Another thing we argue about constantly. She'll tell me something's wrong, I'll try to fix it, and she says, no, I just wanted you to listen! Why? Why tell me if I can't *do* something about it?

"Known that girl since we was kids," Tater said. "I go off to Vietnam, come back, she's married to that no good Calvin Hardy! But I gotta tell you, ol' Calvin was just a fine little ass-kisser as long as Old Man Scoggins was alive. But I swear to you, on the very day Rogene buried her daddy, that son started in on her! And truth be known, that whole thing's Rogene's—the truck stop and the turkey farm! Her daddy left ever bit of it to her! Not like she needs that ol' son for the money! But she's got six young'uns. Sometimes women feel young'uns need a daddy, even if he is a rotten, no good son of a son!"

"Well, I certainly have no answers when it comes to women," I admitted.

"You got a good marriage?" Tater asked me.

I had to think about it. "Okay," I said. "Could be better."

"Name me one that couldn't."

"You married?" I asked.

"Naw. Had me a wedding in 'Nam with this little girl over there, but it wasn't sanctioned by the army. She thought she was pregnant, then it turned out she weren't, so it was no big deal."

"Well, anything I can do to help you with Rogene—"

"Calvin's a mite bigger'n me," Tater said. "I done pulled him off Rogene a time or two, but when he's really worked up it'll take two."

"No problem," I said.

We'd make it to Scoggins Truck Stop by a little after four. I figured I could call E.J. from there. She wouldn't start worrying until after five.

We passed Enchanted Rock and kept on going. I hadn't been this way before. It was much the same as what had come before Enchanted Rock. I found myself turning around in the seat, staring through the back window of the cab, past the turkeys, to get a look at the rock. It had been little more than an hour or two since I'd left it, but just seeing it again gave me a feeling of homecoming.

Tater finally pulled the eighteen-wheeler up to what was nothing more than a wide spot in the road. A dilapidated two-story building stood in the center of a black-topped parking area. Attached to either side of the paint-peeling structure were pre-fab steel buildings.

Tater pulled the big rig through the parking area of Scoggins Truck, dodging a couple of eighteen-wheelers and several smaller trucks, around to the back of the truck stop, pulling up in front of a double-wide trailer. I followed him as he bailed out, running to the front door of the trailer, Dumplin' hot on his heels.

The door was unlocked and we hit it running, stopping as we got inside the big living area of the double-wide. A woman lay on the floor, bloodied and seemingly unconscious. Tater ran to her.

"Rogene, honey!" Tater said, slapping lightly at her face. "Rogene, baby, talk to Tater!"

"Oh, oh," came from the woman's lips. Tater lifted her head.

"Get her some water," he said to me.

There was a wet bar by Rogene's head, glasses in a rack above it. I filled one from the wet bar's tap and handed it to Tater. He had Rogene's head in his lap, and lifted her face to the water.

I squatted down next to them, surveying her damage. Her eyes were swollen with that look they get an hour or so before they begin to turn black. Her lip was cut, and most of the blood appeared to come from that and a tear at her right ear. Her clothes were torn and bloodied, and there was a good-sized bump on her head.

She began to moan as she came to. Squinting at Tater, she said, "He still here?"

"He's gone, baby," Tater said, holding her to him. "Jut hush, now."

"I thought he was gonna kill me for sure this time," Rogene whispered, then moaned again.

"Go in the kitchen and get some ice we can put on this lip, okay, son?" Tater said to me.

The kitchen was an island within the large living area, with waist-high countertops. I went to the opening of the kitchen and stopped short. A leg was sticking out from around one of the counters. I stepped over the leg and got the full view of the body on the floor. A large kitchen knife protruded from the man's chest and blood was congealing on the floor under and around him.

E.J. and I have always had a clear delineation of duties in our married life: I mow the lawn, work on the cars, clean the gutters, and wash dishes; she cooks, vacuums, and finds the dead bodies.

That the man on the floor was dead was easy for me to determine, even without prior experience. I just had no idea what to do from here. Except maybe scream.

"Tater," I said, keeping my eye on the body before me, "can you come here a minute?"

"Son, I'm a little busy here—"

"Yes, sir, I'm aware of that. But I think you should come here."

I heard him cussing me softly under his breath, then heard him say to Rogene, "Honey, now you just lie here on this pillow, okay? Let me go see what that boy needs."

Tater came in the kitchen, his slight intake of breath my only indication that he saw the body lying before us both. "Well, damnation," he finally said.

"Who is it?" I asked, my voice quiet.

Before Tater could answer, Rogene screamed. She had gotten up and come into the kitchen. Her body fell against Tater's. "Oh, Lord Jesus, it's Calvin!"

"What happened?" I asked.

Rogene grabbed Tater's arm. "Tater, what's wrong with Calvin?"

"You do that, girl?" he asked.

"Oh, my Lord, is he dead?" she breathed, still clutching at Tater's arm. "Lordy, Tater, last thing I 'member he was hitting me and I was running for the door! I didn't do this thing, Tater, you gotta believe me!"

I saw a phone sitting on a table next to the sofa. I walked toward it. "We better call the law," I said.

As I picked up the receiver, I heard a growl at waist level. Looking down, I saw Dumplin' standing, legs spread, leaning slightly toward me, her fangs showing.

Tater was beside her, his right arm rigid as he gave the dog silent signals. "Now, son," Tater said. "We ain't calling nobody till we figure out what's going on. Put the phone down, boy."

I turned around, the receiver still in my hand. Tater's hand moved slightly and Dumplin's demeanor changed. Foam began to form at the sides of her mouth, her canines grew in length, and she took a small step toward me. I put the phone slowly, carefully back in its cradle.

Nine

"**These ropes are** too tight," I said, pulling at my hands where they were bound in front of me on one of Rogene's kitchen chairs. My legs were tied, one each, to the rungs of the chair.

"Where are the young'uns?" Tater asked Rogene, ignoring me.

"Little ones are all over to Mama's, but Bubba'll be coming off shift in less than an hour. Tater! What are we gonna do?"

"We gonna find out who done this to Calvin." He took Rogene's face in his hands, looking her square in the eye. "Now, tell me, girl. You do this?"

"No!"

Tater smiled. "Okay. I always could tell when you was lying."

"Tater, I ain't—"

"Girl, I know that."

Rogene looked at me. "What are we gonna do with him?"

"First things first. I gotta go take care of Bubba. Make sure he ain't gonna come in here."

Rogene grabbed Tater's arm as he went toward the door. "You ain't gonna hurt him?"

Tater shrugged her hand off and glared at her. "Who you talking at, girl? I ain't Calvin Hardy, ya know. This is Tater. I never touched that boy in his life, and you know it."

"What're you gonna do?"

"Bubba's always wanted to drive my rig. 'Bout time I let him. Somebody's gotta get them damned turkeys to Houston—and it ain't gonna be me, under the circumstances."

Tater left, leaving me alone with Rogene. She was on the downhill side of fifty, platinum blond hair with two-inch grayish brown roots, ratted and done up like a sixties country-girl singer. She was medium height, maybe five-five or five-six, with the glimmer of a formerly nice body still showing. Her legs, what I could see from the knee-length shorts she was wearing, looked good from the knees down. The thighs had thickened with age and lack of exercise, the breasts appeared to sag, and the stomach was distended. Varicose veins were prominent on the still-shapely calves.

"Excuse me, ma'am," I said, smiling like my mama taught me. "But these ropes are a little tight."

"Oh, hush up, you!" She turned to face me. "Who are you, anyway?"

"Just a hapless motorist drawn into your web of murder and—"

"You talk weird, you know that?"

"Just a joke. These ropes?"

Rogene sat down on the sofa, chewing on a fingernail, a worried look on her face. "You gonna have to take that up with Tater. Oh, Lord," she said, glancing toward the kitchen where Calvin's dead body still lay. "I gotta cover him up. Only seems proper."

"Good idea," I said.

She ignored me as she went down the hall of the double-wide. I took that opportunity to work on the ropes binding my hands. If I had those free, then I could work on the ones binding my feet.

There wasn't much play. Tater Bascomb certainly knew what he was doing when it came to tying up hostages. And then there was the added pressure that every time I moved slightly, testing the ropes, Dumplin', on guard three feet away, would show me her teeth. I thought, stupidly, if I could just get her on the side of goodness and righteousness, I could use those incisors on the ropes.

All I needed to do was get to the phone. If I could call E.J., even if I didn't get away or have much time to tell her where I was, we had caller ID on the phone. If E.J. remembered it. If E.J. noticed I was gone. I stole a look at my watch. Five-thirty.

She wouldn't be worried yet.

Rogene came back in the room carrying a bedsheet. She went in the kitchen and gently covered her husband's dead body. "He was a real asshole," she said, her voice sounding like a eulogy. "But he was a good man.'

I wondered where that came from, but let it pass. Instead, I said, "Who's Bubba?"

Rogene looked at me like she'd forgotten I was there. "Oh. My oldest. Calvin, Jr., but we always called him Bubba. He's nineteen, working at the truck stop."

"Look, ma'am, if I could just call my wife—you know how it is, she's gonna be real worried. If you could just let me call her and tell her I'm running late—"

The door opened and Tater came in. "Hush up," he said to me. "You ain't calling nobody."

"Tater, look," I said, trying to be reasonable. "My wife's really going to be worried. She'll call the law if I'm not home in about twenty minutes!"

''Well, fine, but they won't come looking for you till you been gone forty-eight. That's the law, or don't you watch TV?''

''Tater,'' Rogene whined, ''what we gonna do with him?'' She was pointing at Calvin now, not me. Which was just as well. I'd rather Tater didn't dwell too long on what he was going to do with me.

''Well, you covered him up. That's good. Way I figure it, we wait till everthing's quiet-like late tonight, then we'll figure out what to do with him.'' Tater rubbed his hands together. ''Now, Rogene, Bubba's getting ready to take my rig on to Houston. He wanted to come back here and get him some clothes, but I tol' him you'd bring 'em to him. You also gotta get some clothes for the little ones and take 'em to your mama's. Tell her the kids gotta stay there a day or two. She gets one look at your face, she'll figure the reason why.''

Rogene just stood there, chewing at her cuticle. ''Now, Rogene,'' Tater said. ''Get cracking. And don't say nothing to nobody, girl, you got that?''

Rogene nodded her head vaguely and went down the hall to pack up clothes for her children. I looked at Tater. ''My hands are numb.''

''Count your blessings, son. You're alive.''

''Tater, just let me call my wife—''

''Son, I ain't stupid. You call her and you two got some secret code worked out, you could tell her things I'd have no way of knowing. Uh-uh,'' he said, shaking his head. ''You just sit tight.''

''What do you expect to accomplish with this, Tater? If you call the law—''

''The only law around here is Delbert McKay, and he's stupider than a truckload of turkeys. And 'sides that, he's lazy. He'll take one look at Calvin, and knowing the history of them two, he'll arrest Rogene quicker 'n you can spit cotton.''

''So what county is this? Call the county sheriff and—''

"Worse. At least Delbert knows Rogene. Them boys from the county take a look at how many times the locals got called in on domestic abuse, they'd put Rogene away in a New York minute."

"So what's your plan?"

"Gonna find out who done this. That's my plan. Gonna find me the guilty party."

"Well," I said, leaning my head over to scratch my cheek on the rough rope that bound my hands. "I know a little something about that kind of thing."

Monday

A couple of months ago, E.J. and I had been at the grocery story and something had happened that I knew, I mean *knew,* was wrong. I knew how I was supposed to react to what we'd seen. E.J. was livid. As a card-carrying Liberal, an enlightened and liberated man, I *knew* I was supposed to be livid, too.

A man and woman had walked out of the grocery store, the woman pushing the basket full of groceries, a baby in the carrier seat of the basket, a little girl about two riding, holding onto the front of the basket, and two boys about four and five, walking with her, holding on to the sides of the basket.

The man got in the driver's side of a brand-new Bronco and sat down.

The woman opened the back door and let the three older children crawl in the car and helped them with their seat belts. She took the baby out of the basket and strapped it into the baby seat in the car. Then she went to the back of the Bronco, opened the tailgate, and proceeded to load the seventeen bags of groceries.

Meanwhile, the man, sitting in the driver's seat, lit a cigarette and stared out the window.

I *knew* this was wrong. In every corpuscle of my being

I *knew* this was wrong. But I thought, maybe he's got a bad back, a heart condition, some *reason* why we'd seen what we'd seen. But in my heart I didn't think so.

There had been something about his attitude, his demeanor, that had screamed, "I pay for it. You deal with it."

The days following, I couldn't get it out of my mind. Although I *knew* this was wrong, there was something about it I found satisfying. This guy was indisputably the king of his castle. He said jump and everybody asked how high. His wife probably had an allowance. He probably was in total charge of the checkbook.

He never had to ask if it was okay if he went out to lunch.

He never had to check if it was okay if he bought new clothes.

But sitting in the living room of Rogene Scoggins Hardy's double-wide trailer, my wrists and ankles tied to a straight-back kitchen chair, seeing the clock wend its way to midnight, I began to see what that guy at the grocery store was missing.

There were pluses to being a unit, a team, rather than a patriarchy. How involved was this guy in the lives of his children? Was the woman who loaded those groceries so docilely his partner, someone he could stay up late at night with arguing politics?

In the same circumstances would he have the same worries I had? Like, would E.J. remember that tomorrow, or later today actually, Graham had soccer practice? Would she call Martin and let him know I wouldn't be there in my job as assistant coach?

Would Megan remember to brush her teeth without that being the last thing I said to her every night? Right before "I love you"?

Would E.J. remember to turn on the alarm system, and check all the windows before she went to bed?

Who'd take the trash out if I wasn't home by Wednesday? Would E.J. remember—or even know—that the extra can was full of leaves and needed to be set out, too?

Could Bessie handle losing two daddies?

I was having those wee-hours thoughts, the kind that had been coming to me so regularly lately. All those questions I'd been asking myself about my life had been answered by Tater Bascomb and his sweet dog Dumplin'.

I *had* accomplished something with my life. I had a beautiful, loving, sometimes maddening, wife—who, when all was said and done, at least has never bored me; three pretty sensational kids; a house I liked; a business I wanted and hoped would grow and expand; and a mother who cared about me and, at sixty-two, was still pretty damn spunky.

Okay, the cats I could have done without, but everyone has their crosses to bear.

I wanted my life. I liked my life. I wanted to kiss my kids and watch E.J. undress in the bathroom, thinking I couldn't see her in the mirror. I wanted to sit with her and watch TV, knowing the kids were asleep upstairs and we could say anything to each other we wanted. I wanted to clean the garage.

But most of all, at that moment, I wanted to feel my hands.

Just feel them. That was something I hadn't been able to do in a couple of hours. The door to the double-wide opened and Tater came in. He walked up to me and took a Swiss Army knife out of his pocket. I cringed. He took my hands and used the knife to loosen the knots on the ropes that bound my wrists.

I pulled my hands to my lap, using my knees to rub the circulation back into them. I couldn't use my hands to rub each other; there wasn't enough circulation left for that.

"Untie your feet," Tater said.

I shook my head. "I couldn't scratch my nose right now."

"Oh, for God's sake." Tater knelt down in front of me and untied my ankles. Taking my hands in his he began to rub them. "You okay?" he asked.

"No."

"Hell, son, you wouldn'ta made it a week in 'Nam."

"My feelings exactly," I said. "Are you letting me go?"

Tater sighed. "No, boy, when you gonna understand that just ain't gonna happen? Not until we got whoever done in ol' Calvin hog-tied with a bow for Delbert McKay. Only way Delbert'd know which one was the bad guy."

"Any ideas on a suspect?" I asked.

"Shit if I know. Nobody much liked Calvin, so the list is pert near longer 'n my pecker—and, son, that's long."

I rubbed my feet with my semi-useful hands and tentatively stood up, stretching my legs and back. "So why did you untie me?" I asked.

"We gotta do something with Calvin," Tater answered. "The place has quieted down some, so I figure now's the time to do it."

"What are you going to do?" I asked.

"We, son, we. What are *we* gonna do."

"Okay. We."

"We're gonna haul Calvin's fat ass over to the truck-stop kitchen and put him in one of the deep freezers."

"And in the morning the cook will open the freezer—"

"Not if we put a sign on it saying it's out of order and"—he pulled a hasp and lock out of his back pocket—"we close it with this."

I nodded my head. "Sounds like a plan to me."

"Don't it, though?" Tater walked over to Calvin's body, surveying it. "Well, you grab his head and I'll take his feet—"

"I don't want the head. I want the feet."

"Well, now, boy," Tater said, his right arm beginning to go rigid as Dumplin' came to attention, "don't think you got much say in this."

I grabbed the head, and Tater's right arm and his dog both relaxed. Tater grabbed the feet and we hauled Calvin Hardy's lifeless body off the floor.

Personally, I thought Tater's plan was stupid. I thought the whole situation was stupid. But going along with it meant getting outside the double-wide, and once outside . . .

"And by the by, boy," Tater said, his voice strained from the weight of the bedsheet-shrouded body, "don't you go thinking you can drop ol' Calvin and run off. I told myself when I left 'Nam I wouldn't never take another life, and I won't, boy, I can promise you that. But I can't be responsible for what Dumplin's liable to do. She's got a stay command on you, son, and that means you don't move less I want you to, unnerstand? And the thing is, she probably wouldn't kill ya, but you'd be bleeding something awful and we couldn't call in no doctor, and then you could bleed to death or, at the very least, get gangrene and have to lose some vital organ or limb. We don't want that, now do we, boy?"

"No, sir," I said, "we surely don't."

So Tater wasn't the only one with stupid plans.

It was maybe one hundred yards from the front door of the double-wide to the back door of the truck stop. From the position of the trailer, I could see some of the blacktopped parking lot in front. There was still one eighteen-wheeler left and a couple of smaller trucks.

"Jesus, Tater," I said, "the place is a zoo."

"Naw, them truckers are asleep in the dorms. Nobody in the diner last I looked. Nobody in the kitchen 'cept Rogene."

As if she'd heard her name called, which she couldn't have since Tater and I had been whispering, Rogene opened the back door to the kitchen.

"Y'all hurry up," she whispered loudly.

We moved as quickly as possible with our heavy burden to the kitchen door. The lid was open on one of the large chest-style deep freezers standing against one wall of the truck-stop kitchen. Tater and I moved directly to that, depositing Calvin Hardy's body into its emptied-out depths. Tater shut the lid and attached the padlock, and Rogene taped a handmade sign saying OUT OF ORDER to the front.

The three of us stood back and looked at each other. "Well, that's done," Tater said, stating the obvious.

"Now what?" Rogene asked.

"Now nothing. Anybody asks you where Calvin is, you say you don't know. It ain't like he never took off on a bender before."

"Excuse me," I said. Both turned and looked at me, neither entirely happy with my presence. "But I haven't eaten since a granola bar yesterday morning . . ."

Tater nodded his head. "Boy's hungry, Rogene. Fix him up something. Come on, son," he said to me, taking me through the kitchen door and into the dining room of the truck stop, Dumplin' dogging our steps.

"Dogs aren't supposed to be in food areas," I said.

"*You* throw her out," Tater suggested.

I let it pass. "I could also use a piss," I ventured.

Tater sighed. "Well, come on then." He led me out of the dining area, past several rows of groceries and sundries, down a hall where we passed a door marked TV ROOM, another door marked SHOWERS, and finally to the public bathroom.

"You be quiet," Tater said. "We got truckers down the hall here asleep in the dorms. You wake 'em up, and Dumplin's not gonna like it."

I did my business and Tater marched me quietly back to the diner.

"What's on the other side?" I asked, pointing to another hallway that led in the opposite direction, from which I could hear muted country-western music.

"That's the titty bar," Tater answered. "Maybe got one or two truckers still in there drinking beer. But they wouldn't notice if we dropped ol' Calvin in their laps."

"You actually have a stripper in there?" I asked.

"You bet. Friday and Saturday nights. Brings them truckers in big-time. 'Though I gotta say, the last lady Calvin hired's getting a little long in the tooth. Forty if she's a day. Good titties though."

We went and sat down at a table for four, where Rogene had set out a full turkey dinner—turkey, dressing, giblet gravy, green beans, and cornbread. I must admit, I didn't think once about my cholesterol count or the spare tire around my belly. I ate it all.

The music stopped from the other room and a man came in, nodded at Tater, and opened the door to the kitchen, calling out, "I'm outta here, Rogene. It's after two."

"Bye, Purvis," I heard Rogene say. "See ya tomorrow."

"Tell Calvin we're low on Bud Light and totally out of Seagrams, okay?"

"Uh-huh," came from Rogene.

"Night, Tater," Purvis said, walking toward the front door.

"Night, Purvis."

After the door closed behind him, I asked, "The bartender?"

"Yeah."

"How'd he feel about Calvin?"

Tater shrugged. " 'Bout like everybody else, I reckon. Calvin was a real easy man to hate."

"Any real grudge against him?"

Tater thought for a moment. "Well, now, couple ten years ago, Purvis had him his own bar between the rock and Fredericksburg. Calvin bought up the paper on the loan and called it in. Then he had the place bulldozed." Tater sighed. "Like I told you, Calvin was a real piece of work."

"Why'd he do that?" I asked.

" 'Cause he could," Tater answered.

"And Purvis came to work for Calvin after he'd done that?"

"Calvin offered him a job and Purvis has kids to feed. You bet he took the job." Tater laughed. "Once a month or so, though, ol' Purvis'll put ipecac in Calvin's beer. He thinks he got a ulcer cause he gets sick so regular." Tater laughed again then stopped. "Well, he thought that, anyway. Guess ol' Calvin ain't thinking much of anything now."

"Who else works here?" I asked.

"Well, Rogene works nearly round the clock, poor girl. But Bubba takes it some during the day—that's her oldest boy."

I nodded my head.

"Then there's Ray Maladondo, he does the cooking during the day, from five in the morning till around six at night. Starts the dinner, then Rogene finishes it up. His daughter, Trudy, waits tables noon through dinnertime. Claudia's the barmaid, works seven days a week, five till two A.M. Then there's Salome, she's the dancer, like I told you. Only works on Fridays and Saturdays."

"And this place is open twenty-four hours a day?"

"Seven days a week, including Christmas. Truckers always need a place to flop and they work ever' day of the year. Believe you me."

The front door opened and a man came in, hitting his dusty jeans with his gimme cap, hair pressed down, giving him hat-head. Bowlegged, tall and thin, he looked at Tater and said, "Well, kiss my butt, Bascomb. Thought you was in Houston."

"Got tired of them turkeys. Let Bubba take 'em for me."

"Oo-ee, boy, don't you let the smokeys know that. That boy ain't licensed for that rig of yours."

The man came and sat down at our table, sticking his hand out to me. "Al Grunwald," he said.

Before I could speak, Tater said, "This here's my

cousin Marvin, up from the valley. Say hidy to Al, Marvin.''

I said hidy to Al.

''Now you should let the boy speak for himself, Tater. More'n likely he don't wanna admit no kin to you!'' Al laughed at his own joke.

''Whatja hauling?'' Tater asked.

''Loaded down with rebar from San Antonio to Abilene.''

''Lord, man, stay away from the weight stations,'' Tater said.

''You telling me? Why you think I'm taking these back roads and coming through here two o'clock in the goddamn morning?''

Rogene stuck her head out of the kitchen. ''Hey, Al. Usual?''

''Sure thing, honey, long as you give me a great big ol' kiss to boot.''

''Al, I kiss you, you wouldn't be able to drive your rig for a week.''

''Oo, baby, I love it when you talk dirty!''

Rogene moved back into the kitchen and Al shot Tater a look. ''That son-of-a-bitch Calvin been at her again?'' he asked. Rogene's bruised face was hard not to see.

Tater looked down at his plate. ''Yeah,'' he said.

''Goddamn, don't know why she puts up with it,'' Al said. ''If I done that to my old lady once, she'd wait till I was asleep, roll me up in a bedsheet, and beat the living tar out of me. Leastwise, that's what she tells me.''

Tater looked up. ''It ain't Rogene's fault,'' he said.

''Hell,'' Al said, ''I ain't saying it is. Finer woman never walked the face of this earth.''

''Amen to that,'' Tater said.

Rogene brought out a plate for Al, the food identical to what I'd just finished. Al said, ''Girl, I've done died and gone to heaven. Give me a kiss to make my whole life complete!''

Rogene thumped Al on the ear with her finger.

"Ow!" he said, playfully ducking her. "I don't like it rough, honey!"

"You don't know rough less you mess with me, Al Grunwald. Now, eat and shut up."

Rogene went back into the kitchen.

"Um-um," Al said, "good food and a pretty ass to look at. God's in his Heaven, all's I can say."

I sat quietly while Al and Tater talked about people I didn't know and places I'd never been. Finally Al said, "So, Marvin, what you do for a living?"

I sat staring off into space. "Yo, Marvin," Tater said, jabbing me with his elbow. "Man's talking to you."

He made a face at Al that seemed to signify something to do with my mental capacity.

"I'm a brain surgeon," I said. "That's why I'm up here. Tater's going under the knife tomorrow. We're going to see if there's anything up there."

Al laughed and Tater scowled. "Well, Al," Tater said, "me and Marvin gotta be hitting the road. See you later."

"Back at ya," Al said, laying into a piece of cherry pie Rogene had just brought out.

Tater grabbed my arm and marched me into the kitchen and out the back door.

Ten

Tater pushed me into the living room of the double-wide and pointed at the kitchen chair, from which my bindings lay loosely on the ground.

I turned to face him. "No," I said. "Sic the dog on me. I'm not getting back in that chair. My back hurts, my legs hurt, my hands—"

"You are a real mama's boy, you know that?" Tater said.

"Mama's boy or not, it's three o'clock in the morning and I'd like to get some sleep. Preferably in a prone position."

Tater sighed. "Well, goddamn, you're a pain in the ass. Come on."

I followed him down the hall of the double-wide to one of three bedrooms on that side. This appeared to be the smaller room, only large enough for a single bed and a small dresser. The floor was heaped with dirty clothes, CDs, plates with crusted food, empty soda cans, and assorted unidentifiable debris.

"This is Bubba's room," Tater said. "You can sleep in here."

I looked at the sheets on the bed. I'm not generally a fastidious kinda guy, but even I had my limits.

"I'll take the straight back chair," I said.

Ignoring me, Tater went to the small, very small window of the room and peered, not through it, but at it. Coming back to me, he put his hands on either side of my shoulders, then, walking with his hands spaced at my shoulder breadth, went to the window, finding the spread of his hands to be much greater than the width of the window.

"You ain't getting through there," he said, mostly to himself.

He walked to the door and made hand signals to the dog. Dumplin' lay down across the door's threshold, effectively blocking my exit. "Now, she might doze," Tater said, "but she never sleeps on guard duty. You try stepping over her, and your wife might be looking for a better equipped man, if you get my drift."

His drift was mighty easy to get. I curled up on Bubba's bedspread and was asleep in two minutes flat.

I woke up sometime later when Rogene poked me repeatedly in the stomach with her finger. "What?" I finally said.

"You gonna get up or just lay there all day?"

"Why should I get up?"

"Beats me why, but Tater wants you in the living room."

I got up and went into the bathroom, escorted by my canine companion, did my business, and splashed cold water on my face. My watch said it was seven-thirty in the morning. An hour and a half before Doug would have his meeting with the Branson people. It seemed like an eternity since I'd watched him drive off from the campsite in the Miata. It hadn't even been a full day ago. I took some toothpaste and spread it on my index finger, using that to rub my teeth clean. E.J. would be up by now. And worried. If I'm going to be late for some reason, I call. That's polite. The kids would be worried. I had to find some way to call home—to let E.J. know what's going on.

''Hey, you fall in the commode?'' came Tater's voice from the other side of the bathroom door. Dumplin' whined and wagged her tail at the sound of her master's voice. ''Rogene, you check that bathroom window?''

I opened the door. ''Too small,'' I said, moving past Tater into the living room.

I sat down on a sofa, stretching my legs out in front of me. ''What's for breakfast?'' I asked.

''Well, don't he just make himself at home,'' Rogene said, sending me a glaring look.

''Rustle us up something to eat, Rogene honey, okay?'' Tater said, taking an armchair next to me, Dumplin' happily flopping at his feet.

''Well, all's I can say is I didn't take neither of you to raise,'' Rogene said as she slammed pots and pans in the kitchen.

''Okay, son, tell me what's on your mind.''

I yawned. ''About what?''

''You said yesterday you knew a little something about this here—''

''What here?''

Tater sighed, then leaned forward, whispering, ''About finding out who done in ol' Calvin!''

''Oh, that. Well, my wife and I've been involved in a few things like this.''

''Do tell,'' Tater said, sarcasm dripping.

''Not if you're gonna take that attitude,'' I said.

Tater leaned back in his easy chair. ''You know, I'm beginning to rethink that vow I took back in 'Nam. Some people just surely need killing, and you're beginning to strike me as one of them.''

''Did you or Rogene look to see if anything was taken from the trailer?''

Tater turned to Rogene. ''Rogene, you look to see if anything was taken?''

''When?'' she called back.

Tater sighed again. His trial was having to deal with the likes of Rogene Scoggins Hardy and yours truly. ''When you was out and Calvin got kilt!''

''Oh. Well, no, now, I didn't, but that would be a real interesting idea.'' Rogene walked in from the kitchen. ''You think it was a burglar?''

''Someone could have walked in and then taken advantage of the situation,'' I suggested.

Rogene looked around the living room. ''Well, TV's still here, and so's the VCR and CD player.'' She looked at her hands. ''Didn't take my wedding rings. Let me go check my jewelry box.'' She went down the hall opposite the one with the three bedrooms where I'd spent the night.

''Don't seem like a burglary-kinda killing,'' Tater said. ''What self-respecting burglar's gonna come in a house where a woman's screaming from being beat?''

''Got a point,'' I said.

Rogene came back from the master bedroom. ''Everthing's just fine in there,'' she said. ''Can't see where nobody took nothing.''

''Well, son,'' Tater said, squinting daggers at me. ''You're gonna have to do better than that.''

Rogene put breakfast on the table and Tater and I sat down, Dumplin' at Tater's feet. There were many reasons why I didn't want to spend much time where I was, and it was becoming very apparent that one more reason to add to the list was what my presence in the company of Rogene Scoggins Hardy was doing to my cholesterol level.

Laid out before us were fried eggs, ham, sausage, grits swimming in butter, and the prettiest biscuits I'd ever set eyes on. They melted in your mouth from all the fat contained within them. She completed the meal with a pot of dark roast coffee and mini-glasses of orange drink. (Not, God forbid, orange juice.)

Rogene sat down with us and we all dug in. I'm not about to say I didn't eat everything set in front of me. That would be a lie. It was the best breakfast I'd had in years.

"Okay, Rogene, tell me who all was in the truck stop when Calvin started in on you," I said.

"I really don't wanna talk about this," Rogene said, a pleading look to Tater.

"Honey, you gotta. You wanna find out who did this to Calvin so we can get his fat butt outta that freezer, right?"

"Well, yeah. It would be nice for the kids if we could bury him, I suppose."

" 'Course it would, honey. So you answer Willis's questions best you can, okay?"

Rogene nodded her head. She was still in her housecoat, a lovely thing in shades of hot pink and cobalt blue, and her hair was done up in pink spongy rollers. Her makeup, however, was already artfully applied, covering a lot of the bruising and cuts from yesterday's beating.

"Just tell me everything that happened preceding Calvin's . . . well, before he . . . well," I tried.

"Before he beat me? You can say it, honey. Calvin beat me."

"Okay, before Calvin beat you."

"Well, I was working the diner from about eight in the morning till Bubba came in about three. Him and Calvin were having words, and he hadda get out of the house. Bubba done took the little ones over to my mamma's, he said, 'cause his daddy was acting up. So I told Bubba to take the counter, and I went back to the house to see if I could calm Calvin down some." She stared off into space. "Sometimes I could. If I played it just right." She shook her head. "Didn't work this time, though. Usually don't."

"Who was in the truck stop when you came back here?" I asked.

"Well, now, let me think." She pouted her lips and tapped one long, blood-red nail against her lower lip. "Ray was in the kitchen. Bubba at the counter. Had a couple boys in for a late lunch." She looked at Tater. "Avrell and Cody?"

"Um-hum," he said.

"And by then Purvis woulda been getting ready to open up the bar. We open at four-thirty. I'm not sure if Claudia was there yet. She's been getting in later and later these days. Trudy woulda come in about four, I guess. I didn't see her 'fore I came back to the house."

"Who's Trudy?" I asked, getting confused with the cast of characters.

"Ray Maladondo's daughter," Tater said. "She waits tables noon through dinnertime."

"Okay," I said, pushing myself away from the table. "Which of these people is most likely to have killed Calvin?" Simple question, I thought.

Tater and Rogene looked at each other, their eyes big. Finally Rogene turned to me. "None of 'em," she said. "These people's either my kin or my friends, Mr. Smarty-Pants! I ain't about to accuse none of 'em!"

"Okay," I said. "That leaves you."

"Now, wait just a goddamn minute!" Tater said, coming up out of his chair. At her master's demeanor, Dumplin' rose, the hair on the back of her neck bristling and a low growl emitting from her throat. Both of them were looking at me.

I sat very still and spoke softly when I said, "Somebody did it, Tater. We've already eliminated any chance of a burglar having done it."

"Well, it had to be some serial killer wandering by," Rogene said. "He hears me screaming and comes in and just takes advantage of the situation."

"The steak knife in Calvin's heart," I said, watching Rogene wince, "where did it come from?"

Rogene shrugged. Tater said, "Out of the kitchen. It's one of a set."

"Okay," I said, looking at Rogene, "why would a serial killer come in, upon hearing you scream—a very chivalrous serial killer, I might add—and, having nothing on him for which to imbibe in his blood lust, run to your kitchen and borrow one of your steak knives?"

Rogene didn't answer. Her lower lip came out again and she turned her head away, not looking at me.

Tater sighed. "Rogene, honey, the boy's right. We gotta assume somebody Calvin knew done this to him. And most likely, if it was someone Calvin knew, it was somebody we knew. It probably had to be somebody who was around the truck stop when you came over here." He looked at me. "You could be a little nicer about this, son," he said. "She's had a rough time."

I laughed. "Yes, Tater, she's had a rough time. But might I mention, I'm the one being held hostage here?"

"Son, you do go on, don't ya?" Tater said, getting up from the kitchen table and heading into the living room.

Dumplin' made as if to follow Tater, but stopped next to my chair, watching him, a high whine coming from her throat. She longed to be with the one she loved, but duty came first. And duty appeared to be watching every move I made, ready to kill me if it became necessary.

But only if it was absolutely necessary.

Tater started to sit down but stopped, his head cocked as if listening. I heard it, too. The sound, which I'd been hearing off and on since arriving at Scoggins Truck Stop & Turkey Farm, of a large engine.

"Bubba's back," Tater said.

"How can you tell?" I asked.

Tater looked at me like I was a slightly challenged four-year-old. "I been driving that rig for over ten years, boy. I guess I know what the engine sounds like."

Rogene jumped up from the table and ran to Tater. "What're we gonna do with Bubba?"

Tater scratched his chin. "Well, now, we gonna have to let him in his own house. He's gonna wanna take a shower and all." Tater looked at me. "No reason to change our story, boy. You're my cousin Marvin from the Valley. You let on anything to Bubba and I'll sic Dumplin' on ya."

"Won't that make him suspicious?" I asked.

"Hell, son, even a dog can have discriminating taste," he said as he headed for the door.

Over his shoulder to Rogene, he said, "Make sure he don't go nowhere." Rogene nodded and Dumplin' wagged her tail.

Calvin Hardy, Jr., a/k/a Bubba, was nineteen years old, short, skinny, had a protruding Adam's apple, and bad skin. He was wearing skintight, boot-cut Levis over $200 scuffed and dirt-smeared Nocona boots, a faded black T-shirt from a Travis Tritt concert, and a gimme cap worn backward. He had a missing molar that only showed when he opened his mouth, which he seemed to do in order to breathe. The other teeth were jammed into too small a space, making them overlap and stick out in total abandon.

The two women in the room, Rogene and Dumplin', seemed to find his presence enthralling. Rogene hugged him to her bosom and Dumplin' put her legs on his scrawny chest, tongue lolling and tail wagging.

Tater introduced me as "Cousin Marvin from the Valley."

"No shit," Bubba said, and sniffed, wiping his nose on his bare arm. "Didn't know you had kin in the Valley."

"Just Marvin here."

"Well, hey-dee, Marvin," Bubba said, and stuck out his hand.

I shook, reminding myself I'd slept in this kid's bed only the night before. Made me shudder.

"How'd you do with the rig?" Tater asked.

Bubba did the sniff and wipe number again. "Piece a cake. That baby's a real hummer, Tater." Bubba looked around the double-wide. "Where's Daddy?"

"Don' rightly know, son. Took off yesterday afternoon, ain't seen him since," Tater said.

Bubba's shoulders relaxed and he sank down in a chair. "Where's the young'uns?" the boy asked.

"Over to your grandma's. Your mama said, as how me and Marvin, here could stay at the trailer, so there wasn't room with all the kids."

Bubba shook his head. "Daddy ain't gonna like that." He looked around the room again as if Daddy would walk back in at any moment to show his displeasure at the current sleeping arrangements. "No, Daddy ain't gonna like that a bit."

"Well, I'll deal with Calvin," Tater said.

Rogene sat silently on the couch, looking from one man to the other.

For a fleeting moment I wondered if Tater already had dealt with it, but remembered he'd been with me when Rogene had called to say Calvin was beating up on her.

Unless it had been a setup.

Unless I was Tater's alibi and Calvin had been dead for longer than I thought. No ME had seen him. I had no way of telling by looking if the body I'd seen had been dead for one hour or six.

Okay, I thought, this is good. Tater and Rogene conspire to kill Calvin. Tater knocks Rogene around to make it look good. Then he hops in the truck and takes off, looking for some unsuspecting hitchhiker to use as an alibi.

That's where my scenario fell flat. How did he know he'd find someone like me, standing beside the road with a dead car? There was no guarantee. Unless he'd originally planned on using his stops as an alibi.

Then why did he hide Calvin's body? It didn't make

any sense. If I was his alibi, why didn't they fix an alibi for Rogene while they were at it? Why hide the body?

I wished, for a split second, that E.J. was here. For all her tomfoolery with murder cases, her scenarios always rang truer than what I'd come up with so far. But wishing E.J. here was wishing her into possible danger. Did I want E.J. going through what I was going through? Would I trade places with her? For a second I began to wonder if maybe I was having the easier gig. What would it be like to be at home, wondering where she was?

Tater stood up. "Well, we'll let you get some sleep, Bubba. Me and Marvin'll go on over to the truck stop. See you later."

"Yeah, you guys, see you later. Nice meeting you, Marvin."

Tater elbowed me. "Huh?" I said.

"He said, 'Nice meeting you, Marvin.' " Tater glared at me.

"Oh, right." I slapped Bubba on the back. "Nice meeting you, too."

I followed Tater out the door.

Once outside, Tater whispered, "Marvin, okay? Ain't great but it's all I could come up with in a hurry, so you're stuck with it. Marvin. M-A-R-V-I-N, got it?"

"Why are we going to the truck stop?" I asked.

Tater shook his head and sighed. "You ain't real bright, are you, son? I cain't believe I'm putting all my eggs in a real rickety basket."

"All what eggs?" I asked and yawned. It had been a rough couple of days.

"You're supposed to be my investigator, boy, or did you forget that?" He grabbed my arm and pulled me along. "Goddamn and shit fire, I do believe you are the dumbest engineer I ever heard of."

I pulled my arm away from his grip. "Let me call my wife," I said.

He just looked at me, but this time I glared back. ''I'm not doing shit until you let me call my wife.''

Tater's face split into a grin. ''Well, seems like we're having what they call a Mexican standoff, boy. You don't find out who done this, then Calvin stays in the freezer. Long as Calvin stays in the freezer, your ass is mine. Long as your ass is mine, you ain't seeing or calling your wife. Any of this getting through to you, son?''

We stood there staring at each other for what seemed a very long time, Dumplin' between us, looking from one of us to the other. Her tail did not wag. Finally I turned and marched into the truck stop.

I sat down at a table in the diner, Tater dogging my steps. A girl came up to take our order. Pie was on my mind and the word was almost out of my mouth when I looked up at the waitress.

She was the most stunningly beautiful creature I'd ever seen.

Black hair was pulled away from her face in a braid that went fully down her back, exposing the face of a madonna. Deep olive skin, flawless, large dark eyes, a generous mouth. Words cannot begin to describe how beautiful she was. The swollen, protruding belly didn't detract from the ethereal beauty. I'd always heard women glowed when pregnant. I hadn't noticed with E.J. She'd been alternately belligerent, weepy, and horny—but she never, to my memory, glowed.

This girl glowed. She radiated. She hummed. Or maybe it was just me. I had a quick fantasy about Tater tying me up and allowing this creature to have her way with me. Under the circumstances, surely E.J. would understand.

''Hey, Trudy,'' Tater said, oblivious to the radiance shining our way. ''Give me a piece of that cherry pie and some coffee.''

''Sure thing, Tater. And you?''

She was speaking directly to me. I wasn't sure I could speak, but finally the words came. ''The same.''

She smiled. My knees felt wobbly. The palms of my hands began to perspire. The girl, Trudy, wobbled off, and I turned to Tater. "Who is she?" I asked.

"Son, don't you listen at all? I done told you twice. That's Trudy. The waitress. Ray's daughter. Ray's the cook. You getting any of this now?"

"She's . . . my God, she's . . ."

"Pregnant," Tater supplied.

"That, too."

"Oh," Tater said, and smiled. "I seen guys do that some with Trudy. I always forget. I knowed the girl since she was in diapers. She don't have much effect on me. But she is pretty."

"Pretty? Marilyn Monroe was pretty. Elizabeth Taylor was pretty. Michelle Pfeiffer's pretty. This girl is not pretty."

"Maybe now'd be a good time to call that wife of yours," Tater said, and giggled.

I sobered. "That would be fine," I said.

Tater sobered, too. "It was a joke, son, a joke."

I took a deep breath. Time to get down to business if I was ever going to coach soccer again, tuck my daughters in bed, kiss my wife's neck.

"Seems to me somebody must be wondering where Calvin is," I said, trying to keep my mind on the business at hand.

"Shit. Most people's just glad when he ain't around."

"I mean, whoever killed him must be wondering why no one's made a fuss about finding his body."

"Oh," Tater said. "That makes sense."

"Anybody seem overly nervous?"

Tater looked around. The beautiful Trudy was behind the bar/counter, leaning her back against a wall and slowly rubbing her belly. A man that could only be Ray, Trudy's father and the daytime cook, was sliding plates of food onto a window ledge between the diner's counter and the kitchen.

Two truckers sat at a booth to the side, silently eating. Nobody looked nervous.

"Anybody asked?" I asked.

"About Calvin?" Tater shook his head. "No. Not yet. Too soon, anyway."

"For someone without a guilty conscience."

"How we gonna do this?" Tater asked, leaning forward across the table.

I shook my head. "I'm not sure. Let me think about it."

"Well, think fast. 'Cause you ain't seeing that wife of yours long as Calvin's in the freezer, boy. You understand?"

I understood. I didn't like it much, but I understood.

Eleven

It was getting close to four o'clock. Purvis, the bartender, and Claudia, the barmaid, would be coming in shortly. Tater and I had been sitting for hours in the diner of the truck stop. I'd consumed two pieces of pie, some French fries, three cups of coffee, and a beer. I figured if I ever got out of this alive, I'd have to go on a diet.

"Look," I said, "I've got an idea on how to begin my investigation, but you're not going to like it."

Tater let out a snort. "Yeah, I just bet it has something to do with you going back to Codderville and working from there, huh?"

"No," I said indignantly, although the same thought had crossed my mind. "I need to interview our suspects. And I can't do that with you hovering around me. Nobody's gonna talk to me about Calvin with you around."

"Ain't nobody gonna talk to you about Calvin, period," Tater said. "You're an outsider—"

"Then fine. I'm not doing you much good, am I? Time to take off, I guess." I started to rise from the table.

"Oh, shut up," Tater said, reaching out and pulling me back down to the table. "I wish to hell I never picked you up!"

"That makes two of us!"

We sat there and glared at each other for a while. Finally Tater spoke.

"Okay, what would you say to them?"

I shrugged. "I don't know. Play it by ear. Just start talking and steer it around to Calvin."

"Lordy, I love it when a good plan comes together," Tater said.

The sarcasm was not lost on me. I happen to live with the Queen of Sarcasm. Tater could take lessons.

"The thing is, Tater, I can't have you hanging around while I talk with them."

"Yeah, right. First thing you're gonna do minute I'm out of sight is call either your wife or the cops. I ain't as stupid as you look, son."

"Then I guess we're back to another one of your Mexican standoffs," I said.

Tater rubbed his chin. "Thing is, I don't gotta be breathing down your neck to keep an eye on you. We can be in the same room. That way I can watch that you don't try to make a phone call. And Dumplin' can see to it you don't take off."

We heard the front door of the truck stop open and turned to see Purvis walking in. He waved at Tater and Tater waved back. Show time, I thought.

The Taj Mahal Lounge was fairly quiet in the late afternoon. Tater said the real fun started after dark, when farmers and ranchers and cowboys from the area came in, and the illegal long-haul truckers stopped for the night.

Tater had told me a little of the history of Scoggins Truck Stop & Turkey Farm while we were whiling away the time earlier in the day. The original part of the truck stop, the two-story interior portion, had been a general store built back in the late 1930s to handle the trade of the small community of Oxford, not far down the road. Texas Highway 16 had been the only road through there at that time, and truckers used it to service the small hill country towns. Old Man Scoggins had bought the general store in the early forties, added the gas pumps and the diesel pumps, and took half the downstairs portion and built the diner.

Tater said there was a rumor that in the early war years the upstairs portion of the old building had been used as a brothel for the soldiers from the then newly established Fort Hood—Camp Hood at that time—which wasn't that far away.

After the war, the upstairs had been the bar, but when RR 965 was cut through back in 1962, putting the truck stop smack at the intersection of RR 965 and Highway 16, the traffic had gotten better, and Mr. Scoggins had added the two pre-fab steel buildings, turning one into the Taj Mahal Lounge, the other into the dormitory for the truckers.

Then came the seventies and gas rationing. The independent truckers were hurt bad during those days and, with the independent truckers hurt, Scoggins Truck Stop was hurt.

Old Man Scoggins had been playing around some with turkeys prior to that, but he got serious when the truck-stop business began to dry up. He expanded his turkey operation and Scoggins Truck Stop & Turkey Farm was born.

Since then, except for the few legitimate trucks moving through the hill country to deliver to the small towns there, most of the truck traffic at Scoggins was from overloaded and contraband carriers taking the back roads to avoid the weigh stations and smokeys on the highways.

The barmaid, Claudia, had hustled in about an hour after Purvis had opened the bar. She was a bottle redhead, about my age, fortyish, shaped like an avocado—small shoulders and a large butt. Her face may have once been pretty, but it was hard to tell under the layers and layers of makeup. But her manner was friendly when she took our orders, and she flirted outrageously with Tater, to Tater's obvious delight. She bent down and rubbed Dumplin's head, talking baby talk to the enormous creature, giving both Tater and me a clear view down the front of her blouse.

She straightened and gave me the eye. Tater had already done the introductions. "Now I got kin living in the Valley," she said, smiling at me. "You know the Hoffstedders owned the brickworks out toward McAllen?"

I shook my head. "Nope. Sorry. Don't get around like I should, I guess."

"What high school you go to?" she said, a hand on an ample hip, resting her weight on one leg, as if we were in for a long siege of "who do you know."

I looked at Tater. I had no idea of the names of any high schools in the Valley. Tater looked blank. I was on my own. "Actually, I graduated high school in Austin. Moved with my folks to the Valley right after."

"Oh, so you wasn't raised there?"

"No, ma'am."

"Well, then you probably wouldn't know the Hoffstedders, then. Uncle Merle's brickworks went belly up 'round seventy, seventy-one."

"Before my time," I said, smiling.

The door opened and two truckers came in, found a table, and called lewdly to Claudia. Tater let out a sigh of relief.

"Hold your water," Claudia called to them. "You boys holler if you need anything," she said to us. " 'Specially you, Tater," she said, and chucked him under the chin.

I wiggled an eyebrow at Tater and I left him sitting at a table in the back of the lounge, nursing a Longneck, and moved up to the bar where Purvis was cleaning glasses. Dumplin' was by my side. I attempted to pet her head, but got only a low growl in return. No touchy-feely on duty, she seemed to be saying.

''Hi,'' I said to Purvis. ''Mind if I sit up here for a while? My cousin's beginning to bore me stupid.''

Purvis laughed. ''Tater's a good ol' boy. But he does go on with a story, now don't he?'' He looked down at Dumplin'. ''But hell, anybody can charm that dog of Tater's gotta be a okay fella. Need another beer?''

''No, thanks,'' I said. ''Tell you the truth, after everything Tater's told me about the guy who owns this joint, I was hoping to see him.''

''Calvin? He don't rightly own this place. Rogene, his wife, does. But Calvin likes to think he owns it,'' Purvis said.

''Some men are like that. What's mine is mine and what's hers is mine.''

Purvis snorted a laugh. ''With Calvin you can just keep on going with that line: What's mine is mine, what's hers is mine, what's his is mine, and what's yours is mine.''

''Yeah, ol' Calvin sounds like a real pistol,'' I said.

Purvis put both hands on the table and leaned toward me, a very serious look on his face. ''Calvin Hardy's a no good, lousy, mean son-of-a-bitch, and I hope he dies a slow lingering death sometime real soon.''

''Hell, you sure don't beat around the bush,'' I said, sipping from the beer bottle I'd brought with me from the table.

''Ain't no secret,'' Purvis said, going back to drying glasses. ''I hate his guts and he knows it.'' He stopped drying for a minute and looked at me. ''Actually, now that I think about it, I think Calvin really enjoys the fact that I hate him and wish him dead. Weird, huh?''

''Some people thrive on animosity,'' I said.

''Then no wonder ol' Calvin's doing so good. Ain't

nobody around here feels anything but animosity about him—including his own kids."

"You mean Bubba?"

Purvis laughed, a sneer on his face. "I said his own kids."

"Bubba's his—" I stopped.

I'd carried Calvin Hardy's body from the double-wide to the freezer in the truck stop. Granted, I hadn't seen him standing up, but Calvin wasn't five seven, or eight, like his son. He was closer to my height. At least six foot. And he'd been heavy. Very heavy. His face, in death, had been round and smooth. Maybe, I thought, Bubba took after his mama.

But he didn't.

There was one person Bubba did look like, from the scrawny, bantam-rooster legs to the protruding teeth.

I turned and walked back to my "cousin."

I slammed my beer bottle down on the table and leaned over, glaring at Tater, ignoring the low growl in Dumplin's throat. "If I'm going to find out what the hell happened around here, you can't be keeping secrets from me, you son-of-a-bitch!"

Tater stood up. "Don't you go talking about my mama!"

"Sit down!" I said, pushing him into his seat. Dumplin' went on point, and I quickly sat down opposite Tater. Tater gave the rottweiler a hand signal and she sat down on her haunches, glaring icily at me. "Why didn't you tell me Bubba was your son?" I demanded.

Tater went white. "What the hell are you talking about?" he demanded.

"You're denying it?" I said.

"Denying what? Are you out of your mind?"

I sat down at the table. The beer in my hand was getting warm. I pushed it aside. I'm not enough of a beer drinker to drink one warm. "Didn't you ever notice how much that boy looks like you?" I asked.

"Bubba? He don't look like me! He takes after Rogene's daddy. He was a scrawny so-and-so just like Bubba.''

I shook my head. I had no idea what the late Mr. Scoggins had looked like, but unless Tater was kin to him, I had seen the truth and the truth was a bouncing bundle named Bubba.

''What made you even think of such a thing?'' Tater demanded.

''Something Purvis said.''

Tater snorted. ''Well, that boy don't know diddly.''

I just shook my head. ''Tater, are you trying to tell me that you didn't know Bubba was your kid?''

''He ain't!''

I stood up, dragging Tater with me to the bar. ''Purvis, you wanna repeat what you just said about Bubba,'' I said.

''Not really,'' Purvis said, cleaning out the draft-beer jets.

''What the hell did you say to my cousin to get him all riled up?'' Tater asked.

''Tater, I didn't say squat. If you wanna deny the truth that everybody and their brother can see with their own eyes,'' Purvis said, ''then more power to you, all's I can say.''

''What are you talking about?''

Purvis sighed. ''Okay, first look at Bubba. He's the spitting image of you. Next, how many kids Rogene got? Six? Bubba's the only boy. You know that sex gene stays with the daddy, don'tja? Looks to me like ol' Calvin's shooting nothing but girl bullets.'' He leaned forward on the counter. ''And let me ask you the $64,000 question, Tater Bascomb: You ever been with Rogene? Like maybe twenty years ago?''

Tater got a strange look on his face, turned, and marched toward the door into the other part of the truck stop. I was busy planning my escape route when Tater did a quick about-face and marched up to me at the bar, taking me by the arm.

"Bye, Purvis. Marvin, come along."

"Where are we going?" I asked.

"Marvin, just shut up for once in your life, okay?"

"Don't call me Marvin."

We headed through the kitchen of the truck stop, out the back door, and to the double-wide behind. Tater tapped lightly on the front door and, without waiting for a reply, walked in.

"Now you behave yourself," Rogene was saying into the phone. "I don't want you givin' your gramma any grief, girl, you understand? No, now I told you, your daddy's acting onry, and I think you girls best stay with your gramma . . . I don't care if she does. 'Bout time you got some table manners!" Looking up at us, she said, "Vandella, you behave. You're the oldest. You watch the little ones, you hear? I gotta go. No, I gotta go. I tol' you no. I'll call you later."

Rogene hung up the phone and looked at us. "Well, hey, boys, find out anything?"

Tater just stared at her.

"What?" Rogene said. "I got a booger or something?" She wiped at her nose. Still Tater stared. "Tater Bascomb, you stop that and tell me what's going on!"

"Is Bubba my boy?" Tater said, not one to beat around the bush.

Rogene turned white, then slowly turned red. She stood up, walked into the kitchen and got a bottle of Wild Turkey out of the cupboard, and poured herself a stiff one. She downed it in one gulp. Turning, she said, "Whatever gave you that idea?"

"Well, shit fire and damnation, excuse my French. I don't think I ever saw you take a drink in your life, girl. And I think you just answered my question."

Rogene walked back into the living room area and sank down on the Early American couch. "Tater . . ."

He sat down on the coffee table in front of her, taking her hands in his. "Why the hell didn't you tell me, girl?"

Rogene hung her head. "You went off to Vietnam and I didn't know if you were coming back." Tears began to splash her legs.

I was standing by the front door, by the hallway that led to the master bedroom and the back door. I heard a sound and turned. Bubba was standing two feet behind me.

"Ah, Tater," I said.

Bubba walked past me into the living room. He looked from his mother to Tater. "Is it true?" he said.

Tater and Rogene both stood up. "Yes, son," Rogene said. "It's true."

Bubba looked at Tater and slowly his face broke into a huge grin. "Well, hot damn!" he said, and threw his arms around Tater.

Tater, off balance, almost fell over backward. I ran forward, offering physical support. The boy had a stranglehold on Tater's neck. Finally he pushed himself away from his newfound father and, still grinning, said, "Wait till ol' Calvin hears about this!"

"He knows," Rogene said quietly.

All three pairs of male eyes turned her way.

"Calvin knows?" Tater said.

Rogene sat down on the couch, tears springing to her eyes again. "I was all alone. You'd gone off to Vietnam, and you never did write. And then Calvin came to work for Daddy. And he was always after me to go out with him, then I found out I was pregnant. I didn't have nobody I could talk to about it—except Calvin. He said he'd marry me. And Daddy liked him, and he never did like you. And Daddy wanted me to marry him, so . . ."

Tater shook his head. "You always did do what your daddy told you to do," he said.

"Yeah," Rogene said, a bitter sound to her voice. "And it plumb near ruined my life."

Bubba sat down heavily on a chair. "So that's why Daddy's always hated me," he said softly. "I thought it was just 'cause I wasn't good enough. He always did tell me that."

Tater turned to his son, paternal pride swelling his chest. "Boy, you are now and you always been good enough to do anything you set your mind to. And Calvin Hardy be damned."

Which, I thought, was appropriate.

Twelve

"When's Daddy coming home?" Bubba asked, looking around him in a daze.

Tater looked at Rogene and Rogene looked at me. I decided not to look at anybody.

Tater took a deep breath. "Son," he said, squatting down in front of Bubba where he sat in his armchair, "I got some bad news to tell you."

Bubba focused on his newfound father, his mouth slightly open, his face as vacant as it had been prior to his newly acquired ancestral knowledge.

"Something happened to Calvin," Tater said. "Something pretty bad."

Bubba's beady eyes narrowed. "He dead?"

"Well, yeah, son, I guess he is."

Bubba leaned back in his chair. "When'd y'all find out?" he asked, looking at his mother.

Rogene crossed and recrossed her legs, her fingers fiddling with the hem of her oversized top. "While ago," she finally said.

Bubba thought on this for a moment. "While ago? In the morning?"

Tater straightened up and sat down on the couch opposite Bubba, leaning forward. "Son, we got us a real problem here, and we need your help. We're trying to keep this quiet, you unnerstand?"

Bubba chewed awhile on Tater's statement. Then he said, "Why?"

It was the slowest conversation I'd ever witnessed.

" 'Cause Calvin got himself murdered, boy. The way it came down made it look like your mama done it, and we're trying to figure out who did 'fore anybody finds out and tries to throw your mama in jail."

Bubba slowly stood up. "I done it," he said. "I kilt Daddy."

"You done *what?*" Tater said, staring at his new son.

"I done kilt Daddy—I mean Calvin," Bubba said.

"Oh, Lord!" Rogene wailed, clutching her head.

"How?" I asked.

All three heads turned to me. Tater nodded his head a fraction. "That's a good question. Boy, how'd you do it?"

"Whadaya mean, how? I kilt him."

"You shoot him?" Tater asked.

"Yeah. I got one of Daddy's—I mean Calvin's—guns, and I shot him with it!"

"Uh-huh," Tater said, "And when'd you do this?"

"When?" Bubba repeated.

I sat down. Listening to any conversation that included Bubba was a marathon event.

"That's right, boy. When did you shoot Calvin?"

"Ah, yesterday?" Bubba sank back into his chair. "Like last night, maybe?"

"Good trick, son," Tater said, walking up to Bubba's chair and placing one hand protectively on his shoulder.

" 'Cause Calvin's been dead since Sunday and he was kilt with a knife."

Bubba looked at his mother. "Mama—"

Rogene wiped a tear from her eye and smiled at her son. "That's the sweetest thing you ever did do for me, Bubba. And I really appreciate it. But I'd confess my own self 'fore I'd let one of my children say they did it."

"Did you do it, Mama?" Bubba asked, his voice a whisper. "Not that anybody in their right mind would blame you . . ."

Rogene shook her head. "No, honey, I didn't. Calvin was knocking me around something awful and I lost consciousness. When I come to, Tater and this guy"—she said, pointing at me and giving me a not-altogether-friendly look—"were standing here and we found your dad, I mean Calvin, on the floor of the kitchen with one of my kitchen knives in his chest."

Bubba stood up quickly from his chair, both hands in fists. "Well, I ain't sorry he's dead, all's I can say!"

"Well, son, I don't think anybody is," Tater said. "Boy, I need you to go on to the truck stop and help out Trudy. Me and your mama's gotta talk."

I stood up. "I'll go with Bubba. I know you two need to be alone."

Bubba was out the door and I was fast on his heels when I felt a thrust of momentum from behind and found myself holding up a wall. I could feel paws on my back and hear the low growl.

"Whoa, boy. You just stay here with me like you're supposed to. We ain't no closer to solving this thing than we were twenty minutes ago. And you ain't no closer to getting home than you were then neither."

The pressure was released and I turned around and sank back into my chair. "Anybody have any earphones?"

"Just shut up. And stay out of it," Tater said.

Tater turned to Rogene. "Why didn't you tell me when

I come home from 'Nam? I came right back here. I came back to you."

"And I was eight months pregnant with Vandella." Rogene lowered her head. "That's the first time he hit me, when you come home. He kicked me in the belly. Said, I went back with you, he'd kill me and the baby." Tears leaked out of her eyes. "Calvin was all things bad in this world, but he sure didn't lie when it came to threatening me."

"If I'd known about Bubba, neither Calvin nor your daddy coulda stopped me from taking you both away. You know that, don't ya?"

Rogene looked into Tater's eyes. "I do now. But back then, Calvin had me convinced I was a dead woman if I ever . . ."

Tater's hand touched Rogene's face. "If that boy weren't already dead, I'd kill him right now."

I closed my eyes and hummed a couple of stanzas of "In-A-Gadda-Da-Vida." There were some things strangers shouldn't intrude upon, even if they couldn't help it.

Tuesday

I'd spent the night in the same room as Bubba. His mouth remained open while he slept, and I spent most of the night listening to him snore. Needless to say, under all the circumstances, I was not in a jovial mood the next morning. Tater, however, who'd managed to sleep in another part of the trailer, seemed to be in amazingly good spirits. He led me out of the trailer toward the truck stop.

It was one of those mornings we dream about in Central Texas—clear azure blue sky, not a cloud in sight, temperature in the midsixties, cool and crisp, humidity low. I could see Enchanted Rock in the distance, beyond the turkey farm, its massive bald head thrusting upward into the sky itself. From somewhere, I could hear the fractured cry of a mockingbird.

Tater made a hand signal to Dumplin', who wagged her tail, grinned, and took off, barking at nothing in particular and everything in general.

"Don't make me call her back," he said, taking my arm and ushering me into the back door of the truck stop.

The place was crowded. Several truckers had spent the night, and there were climbers from the rock there for a quick breakfast as well. We found a booth against the wall and sat down, checked the menu, and gave our order to the beautiful Trudy, who looked even better today, if that was possible.

"Why'd you hang around here after you came back and Rogene was married to Calvin?" I asked as we sat, waiting for our food and sipping our coffee.

Tater shrugged. "Only place I knew, I guess. My mama was still living then. Wanted to be near her. Hell, boy, this is my home. Been a Bascomb living in these parts since the mid-eighteen-hundreds."

"And you wanted to be near Rogene?"

Tater shrugged again and looked off beyond the people in the diner. "Never did stop loving that little girl. Guess I never will."

"Why—"

"Why didn't I take her away from Calvin? Hell, boy, you just didn't know Old Man Scoggins. He hated my guts. Him and my daddy had a beef about something years back. After my daddy died, the old man just decided to keep on hating, and I became the one he fixed on. Come to think of it, Calvin and the old man were a lot alike. Sometimes I think the reason the old man had me hauling for him all those years was 'cause he liked the thought of Lafayette Bascomb's son being obliged to him.

"But the old man had that little girl tied up in knots; ever since we were little kids together he was on her. He'd say jump and Rogene'd look like she had the Saint Vitus' dance. When we was teenagers, she'd sneak away from him and we'd be together, but only a few times. Then when I come home, she had both her daddy and Calvin keeping her down. Me and her never even said hidy when either of them was around. Her old man never beat her to my knowledge, but there's other ways of abusing a child other than just that, you know?"

I nodded my head. I knew. "Tater, I want you to know that I don't think either you or Rogene had anything to do with Calvin's murder. All I'm saying is that, although I think you're both innocent, the fact that you're together now, the fact that it will probably come out that Bubba's your son—"

"You bet your ass it's gonna come out! I'm gonna shout it from the rafters!"

"Put those two things together and it's gonna look like the two of you conspired to kill Calvin."

"Well, damnation, son, we didn't do no such thing . . ."

Tater's voice was rising. I laid a hand on his arm, shushing him. "I know you didn't. At least I believe you didn't. I'm talking about the authorities."

"So now we're in a worse fix than we was on Sunday, right?"

"Oh, yeah, considering you've been hiding a corpse for three days."

"Well, what the hell did you want me to do? Throw Rogene to the wolves? She's the only thing in this world ever mattered beans to me, son. Ain't no way she's going down for this. Even if she'd a done it, which she didn't."

I looked around the diner. "Well, somebody did."

Trudy came to refill our coffee cups. "When's your baby due?" I asked her.

"Less than a month," she said, smiling at me. She was even more beautiful when she smiled.

I smiled back. "Good luck to you," I said.

She smiled, nodded, and walked off. Tater grinned at

me. "Guess you don't mind so much hanging around here long's you got her to look at, huh, boy?"

I sipped my coffee. "Rather be home doing honey-dos, truth be known, Tater."

Tater sighed. "I'm really sorry about this, Willis. When it all come down, I didn't know what else to do. You gotta know I'd protect that girl with my life."

"I know that, Tater. And I understand. But keeping me here isn't doing either one of us—or her—a bit a good."

Tater let out a snort. "You're telling me! You ain't done squat about finding out who done it!"

"Well, I'm trying, for God's sake!"

We were hissing at each other, trying to keep our voices down so we wouldn't be overheard, but still angry with each other because we didn't know who else to be angry at.

Tater sighed. "Maybe we should haul the body down to the Perdernales River and dump it," he said. "You sure ain't Sam Spade and I ain't no Mike Hammer."

Part of me thought it wasn't a half-bad idea. No one would report Calvin Hardy missing until it was absolutely necessary, and there was a good chance it would never become necessary. No one would miss him. Oh, maybe his daughters, the younger ones, for a little while, but with Tater around to love them, it wouldn't take long to forget him. Calvin was known for taking off on binges, drunken and sexual. He could have taken off for good. He hadn't been the type to leave a note of goodbye.

But in my head I could hear my wife. *Sure, fine. There's a murderer out there, and you're not only going to let him go Scot free, you're going to clean up his mess for him. Aren't you the little boy scout?* But what else can I do? I know Tater didn't have anything to do with it, and I'm pretty sure Rogene's innocent, too. *Okay, fine. But somebody did it. Or did Calvin just impale himself on that kitchen knife?* Well, now, I hadn't thought about that—*He was on his back, numb nuts! How'd he roll himself over?* Okay, okay. I just thought—*No, actually, you're not think-*

ing at all. Look at your suspects. What do you know about them? Next to nothing. *My point exactly. What are the reasons people murder, my darling?* No need to get sarcastic. The reasons—love or money or variations on those two themes, right? *Very good, dear. Who stands to gain financially from Calvin's departure?* Nobody that I know of. Calvin didn't own anything. Rogene owns everything. *But Calvin ran it as if he owned it, right? How can it really be Rogene's when he has total control?* Okay, so now you're saying Rogene did it. *Not necessarily. Who stands to gain from Rogene?* Her children. Bubba's too dumb to have pulled it off. You think one of the little girls did it? I haven't even met them, and besides, they were over at their grandmother's during all this. *Okay. Next on the list. Love.* Again, we go back to Rogene. *Not necessarily. There are three other women on our suspect list, my precious. Including your new little girlfriend.* What new little girlfriend? *The pretty pregnant one.* Trudy? *Then, of course, there's Claudia and the stripper. What was her name?* Salome, or something like that. *Don't we have the impression that Calvin wasn't real big on his wedding vows?* Oh, we definitely have that impression. *So maybe he was having his way with the help.* Claudia, maybe. She looked a little eager for love to me. *Why, because she's overweight and over-age?* Don't get snippy, my sweet. She was flirting big time with every guy in the joint. *Tips, precious. Tips.* Why are you defending Claudia? *Why are you avoiding any discussion of Trudy?* I'm not avoiding—*Yes, you are.* No, I'm not.

I looked over at Tater. My internal fantasy was getting me nowhere in a big hurry. I leaned toward Tater. "Okay, we know Purvis hated Calvin's guts and admitted he would like to see him dead. Could he have done it?"

Tater scratched his head. "Well, now, you mean has he got the wherewithal or the opportunity?"

"Either."

"Well, then, both."

''Wherewithal and opportunity?''

''Sure, son. Purvis was in 'Nam just like me. Uncle Sam's real good about teaching his boys to kill. Sometimes that's the only thing he does teach 'em. Purvis was a grunt just like me. He was there couple years later than me, but they was still shooting each other then, too.''

''Okay. Wherewithal. What about opportunity?''

''Rogene says he was here, opening up the Taj Mahal. He coulda slipped out, come back to the trailer for some reason. Yeah, I'd say he's got opportunity.''

''Okay, good. We got one suspect with motive and opportunity. And since the knife was right there in the kitchen, everybody had the means.''

Tater grinned. ''Hell, boy, you sound just like Perry Mason. Keep it up.''

I grinned back. ''Okay, Claudia.''

''Wherewithal,'' Tater said. ''Saw her slam a drunk into the wall once and put a knee to his gonads. I'd say the girl's got the wherewithal. Opportunity same as Purvis's.''

''What about motive?'' I asked.

Tater shrugged his shoulders. ''Well, I know Calvin bedded her a few times, leastwise he said he did. But if anything, she seemed relieved when it was over.''

''Ray Maladondo.''

Tater thought for a moment. ''Well, now, I gotta say he'd have the wherewithal. Never seen Ray lose his temper or touch nobody, but there's something in the guy's eyes tells me, push come to shove, he'd be one to reckon with. 'Sides, you ever see them forearms of his?''

''Opportunity?''

''Kitchen door leads right to the front door of the double-wide.''

''That it does. Motive?''

Tater shrugged again. ''Lousy pay? Bad working conditions? Just plain old general principles?''

''What about the stripper?''

"Salome? She usually goes home to Wimberly of a Sunday. Her daddy preaches down there, and she helps him with the service."

"Her daddy know what she does?"

Tater grinned. "I ever tell you 'bout Salome's act?"

I shook my head.

"She does Salome's dance from the Bible, with the veils? All to the music of Willie Nelson doing 'Amazing Grace.' And she quotes Bible verses while she does it."

I raised an eyebrow. "How far does she go?"

"Bare boobies and a G-string. It's very spiritual." He grinned.

"We have no way of checking anybody's alibi, since nobody's supposed to know anything happened. So we need to treat Salome just like any other suspect," I said.

Tater nodded his head. "Okay by me. Don't know about wherewithal, but I'm one to believe anybody could kill given the right motive."

"So what about motive?"

He shrugged. "Well, now, Calvin may a been sleeping with her. Hard to tell. But Calvin'll try to bed anything's got the right equipment."

Trudy came by to pick up the remains of our breakfast. I stopped talking for two reasons: One, I didn't want our conversation overheard. Two, it was hard to talk while I was staring at Trudy.

She was an exceptionally beautiful woman, and her beauty didn't diminish with exposure to it. If anything, it struck me harder.

I've never messed around on my wife. You say, right, sure, but maybe just that once? Nope. Never. And it's not a moral thing. My theory on the subject is this: Why jeopardize your entire life, your marriage, your house, your kids, all your stuff and your way of life, simply for a piece of ass?

Now that may sound harsh, crass, unfeeling. Okay, fine. But it's what it all boils down to. Some people try to justify themselves, saying they've got this great passion and they just couldn't help themselves. You see that in movies all the damned time. Bunk. It's a choice. You either choose to put your entire way of life at risk. Or you don't.

Some guys say, "Yeah, but what if it walks right up to you?" Excuse me, but I'm not the Hunchback of Notre Dame. It has walked right up to me. In the fifteen years I've been married to E.J., I have been flirted with by good-looking women on numerous occasions, and on one particular occasion I had a woman come right out and suggest a nooner.

Okay, I'm not a totally stand-up guy. I didn't turn her down by saying I loved my wife and would never think about cheating on her. I didn't tell her my theory about fucking up your life. I didn't tell her I found it morally reprehensible or just plain wrong.

I told her I had herpes. It worked.

But the point I'm trying to make here is that for the first time in my fifteen years of marriage—hell, in the seventeen years I've known E.J.—for the first time I thought about it. Seriously thought about it. And with a woman so pregnant she could barely navigate between the tables of the diner.

I watched her walk away, balancing the tray of dirty dishes on her swelled belly.

Tater said, "Get your mind off it, boy. I know of at least two men'd gut you like a turkey for even thinking about it."

"Two?" I sipped at my recently refilled cup of coffee, trying to hide the heat in my face.

"That's Ray's baby girl you're gawking at. Then there's Roberto Vega, Trudy's husband. He wouldn't much appreciate you looking at his wife that way none either."

"I'm being good," I said.

Tater got a look on his face. "Well, now, boy, here's something I ain't thought of before. When we was talking about who was at the truck stop and had opportunity the day Calvin was murdered, it plumb never occurred to me to think about somebody at the turkey farm having quick access to the trailer.''

''At the turkey farm?''

''You ain't noticed that smelly, noisy building about two hundred yards behind the double-wide?'' he asked.

I nodded my head. ''So who could have been there?''

''Ray's two boys, Jimmy and Joe, both work there. And Ray's son-in-law Roberto's the foreman. That's how he met Trudy in the first place.''

''Were they working Sunday?''

''Hell, boy, them turkeys don't stop eating just cause it's the Lord's day.''

''Shit,'' I said, setting my coffee cup down with a rattle. ''Like we didn't have enough suspects.''

''Well, son, I'm really sorry. Think maybe we should just ignore them three?''

''I swear to God, you're as sarcastic as my wife,'' I said.

''Must come from being around you too damn much.''

''Okay, skip wherewithal. We've already decided anybody's capable of murder given incentive. Let's just go straight to motive. Why would Ray's sons or son-in-law kill Calvin?''

''Same reason as anybody else,'' Tater said. ''Calvin was an asshole and sometimes assholes just plain need killing.''

''Yeah, but Calvin was an asshole for a long time. Why kill him Sunday? What happened to make somebody kill him Sunday?''

Tater thought, his narrow face pinched, his brow furrowed. ''Okay. Sunday was pretty normal, I'm thinking. I got over here around ten-thirty in the morning to get the turkeys loaded in the truck. Had me some breakfast while Jimmy and Joe were loading up. They was fussing at each other, but then they always do that. Never seen brothers fight the way them two do.''

''And?''

''And what? I ate breakfast. Ray cooked it, Trudy served it, and Rogene took my money when I paid for it.''

''Where did you come from?'' I asked, wondering why I never thought about where Tater actually lived.

''My house,'' he said, looking at me as if I were stupid.

''You live near here?'' I asked.

He frowned at me. ''Up the road a piece. But, excuse me for saying so, boy, if you're thinking about interrogating me, I was with you when Calvin met his maker.''

I shook my head. ''No, I wasn't interrogating you. I just realized I had no idea where you lived.''

''Well, tell you what, I'll invite you to tea soon's this is all tidied up, okay, son?''

I was beginning to wonder if there *was* something about me that invited sarcasm.

Thirteen

It's hard to investigate when no one else knows there's anything *to* investigate.

Why are you asking all these dumb questions?

What business is it of yours?

I was beginning to think Tater knew as much about these people as I did. Considering Purvis the bartender had been the one to tell both of us that Bubba was Tater's son, Purvis might be the better partner. The only problem was, Purvis was a suspect. But if he was willing to tell me, Tater's "Cousin Marvin from the Valley," about Bubba's parentage, maybe he'd be just as forthcoming with dirt on the others.

Tater and I kicked it around for a while, considering Purvis as a source of information.

"Well, what are you gonna ask him?" Tater wanted to know.

I shrugged. "I don't know. Play it by ear."

Tater snorted. "You always say that. What we need, boy, is a plan."

The great plan was interrupted by a trucker coming up to our table.

"Hey, Tater," he said.

"Hey, Eugene, this here's my cousin Marvin from the Valley."

I shook hands with Eugene. "Hope to hell you're a mechanic in the Valley, Marv," Eugene said.

I shook my head to the negative.

"What's the problem?" Tater asked.

"Jammed air brake."

Tater sighed. "Need a hand, I guess?"

"If you got the time," Eugene said.

"Be with you in a jiffy," Tater said.

Eugene left and Tater stood, indicating I follow. We went back toward the double-wide. Tater whistled and Dumplin' came running from near the turkey farm, tongue lolling, grin wide at seeing her master.

"You go on in and wait for me in there," Tater said. "Clearing an air brake takes too much concentration to worry about you." He made a hand signal at the giant dog. "Dumplin', on guard."

She and I went inside the double-wide. Rogene was sitting on the couch, staring out the window. When she turned as I came in, I saw tears streaming down her face. I walked over and sat down on the sofa next to her.

"You okay?"

Rogene wiped her face with the back of her hand. "Just dandy. Go away."

"You want to talk?" I asked.

"Why in the world would I want to talk to you? You're a perfect stranger!"

"Sometimes it's easier to talk to a stranger than a friend. I've got nothing to gain—you've got nothing to lose."

Rogene sighed. "Just sitting here thinking about that no-good Calvin Hardy."

"Why wouldn't you be? You were married to him for a long time."

"Twenty of the longest, worstest years of my sorry life."

I didn't say anything. Rogene sighed again, the tears beginning to flow. "Bet you must think I'm some kinda scummy thing living with a man all that time when he beat me like he did."

"I have no room to judge anyone, Rogene. Besides, I don't know a lot about it, this is my wife's territory, but I've read some books. I know about the battered-wife syndrome."

Rogene nodded her head. "Seen all about that on 'Oprah.' " She looked out the window, not at me. "What I shoulda done is, I shoulda said just hell on everybody when I found out I was pregnant with Bubba and just took off for California. Wrote me a letter to Tater telling him, and wait for him to come get me there. That's what I shoulda done."

"Then you wouldn't have your daughters now," I said.

She looked at me, her eyes big. "Well, now, you're right about that. Something good did come out of being with Calvin Hardy. I got me them beautiful little girls." She looked out the window again. "It weren't all Calvin's fault, ya know. I didn't love him and he knew it. If I coulda loved him, he probably wouldn't a beat me."

"So now it's your fault? What did you do? Say, Calvin, I don't love you. Why don't you beat me up?' "

She gave me one of her full-force glares. "Don't get snippy with me, Marvin. I'll sic that dog on you."

"Yes, ma'am," I said, and grinned.

She grinned back. "Okay, so it weren't my fault Calvin beat me."

"No, ma'am," I said, my face serious.

Rogene sighed again. "Sometimes I felt like I couldn't

do anything right. Not even fry a pork chop. Or clean a toilet. Only time I ever laughed was when I was alone with my kids.''

''You're free of that now,'' I told her.

She cocked her head. ''Really? You think I can ever be free of what he done?''

''If you try real hard. Tater's a good man—''

''Tater's the best man ever walked the face of this earth,'' Rogene said.

''Maybe get some counseling . . .''

Rogene shook her head. ''Well, my family don't truck much with psychiatry.''

''Your family's what got you into this,'' I said.

Rogene sighed again. ''You mean my daddy.''

''Yes, ma'am.''

''My daddy made Calvin look like a Catholic saint.''

''Maybe you need to talk about all this with someone.''

''You think maybe somebody like that would be able to help me figure out why I kinda miss ol' Calvin?''

I patted her hand. ''Probably.''

''You think that's pretty stupid, huh?''

I shook my head. ''No, ma'am. He was your husband for twenty years. You have a toothache for that long, you'd miss that, too.''

''At the beginning, he was a good man. He loved me. It weren't just the money he was after at the beginning. But I couldn't love him back, and he knew it and it turned him mean.''

''He turned himself mean, Rogene, not you.''

The door to the trailer opened and Tater walked in, wiping his hands on a red grease rag.

''Hey, you messing with my woman?'' Tater said, grinning to take the sting out of the words.

''She won't have me, Tater, much as I tried.''

''Always said she was a smart woman,'' Tater said.

''Well, you two can go on like nobody I ever seen,'' Rogene said, getting up from the couch. ''I think I'd rather go sling hash at the truck stop than listen to the likes of you.''

She headed for the door, stopping to give Tater a kiss.

Once the door was closed behind Rogene, Tater went to the kitchen and removed the bottle of Wild Turkey from the shelf above the refrigerator. Grabbing two glasses, he came back into the living room.

''Don't reckon Calvin's gonna miss this much,'' he said, pouring two double shots. Holding up his glass, he winked. ''Here's mud in your eye,'' he said, slugging back the whiskey.

I followed suit, and before long the bottle was getting low and we were more than high.

''You know the rock,'' I said, staring at the amber liquid in my jelly glass.

''What? That little ol' thing outside the window there?'' Tater said and giggled.

I giggled back. ''Yeah, that'd be the one. About the rock—''

''Uh-huh?''

''Well, have you ever heard anything, well, strange, I guess, about it?''

''You mean like the drums?'' Tater said.

''Drums?''

''Oh, hell yes. Drums, chanting, you name it. Regular old hullabaloo over there some evenings.''

''What are you talking about?'' I demanded.

''What are *you* talking about?'' he demanded.

So I told him about the pressure. I told him about my calling—my, at that point I decided, religious calling—to climb the rock.

Tater poured himself another shot and leaned back in an almost prone position on the couch, his finger making music on the rim of his jelly glass.

''Well, now, knew this one lady went up there and the rock started spinning around on her. Weren't no, what'd you call it, vertigo. Yeah, that's the word. Weren't no vertigo either, she said. Said she'd been atop the Empire State Building and never had no vertigo problem. But mostly I hear about people hearing the drums and the chants."

"You ever hear it?" I asked.

"Oh, hell yes. Scared the piss outta me one night when I was only about twelve, I guess. Me and this buddy was camping out on top of the rock, and I woke up hearing these drums. Woke my buddy up, and he swore he didn't hear nothing. Then years later I was taking some tourists up the rock and one of 'em asked where the drumming was coming from. I didn't hear it that time, but that boy sure did. Then, of course, there's the spirits."

"What spirits?"

"Indians. Mostly men, but there's been this one squaw seen a couple of times."

"Enchanted Rock. Guess that's where it got its name, huh?"

Tater shook his head. "That names older'n God, son. Nobody knows where it come from really, but I got a friend who's studied on it, and he says the rock was called, in Spanish, Hill of the Sacred One. In Spanish, sacred one is *santiago,* which also means godlike man. Which could mean medicine man. Which could mean the original name of the rock was Medicine Man Hill. But that's just his opinion. But that old thing's been a sacred place to the Apache, the Comanche, and the Kiowa at different times over the years. And you see that plaque on the top of the rock about the big battle that was fought up there? Lotta white men bit it, but a bunch of Indians, too. Cain't remember which tribe that was, but their leader, some big muckity-muck, died up there. Maybe that's why things can get a little strange on Enchanted Rock."

"My wife didn't feel anything," I said.

"It's like that," Tater agreed. Then he said, "Ah, shit, son, pardon my French, but I really hate it that you're being kept from your family this away. But, Lord, son, I don't know what else to do!''

I thought for a moment he was going to cry, but he belched instead. '' 'Scuse me,'' he said.

''It's okay, Tater. I unnerstand . . . understand why you gotta protect Rogene. I mean, my God, man! She's the love of your life!''

''To the love of my life!'' Tater said, pouring two more double shots.

''And to the love of my life, Miss Eloise Janine,'' I said, holding my glass up to his. Some of the bourbon sloshed out and I giggled.

''That's a purdy name,'' Tater said. ''Eloise Janine. Eloise Janine.''

I belched. ''I hate it.''

''No shit?''

''Yeah, shit! I hate it. I call her E.J.''

''Well, son, that makes her sound like a boy!''

I shorted. ''Ha! You've never seen my wife's titties!''

Tater nodded his head up and down. ''Man don't take pride in his wife's titties, son, he ain't a man!''

''To being a man!'' I said and poured another shot.

The rest of the evening was pretty much of a blur.

Wednesday

Rogene woke us up around seven o'clock in the morning. ''Well, aren't you two just the living end!'' she said, hands on her hips, mouth set in wifely disapproval. ''Drunk as hoot owls and me worried sick about being arrested. I just want to thank you both *sooooo* much for all the help you been! I mean that from the bottom of my heart.''

She stomped off to the bedroom. I held my head from the pain, wondering if I'd ever meet anyone in my whole life whose words didn't drip with sarcasm.

Tater scooted up to a sitting position, holding onto the couch for support and moaning. Trying to rise to a standing position, he said, "Rogene, honey, it's not what it looks like."

From the bedroom came the loud, oh so loud, retort: "It looks like you two is drunk as skunks." She came back in the living room, arms akimbo, a mean glare on her face. "Am I wrong?"

I wondered where Rogene had learned this wifely attitude. I'm sure it's not one she'd used with her husband of twenty years. Calvin wouldn't have gone in much for sarcasm. But, except for the language and the hair roots, she reminded me a great deal of my own wife.

"No, now, we just had a couple while we were making plans," Tater said, a decided whine creeping into his voice.

"Making plans," Rogene said. "My, my. Making plans."

"Yeah, honey, listen. We're gonna go get Calvin's body and dump it in the Perdernales."

"Humph," she said, stomping back out of the room. Over her shoulder she said, "Hell, y'all coulda done that three days ago."

"I gotta shake the dew off the lily, then we gotta make plans," Tater said, stumbling toward the bathroom.

"Now, Tater, I don't know how good an idea moving the body is," I said.

"Better'n any idea you come up with so far," he said, shutting the bathroom door behind him.

I sat there thinking how good it would feel to pee. I got up and leaned against the hall wall opposite the door. Tater came out and it was my turn, and I had been right—it did feel damn good to pee.

Then the three of us—me, Tater and Dumplin', my guard dog—headed out the door of the double-wide to the kitchen door of the truck stop. Ray was cooking bacon and ham and grits and flapjacks, and the smells were enough to make me want to puke.

We went quickly through the kitchen and into the dining room, where I ordered black coffee and half a grapefruit. Tater, however, ordered just about everything on the breakfast menu.

"Only way to cure a hangover is to eat it to death," Tater said, sitting back with his coffee and sighing.

"Moving the body's a dumb idea," I said.

"Says you," Tater said.

"That's right, says me!" I said. Hangovers make me belligerent.

"So what's your big idea?"

"Talking to Purvis. Like we talked about last night."

"Purvis is a suspect!"

"I know that!" I hissed at him. "But we can find out what he knows about the others, and maybe something about him, too, while we're at it."

"Moving the body'd be simpler," Tater said, half to himself.

"We gonna bring it through the dining room?" I asked, looking around at the ten or so truckers eating breakfast.

"You're a real pain in the butt, Marvin," Tater said, grabbing the check.

We borrowed Rogene's car, a three-year-old Buick Regal, and drove to Purvis's house. He lived on the other side of the rock, toward Fredericksburg, in a one-story brick house built to look like a track home, except it was in the middle of about forty acres of scrub oak and Angora goats. We got out of the car and rang the bell. A woman came to the door, about three hundred pounds of dimples, a baby on one hip and a toddler hugging her knee.

"Hey, Arnetta," Tater said. "This here's my cousin Marvin from the Valley."

"Hey, Tater," she said, then she nodded at me, smiling shyly, and said, "Hi."

I smiled back and nodded.

''Purvis around?'' Tater asked.

''He's running errands down to Fredericksburg?'' Arnetta said, a question in her voice.

''When you expect him back?'' Tater asked.

''Oh, Lord, Tater, you know Purvis. If he finds somebody to talk to, maybe see him come Christmas,'' she said, and laughed.

''Where all was he headed?'' Tater asked.

Well, now, let me think.'' She looked down at the little one clutching her knee. ''Travis, let go a Mama for a minute, honey, wouldja?'' The toddler just held on tighter. ''I know he had to go to the auto parts, and I ast him to pick me up some formula at the drugstore. Oh, and I think he was going by Miz Ketchum's for some of that strudel she makes so good. We got company coming by this evening.''

''Well, thank you kindly, Arnetta.'' Tater tipped an imaginary cap and I smiled. Arnetta smiled shyly back and we walked to the car.

''Nice woman, that Arnetta,'' Tater said as he headed the Buick toward Fredericksburg.

''Seems like it,'' I said.

''Lost three young'uns 'fore she had those two. Had a real hard time carrying a baby to term. Rogene says her mama lost a bunch a babies 'fore she ever had Arnetta. Arnetta was an only child.''

''That's interesting,'' I said, wondering when I'd left the world of Scoggins Truck and ended up at my mama's, listening to endless stories concerning the health of people I didn't know.

We drove into Fredericksburg. We'd left the dog at the truck stop. There had to be a way I could get away from Tater in town. Just long enough to make a phone call.

We pulled up in front of the auto-parts store. Reading my mind again, Tater took my arm as we entered, and held on tight.

''Hey, Curtis,'' Tater said to the man behind the counter at the auto parts, ''Seen Purvis?''

"Yeah, you just missed him. He was in here about twenty minutes ago."

"Okay, thanks," Tater said, heading me back out the door and to the Buick.

We got the same story at the drugstore and at Miz Ketchum's bakery. We were walking back to the car when I spied the German restaurant. The thought of something to eat other than turkey and chicken-fried steak was very appealing after my breakfast of black coffee and half a grapefruit.

"I'm hungry," I said. "My treat."

"Well, hell, I can get behind that," Tater said.

We went in and ordered, then I said, "I need to use the restroom."

I got up and found Tater hot on my heels. "I ain't as dumb as you keep thinking I am, Marvin," he said.

We walked together past the pay phone and into the restroom.

When we got back, our food had arrived. It was a good meal and I enjoyed the break from Rogene's cooking, but it didn't do anything to lower my cholesterol count. When the waitress brought the check, I took out my wallet and started to hand her my American Express card.

Tater's hand went out to cover it. "No, we'll pay cash," he said, smiling at the waitress while glaring simultaneously at me. Neat trick.

"Tater, I don't have that much cash," I said.

He sighed and reached to his back pocket for his wallet. "I shoulda known," he said.

We got back in the Buick, Tater mumbling the entire time. "I'll pay you back," I said. "Geez."

"You trying to let your wife know where you are by using that credit card, huh?" he said.

"Damn, Tater, the bill wouldn't come in for a month!"

"Like she's not gonna call the credit-card company and tell them to be on the lookout for you using that card? How dumb do you think I am?"

Not as dumb as me, obviously. The thought hadn't crossed my mind.

The drive back was quiet. I had to wonder at myself. Dumplin' had not been with us in Fredericksburg. Tater is about half the size I am. There was no way he could have stopped me if I'd taken off screaming, "Help, help, I'm being held hostage."

Why didn't I do it?

Because it would get Tater in trouble.

I leaned my head against the Buick's headrest and thought about that one. I'd become so involved in the lives of these people that I did care about them. I knew Rogene hadn't killed Calvin. And I knew blowing the whistle now would do nothing but incriminate her. But I had my own life to live.

I should have done it, I finally decided. I should have taken off when I had the chance.

Thursday

By midnight we'd come up with nothing better than Tater's plan to move the body. Our search to find Purvis had come to naught, and by the time Purvis had shown up for work, Tater and I had been seriously into nap time. So, at midnight, the three of us, Tater, Dumplin', and I, went to the kitchen of the truck stop. Bubba was the only one in there.

"Hey, son," Tater said as we came in. He put his arm around the boy's shoulder and smiled at him. "How you doing, boy?"

Bubba grinned. "I'm fine, Tater, how're you?"

Tater patted his cheek. "Got it in your heart to call me daddy?"

Bubba lost the grin and looked at the floor. "Maybe in a little while, okay?"

Tater dropped his arm and backed away, his face sobering. "Sure, son, sure. Don't mean to rush you none." He cleared his throat and said, "Why don't you go on out to the diner and do whatever you gotta do out there, boy? Me and Marvin got some things gotta be done in here."

Bubba said, "Ain't nobody in the diner, Tater. Done bused all the tables."

"Well, then, just go out there and put your feet up and rest awhile. Look at one of them girlie magazines you always looking at, okay, boy?"

Bubba sneaked a look at the freezer with the out-of-order sign on it. The boy wasn't as stupid as he looked. "Yes, sir," he said quietly, and left us in the kitchen alone.

"Tater, are we going to carry him all the way to the river by ourselves?"

"Huh?"

I sighed. "Transportation," I said, enunciating each syllable. "We need transportation."

"Well, shit fire, I reckon," he said. "Good thinking, son. Hum," he scratched his chin. "All's I got over here's my rig. Left my pickup back at the house. Maybe we could use Bubba's—"

"To transport the body of the man he called Daddy for nineteen years?"

Tater sighed. "Yeah, you got a point. Let me go get the keys to Rogene's Buick. We'll just put him in the trunk."

He made a hand signal to Dumplin', who stood point at my left heel. I leaned against the "working" freezer and waited.

Tater was back in about five minutes. We opened the trunk, where he'd laid a shower curtain down to keep any blood from smearing, then we went back in the kitchen and Tater dug in his pockets for the key to the lock and hasp.

Finally finding it, he inserted the key and unlocked the lock, lifting the lid of the freezer.

It was empty.

Fourteen

"What the hell?" Tater said, staring in the empty freezer.

I stood next to him, looking at nothing. Dumplin' joined us, her paws resting on the side of the freezer, her head pointed down, peering inside.

"Move, girl," Tater said irritably, and slammed the lid shut.

We looked at each other. "When'd you move him?" I asked.

"When'd you do it, boy?" Tater asked back, a mean-looking frown creasing his narrow face.

"I didn't move him," I said. "When could I have possibly done it?"

"Well, I sure as hell didn't do it!" Tater said.

Simultaneously we both looked at the door into the diner, where Bubba was supposedly resting his feet and perusing girlie magazines.

"He didn't do it neither," Tater said, glaring at me.

"Why don't we go ask?"

I walked to the door between the kitchen and the diner, slowing when I heard Dumplin' growl. I looked back at Tater, and he made a hand motion that settled her down.

"Well, go on," he said irritably, pushing me ahead of him.

We all three went into the diner.

Bubba was doing what he'd been told to do. Being a well-brought-up young man, he'd taken his boots off before resting his feet on one of the tabletops. His left sock had a hole in the toe; his right, a hole in the heel. His mouth was open, and a slight bit of drool was working its way down his chin as he stared, his head cocked to the side, at the centerfold of the magazine.

"Bubba," Tater said softly.

Bubba jumped, his feet falling off their perch on the table; the chair, which had been tilted back on two legs, slipped, landing Bubba on his back on the floor.

"Geez, Tater," Bubba said, righting himself, "you scared the shit fire outta me! Thought it was Mama for a minute."

Tater helped the boy to his feet. "Son, you mess with the bod . . . with what was in that freezer?"

Bubba's eyes got big. "You mean Daddy?" he whispered.

"You mess with him, son?"

"No, sir! I ain't even touched that thing! Gives me the willies just thinking about it!"

Tater looked at me and I looked back at him. "Rogene?" I asked.

Tater shook his head. "No way that girl'd touch it," he said.

"What's wrong?" Bubba whispered.

Tater shook his head. "You stay here, boy. Keep an eye on the kitchen. Me and Wil . . . Marvin's gonna go back to the double-wide."

I led the way to the trailer, Dumplin' close enough behind me to sniff my pants.

Once outside, I said to Tater, "That's it. I'm outta here. The body's gone. My work is done."

"Hell you say, boy." Tater pushed me toward the door of the trailer. "I ain't liking none of this, I gotta tell you. Something is fishy, and it sure ain't dinner."

Rogene was in the living room, reading a two-month-old *Woman's World.* She glanced up when we came in. "Well, you move him?"

"Kinda hard to do that, Miss Rogene," Tater said, "seeing as how you already beat us to it."

Rogene frowned. "Huh?" she said, a perfect imitation of her son.

"Ain't no body in that freezer, Rogene. Or did you already know that?" Tater said, staring at his beloved with his hands on his hips and a frown on his face.

Rogene slowly stood up. "Are you accusing me of something?" she said, her tone belligerent.

"Did you move him?" I asked her.

She glared at me. "You know, I've had about as much of your sass mouth as I'm likely to be able to take, Mr. Whoever-in-the-world-you-are! You come in my house and expect me to feed you and give you a bed, and truth be known, I don't know you from Adam! Now as far as I'm concerned, you can just take a hike.

"And as for you, Mr. Tater 'Baby-I-love-you-so' Bascomb, I've had near twenty years of a man bullying me around and if you think for one itty-bitty minute that you're just gonna walk in and take over where Mr. Calvin Hardy left off, you are sadly mistaken. Now, what in the world are you boys talking about, and I want you to keep it simple and to the point!"

She took a breath and glared at us both.

"The body's gone," Tater and I said in unison.

"Well, it can't be," Rogene said.

"Well, it is," Tater said.

"Did you look real good?" she asked.

Tater rolled his eyes. "Rogene, he was the only thing in there!"

"I don't believe you two. You're making this up!"

Rogene marched out of the trailer and across the dirt area to the back of the truck stop, barging in the door with Tater, Dumplin', and me not far behind.

Bubba was in the kitchen, leaning against a counter as far away from the empty freezer as possible, staring at it like it was his father's last resting place. Which, unfortunately, it obviously wasn't.

Rogene went to the unlocked freezer and opened the lid, looking inside. She shut the lid firmly and looked back at us.

"Where is he?" she asked.

"My point exactly," I said.

"Shut up," Tater and Rogene said.

I leaned against the still-full freezer and commenced to shutting up.

"Somebody moved him," Tater said.

"Who?" Rogene asked.

"Maybe the killer," I offered.

Three pairs of eyes looked at me. "Who has access to the kitchen?" I asked.

"Anybody who walks in here," Rogene said. "All the staff come in here, and even some of the truckers when the staff's busy and they're looking for something quick-like."

"Who'd be in here alone long enough to move the body?" I asked.

Screams came from the front of the truck stop and we all ran through the door to the diner.

A young Mexican man, short and squat, with ugly jug ears, was standing by a row of canned goods, leaning against it, trying to catch his breath.

Seeing us, he said, "Rogene! It's Trudy! The baby's coming early! I tried to get her to the hospital, but she's in the car having it now! Right now!"

All of us ran for the front door. Rogene opened the door to the Taj Mahal Lounge as we ran and yelled, "Purvis! Call 911! Trudy's having her baby in the parking lot!"

I got to the car first. Both back doors were open and Trudy lay on the backseat, knees up and panties off, her beautiful face contorted in pain. I stopped, three feet from her, unsure what to do. I'd never delivered anything in my life. I'd taken the Lamaze course for both of our kids, and I'd stood firmly by E.J.'s shoulder when she delivered, but just between you and me, I kept my eyes closed the whole time.

Rogene shoved me out of the way. "Move!" she hollered, and I did, stepping back so far I almost stepped on Purvis's toes. He and Claudia and three rather drunk truckers were standing behind us. "I delivered two of my babies my own self," Rogene said, "I think I can handle this."

She moved into the backseat of the car, and it seemed like only minutes before her head was back out and, with a grin, she said, "It's a girl! Mother and daughter doing fine!"

A cheer rang out, and I was smiling and clapping my hands with the rest of them.

"Like I said," Purvis said behind me, "he always did shoot girl bullets, huh Claudia?"

Claudia whirled around and headed at a rapid pace back to the truck stop.

Tater was standing next to Rogene at the door to the car. Sirens sounded, coming from the direction of Fredericksburg, and Dumplin' ran to the road, barking at all the excitement.

I slowly walked back to the truck stop. Alone.

It was close to two o'clock in the morning when I quietly made my way into the empty diner and found the pay phone next to the cereal aisle. I found a quarter in my pocket and my long-distance card and dialed my home number.

E.J. picked up on the third ring. "Honey, it's me," I whispered.

"Willis! Oh, my God, where are you?"

"E.J., listen—"

"Are you all right? What in the world's going on—"

"E.J., shut up and listen—"

"My God, Willis—"

"Honey—"

I heard a growl and felt the hand on my shoulder simultaneously. Tater wrestled the phone out of my hand and hung it up.

I was at least a foot taller than Tater, but he had a grip of steel. He pushed me up against the wall and glared up at me.

"You son-of-a-bitch!" he said. "I thought maybe I could trust you just a little bit, but *noooo!* You son-of-a-bitch!" He punched me in the solar plexus and I doubled over, coughing.

"Geez, Tater," I wheezed.

"I don't have enough trouble I gotta deal with you, too?"

He whacked me on the arm so hard I knew I'd bruise. All the time he was manhandling me, Dumplin' stood in her attack stance, baring her canines at me. She looked as if one small finger move from Tater would be all it would take to tear me to shreds.

Or one small defensive move on my part. Much as I wanted to, I knew hitting Tater back would just give Dumplin' a taste of my liver.

"What's going on, Tater?" Purvis said behind us.

Tater turned, trying to compose his face. I stood against the wall with Dumplin' still glaring at me. Tater gave a hand signal at his side, and Dumplin' sat down and smiled, her tongue lolling.

Tater smiled at Purvis. ''Nothing. Me and Marvin's just messing around.''

Purvis snorted and turned back toward the lounge. ''You two try to act like grown-ups, okay?''

''Wait, Purvis,'' I said, my voice coming out in a croak. I cleared my throat. ''What'd you mean back there when you said Claudia should know about shooting girl bullets?''

''Didn't Tater tell you?'' Purvis said.

''Tell him what?'' Tater asked, clearly exasperated with the conversation.

''Claudia's little girl, Rachel. I told you before, ol' Calvin didn't shoot nothing but girl bullets.''

''Ah, come on,'' Tater said. ''Rachel's Junior's girl, right?''

Purvis shook his head. ''Tater, you just don't get around much, do you, boy?''

Purvis headed back for the lounge.

Tater and I looked at each other. ''Motive,'' I said.

''Okay, so what if Rachel's real daddy is Calvin? Junior and Claudia broke up three years ago, right after the little girl was born. He'd have no reason to off Calvin now,'' Tater said.

''I'm not talking about Junior, whoever the hell he is—''

''Used to be Claudia's old man. Works over at Renfroe's Tire Works.''

''That is not the point,'' I said in a whispered hiss at Tater. ''I'm talking about Claudia! You said you thought maybe she bedded him a couple of times—now it looks like she's got a kid by him. Maybe he was stiffing her on child support—''

Tater hooted. ''Child support? Come on! Calvin Hardy's idea of child support is letting the mama whip 'em instead of him.''

''Let's go talk with Claudia,'' I said, heading for the bar.

Dumplin' growled behind me. I turned and gave her a look. "Oh, shut up," I said, and kept walking. I felt her nose nudge me in the ass, and we continued in that fashion to the Taj Mahal Lounge.

As it was after two A.M., the bar was closed. Purvis was tallying up the receipts, and Claudia was long gone.

"Let's get some sleep," Tater said. "And don't even think about any more phone calls, 'cause Dumplin's gonna sleep on your chest tonight, son."

Part III

Finding Willis

Fifteen

Thursday
E.J.'s story

I sat staring at the phone.

He was alive. But where was he?

Then I remembered—caller ID. I jumped out of bed, running downstairs to where the little contraption was affixed to the kitchen phone. I knew nothing about the mechanics of the damned thing.

Would it have the number from a call taken on another phone? Had I waited too long?

I rushed into the kitchen and hit the button that would display the caller ID on a little screen. It was there, big as life. A 210 area code. San Antonio. I picked up the phone, starting to dial the number, but then hung up, dialing Luna's number instead.

A sleepy ''hello'' answered the fourth ring.

''Luna, it's E.J. Wake up.''

''I'm awake. Jesus, what time is it?''

''Willis just called.''

''What? Is he okay? Where is he—''

''Shut up and listen to me,'' I said. ''He didn't get a chance to tell me where he was—something happened with the phone and we were disconnected. But we have caller ID. I have the number!''

''Okay, this is good.''

''I started to just call it back, but—''

''No. No, don't do that. Let me think.'' I could hear her adjusting herself, probably moving into a sitting position on her bed. ''Look,'' she finally said, ''how did he sound?''

''Sound? I don't know . . . Well, he was talking very quietly. Kept telling me to shut up and listen—''

''Like he was trying not to have someone overhear him?''

''Yeah,'' I said reluctantly. ''Something like that. You think he's with another woman, don't you?''

''No, I don't. I think maybe he's being held somewhere—''

''Held? You mean like a hostage?''

''Maybe,'' Luna said. ''Maybe. What's the number?''

I read her the number I'd written down from the caller-ID display.

''That's San Antonio,'' she said.

''Yeah, I know.''

''I'll call you right back. I have a Crisscross downstairs. I'll look up this number.''

She hung up in my ear. I wished to hell I hadn't eaten all the chocolate earlier. Now would have been a good time.

''It's a place called Scoggins Truck Stop & Turkey Farm, east of Fredericksburg, between Enchanted Rock and Llano. You ever hear of it?''

''No.''

"Well, that's the number," Luna said.

"Now what?" I asked.

"Well, I guess we wait."

"Wait, hell. I'm going there now."

"What about the kids?"

"You can get yours over here, and I'll call Vera . . ."

Luna sighed. "Okay, just do it."

I hung up and dialed Vera's number, explaining to her what had happened. When I asked if she'd come stay with the kids while I drove over there, she said, "Give me five minutes."

"Vera, it'll take you fifteen just to drive here."

"Not when my boy's missing it won't."

We split the difference. She was ringing my front-door bell in ten.

It was a beautiful night—a trillion stars shown above us, the asphalt of the highway shimmered beneath us from an earlier rain.

"Let me do the talking," Luna said.

"Did you bring your piece?" I asked.

Luna snorted a laugh. "We are not Cagney and Lacey, okay? You understand that? We are not going in there guns blazing." She turned her head to look at me. "Do you understand?" she said, clearly enunciating each word.

"If somebody is holding my husband hostage—"

"I said maybe. Okay? Maybe. We're going into this cold. We need to contact the locals."

"Do you know anyone personally in that area?" I asked.

"No, but—"

"So we have no idea how they'll react. What they'll do."

"They're professionals."

"Wouldn't it be better if we tried to figure out first what's going on?" I asked, pleading with her. "Size the place up, then call in the locals."

"We have no idea what's going on, why Willis is there—"

"He could be there with some bimbo," I said, staring out at the night sky.

"You wanna know what I think?" Luna said, her voice tight.

I thought about it. "Okay," I said.

"I *wish* he were with some bimbo. Unfortunately I don't think that's what's going on."

"What do you—"

"I don't know," Luna said, shaking her head. "I just don't know. But we'll wait before we call in the locals." She gave me a look. "But when I decide it's time to do it, it will be done."

My mood matched the spirit of the town of Fredericksburg at five A.M.: bleak, deserted, and not terribly friendly.

We made the turn on to Ranch Road 965 and headed for the rock. Shortly after hitting the first cattle guard, Luna's foot hit the brake.

"What the shit is that?" she breathed.

It was the rock, looming before us in the still-dark night like a giant Mr. Potato Head.

"Enchanted Rock," I said, my voice giving away my newfound distaste for the overgrown slab of granite.

I hated it. It had taken my husband away and I hated it.

I wanted to go in there with a crew and do the one thing most Central Texans feared the most—chop the damn thing into building stones, and headstones, and paving stones. Tear it to pieces until it was just a flat place on the landscape.

"Damn, that's big," Luna said, craning her neck forward to peer out the front window of the car.

"Are you going to move this thing or are we just going to sit here and stare at that stupid slab all night?"

Luna looked at me. "Okay," she said carefully. "Didn't mean to sound like a tourist."

She put the car back in gear and we began to move. I

didn't look at the rock as we passed, but I could feel it, hear it.

It was laughing at me. The damned thing was laughing at me.

By a little after five in the morning, we pulled into the black-topped parking area of Scoggins Truck Stop & Turkey Farm. It was a huge place, the lot sporting only a couple of the big rigs and a few smaller ones. Luna pulled her car into a spot and cut off the engine. We sat staring at the one lit window of the place, seeing through the plate-glass rows and rows of grocery supplies and an area beyond that had to be the diner area: tables and chairs, booths, a counter with stools.

''Now what?'' I asked.

''Let me think,'' Luna said.

We sat quietly.

''Okay,'' she finally said. ''Sign says this place is open twenty-four hours a day. I would assume it is now open. Which means it would not seem strange if we went in there.''

''Just walk in?''

''We could crawl, but that might bring us unwanted attention.''

''Sarcasm is one thing I don't need at five A.M.,'' I said.

''Then don't say stupid things.''

''What did I say?''

''Let me think.''

''Yeah, right,'' I said, folding my arms and staring out the side window of the car. ''You've been doing such a splendid job of it.''

''Well, you may not need it, but you are certainly full of it, aren't you?'' Luna said.

''Think!''

We sat staring out opposite windows.

''Okay,'' she said again. ''We walk in. We order food. We say we're on the road. Business. Antique dealers. Have to make it to Fredericksburg for a seven A.M. meeting. That's why we left Austin so early.''

"Then what?"

Luna surveyed the large structure of the truck stop. "Play it by ear. You keep the waitress busy and I'll say I have to go to the bathroom. See what I can find."

I nodded my head in the darkness. "Okay, I guess," I said, wondering what kind of businesswomen we looked like in our T-shirts, jeans, and tennies.

We got out and walked toward the front door of the truck stop. To the west the rock loomed, in plain sight of the truck stop. I refused to look at it as we made our way toward the building.

It was an old, two-story structure with peeling paint and a porch hanging at an odd angle. Two huge pre-fab steel buildings had been affixed to either side of the original structure. We went in the front door. On our left was a double door, closed, no light showing underneath, with flaked gold lettering on the door, proclaiming the room to be The Taj Mahal Lounge.

Straight in front of us was the grocery store. The lights beckoned. After row upon row of overpriced food stuffs and over-the-counter drugs, we saw the diner. Steep stairs along the left wall led to the upper story. We went to a table in the diner and sat down. No one was in sight.

After about two minutes of total silence, a door behind the counter opened and a man came out carrying a plastic rack full of glasses.

"Oh, hey, ladies, didn't hear you come in. Be right with you."

We nodded. He appeared to be in his fifties or early sixties, Mexican, with black hair liberally salted with gray. He had a huge mustache over his upper lip that had not succumbed to the aging process: It was as dark as his hair must have once been. He was no more than five-six or seven, but square of body, with forearms that would make Popeye envious. The white pants, white T-shirt and white apron set off his olive complexion well.

Scoggins Truck Stop had no decor to speak off: The

floors were uncovered cement, a food-spotted dull gray in color. The tables and chairs were mismatched, as if they'd been bought without a lot of thought at flea markets and garage sales to replace the originals one-by-one as they fell apart. The four booths were alike, even to the gray duct tape covering holes and rips in the dark red Naugahyde.

The man brought us menus and coffee. He put two cups down and held up the pot, a question on his face.

"Please," Luna said.

I nodded my head.

He handed us the menus and poured, saying something in Spanish to Luna. She laughed and replied. I used to know a smidgen of Spanish I'd learned in our two years in Mexico, but had forgotten most of it in the twelve years since. I had no idea what they were saying to each other.

The waiter left, going back through the door to what I presumed was the kitchen. I asked Luna, "What did he say?"

"He asked me what a beautiful *guapa* lady like myself was doing with a *gringa* redhead."

"He did not!"

"Did so."

"What did you say?"

"I said we all have our crosses to bear, or words to that effect."

"You did not."

"Did so."

A plan was coming to my mind. "Listen," I started, but the waiter was back, coming to our table for our order.

I quickly opened the menu, found something that appeared edible, and quickly ordered. Luna was taking her time.

"Could you point me to the rest room?" I asked the waiter.

Luna glanced up, giving me a dirty look.

"Down that hall to the right. At the back," he told me.

I smiled my most *gringa* smile and got up from the table as the waiter started in again in Spanish. I heard Luna laughing as I made my way down the hall. This was obviously the pre-fab steel building to the right. The bare concrete floors were newer, but in just as bad a state of repair.

I saw a closed door with lettering on it reading TV RO M. I tried the knob and it turned easily in my hands. I peered around the door. The room was dark. Moving in and shutting the door behind me, I felt around for a light switch. I found one awkwardly placed on the wrong side of the door. I flipped the switch.

"Hey, what the hell?" came a sleepy voice.

I jumped about three feet. A man with dyed black hair and a very large nose peered around the side of a reclining chair facing a dark, big screen TV. "Well, hey, baby," he said, "come to make me happy?"

"No," I replied. I moved toward him, checking the other reclining chairs—there were five of them—to make sure no one else, namely Willis Pugh, was asleep in them.

"Come on over and sit on my lap, baby," big nose said.

"Go to hell," I said, and stomped out of the room.

"Oh, baby, you're breaking my heart . . ."

I switched off the light and went back into the hall. Two steps farther and on the other side of the hall was a door marked SHOWERS. I didn't really want to interrupt big nose's twin in the buff, but I had to know.

I opened the door. This room too was dark. I figured, rightly, that no one would be catching a few winks in the shower stalls, but I turned on the light and checked out the long, smelly room. As I walked down the cement-floored center hall, pushing open stalls to make sure they were all empty, I prayed athlete's foot germs didn't have the wherewithal to penetrate my thick-soled tennies.

The room was empty. I went back into the hall, finding the men's room next. The light was on in there, but it was empty. The smell was enough to send me out of the room in a hurry. I tried the ladies' room, using the facilities quickly and efficiently, then found myself back in the hall.

The hall turned at this point, and there were no lights shining in this new section. I turned the corner, wishing I'd thought to bring a flashlight. From the trace of light showing from whence I'd come, I could just barely make out two doors, one on either side of the hall. I opened one.

It was very noisy inside that room. Gurgles, spurts, snores, grinding of teeth all led to a cacophony of sound not unlike that of a large electric tool used for cutting down naughty trees. If I had a flashlight I could have shined it quietly on each noisy face. But I didn't have a flashlight.

I found the light switch and turned it on. There were two rows of seven cots lined up in the room; two ceiling fans moving the dense air. Heads, eyes squinting, looked up at me; more remained where they were, mouths opened, ungodly noises emitting. Of the fourteen beds, six were occupied. None of the six faces, squinting or reposed, belonged to my husband.

I turned off the light and left the room, walking across the hall to the other room. This room, when I turned on the light, I found was much larger. Three rows of cots, about ten each, lined each wall with one going down the middle. But it wasn't nearly as occupied as the other room. There were only two men asleep, or formerly asleep, in the beds in this dorm.

"What the . . ." one squinty-eyed man asked.

"Go back to sleep," I said, softly. "I'm an angel."

"Okay," he said, turning over.

Neither of the faces belonged to Willis.

I went back into the hall. There was a door at the end. I opened it. It was a closet full of bedding and other supplies. I'd hit a dead end.

Sixteen

"What's back there?" Luna asked.

We were finally alone. The waiter, whose name was Ray, according to Luna who'd gotten quite chummy in the time I'd been gone, had brought our food and had gone back to the kitchen. We were still the only patrons in the place. I told her about the TV room, shower rooms, bathrooms, and dorms. And the fact that my husband had not been anywhere back there.

"So maybe he's gone," Luna said.

"Gone where?" I looked at the stairway leading to the second floor. "Wonder what's up there?"

"According to Ray, just the office and storage rooms."

"So would you keep a hostage in a dorm with a bunch of truckers—or someplace those truckers are not likely to go?" I asked.

Luna shrugged. "A thought." She looked beyond the

rows of groceries to the front door of the truck stop. "Wonder what's in the lounge?"

I followed her gaze, then looked toward the door to the kitchen. "Keep him occupied if he comes out," I said, getting up from the table.

"You take the lounge and I take the stairs?" she said.

"So what do we do when Romeo comes back?" I countered.

"Hey, I'm the professional! You got to go last time!"

"He doesn't have a crush on me," I said, leaving her sitting at the table.

Figuring that the door to the lounge was out of sight if Ray the waiter should walk back in from the kitchen, I decided to try that first. I had no really good idea on how to make it up the stairs.

I scooted quickly to the front doors and beyond to the door of the Taj Mahal Lounge. The doors were locked, but they looked flimsy. I pulled a credit card out of my purse and slipped it between the two doors. The lock snicked back and I opened the door, quickly shutting it behind me. My first experience with B&E.

The sun had begun to rise outside, but not enough to shed any light in the windowless bar. I felt along a wall, not finding any switch at all. Hugging the wall, I walked toward the back of the room, finding the bar by touch. Feeling under the bar I found two things: a sawed-off shotgun and a flashlight. I put the sawed-off down and switched on the flashlight.

The room was totally empty. Chairs rested atop small tables, stools atop the bar. There was a stage opposite the front door with threadbare red velvet drapes behind it. I went to those, pulling them back. Stairs led down three steps.

I let the drapes fall behind me as I followed the steps down. A window let in a little light there, but I still needed the flashlight. Another curtained-off area appeared to be a small dressing room, with a mirrored dressing table covered in jars and tubes of makeup, a small rack holding feather boas and sequined G-strings.

Beyond the dressing area, there was a unisex bathroom, and beyond that a storeroom loaded with boxes of Jim Beam, Coors, and mixers. The storeroom did have one very interesting item—a stairway going up.

Keeping the flashlight aimed at the steps, I made my way up, hoping this stairway led to the same place as the one in the main room. I hadn't noticed either pre-fab building being two-story, and I thought it was possible I'd worked my way back to the wall where the two buildings adjoined. I'm not real great with directions.

I could tell by the smell that I'd made my way back into the older main building; mildew and rotting wood permeated the dining room and grocery store.

Without the covering odors of food, the upstairs reeked of age. Light spilled upward from the stairway that led down to the dining room. I turned off the flashlight, hoping Ray was in the kitchen and hadn't seen it. Then I heard Luna's laugh and Ray's deep bass chuckle and knew he was back in the dining room.

There was a door almost opposite the head of the dining-room stairs. I wanted in the room beyond. I had to see inside that room. I crept close to the wall by the head of the stairs and inched my face around the edge, trying to see if I could see the two below. I could see Luna's head where she sat, but only Ray's leg as he stood over her. Unless I made enough noise to make him bend over and look up the stairwell, he wouldn't know I was there.

I moved quickly to the closed door opposite the stairs and tried the knob. It was locked. I grabbed my credit card again and tried that. It broke in two in my hands, one half falling to the linoleum-covered floor, making a clacking sound as it landed. I threw myself out of the line of sight of the stairwell, huddled up against the wall. The talk and laughter continued from below. The sound of the plastic hitting the floor had been deafening to me, but my clearer mind decided it probably hadn't made much of a noise.

I looked farther down the darkened hall of the upstairs. There was another door at the end. I made my way to that and tried the knob. It too was locked. I pressed my ear to the rotting wood of the door and listened. If Willis was tied up inside, I'd be able to hear him breathing, maybe, or squirming, or something.

I heard nothing. I pushed at the door. It was thick wood, the way they used to make them, but the doorjamb was made of less sturdy stuff, and termites had done their damage. I knew one swift kick from my size ten shoe would send the door sailing inward. And Ray sailing up the stairs.

Feeling frustration down to my kneecaps, I went back the way I'd come. I made my way to the diner, glad Ray had gone back in the kitchen. Luna had finished her breakfast. I took one look at the cold yolks staring up at me from their bed of congealed grease and lost any appetite I might have had.

''Anything?'' Luna asked.

''No.'' I stared off into space. ''There's two rooms upstairs I couldn't get into.'' I sighed. ''Or maybe I got the phone number wrong.''

''Great time to think of that.''

''Or maybe you looked it up wrong.''

She glared at me and I glared at her.

''Now what?'' I finally asked.

Luna sighed. ''Let's pay up and regroup outside.''

She called to Ray, who came out of the kitchen and rang up our check on an almost-antique cash register. Luna paid and he said something in Spanish that again made her laugh.

As we walked out the door, I asked, ''What did he say?''

''Learn Spanish, okay?''

We walked toward the car. The sun was coming up and

I looked around, trying to see where else in the building my husband could possibly be.

I stopped, grabbing Luna's arm. "Look," I said.

"What?"

"The double-wide trailer back there."

"Interesting," she said.

We found a small dirt road that led out of the parking lot at the back of the lot to the turkey farm beyond. We drove slowly over the mud holes and dried humps of dirt to the building that housed what sounded like thousands of angry birds.

We sat in the car, first with the windows rolled down, then with them up to keep the stench of the turkey quarters at bay.

"Now what?" I said for what seemed the thousandth time.

"We need to get in those rooms on the second floor. And we need to see what's in that double-wide. Not to mention that," she said, pointing at the turkey building. "But I definitely think it's time to call the locals. We need backup."

I nodded my head, staring through the windshield of the car. "If they're keeping Willis in there," I said, nodding toward the dilapidated turkey barn, the stench of the birds still fresh in my nostrils, "I'll kill them slowly."

The sun was fully up and it promised to be one of those days so typical of a Central Texas September—hot and muggy. I was already beginning to weigh the merits of the current situation: die of heat prostration with the windows up; gag to death on the smell with the windows down.

"Can we park someplace else?" I asked.

"Good idea," Luna said, leaning forward to start the car. Her hand was on the key, ready to turn it when the driver's-side door was jerked open.

A man grabbed Luna's arm and pulled her out of the

car. As I reached for her, my door was yanked open and an arm grabbed me. I stumbled out of the front seat, my free arm coming up swinging. I got the guy on the side of the head and he fell back, momentarily stunned.

I ran for the back of the car, but the man who'd grabbed my arm caught me again, this time pinning both of my arms behind me. He said something in Spanish to the man holding Luna.

I twisted and squirmed, trying to get away, until I heard Luna say, "Easy, Pugh. Let's find out what they want."

She spoke to her captor in Spanish. He let go of her, pushing her up against the car. A knife was suddenly in his hand, pointing at the underpart of Luna's chin. She held up her hands in a conciliatory manner, speaking softly in Spanish. I understood the last line. *"Habla ingles?"*

"Yeah," he said. "I speak English." He had little accent, the words were clear. "You wanna tell me what you're doing here?"

"We got lost," Luna said, smiling. "I'm sorry if we're trespassing. We just had breakfast over at the truck stop and must have taken the wrong turn—"

"Yeah, this old dirt track really reminds you of the highway, huh?" he said.

He reached inside the open car door and pulled out both Luna's purse and mine, spilling the contents on the ground. Luna's gun lay amid the mess.

My captor still had my arms pinned behind me. My shoulders were beginning to ache from the strain. "Please," I said, pulling lightly against the pressure. He just pulled harder. I suppressed a cry of pain as he jerked my arms backward.

Luna's fella was squatting on the ground, rummaging through the contents of the two purses. He'd stuck Luna's gun in the waistband of his pants, at the back. He pulled up a wallet, looked at the ID, and threw it back down. He picked up the second wallet and opened it. He jumped up and spat on the ground, not far from my address book.

"*Policia!*" he yelled.

Luna started to move, but the guy was quick. He pushed her up against the car, the knife now touching her throat.

A third man came out of the turkey enclosure. His Spanish was quick and guttural as he addressed the man holding Luna. He slapped the hand away that held the knife to Luna's throat.

"What are you doing here?" the third man asked Luna.

"Honest to God, we just got lost—" Luna started.

"Shut up," he said. "You a cop?"

"Off duty. My friend and I are on our way to the rock to try some climbing. We're on vacation."

"You always carry your piece when you're on vacation, lady?"

"Regulations," Luna said.

The third man looked in the backseat of the car, then he said, "Open the trunk."

"The keys are inside."

"Get the keys," he said to the man with the knife.

He pulled the keys out of the ignition and handed them to the third man, who walked to the back of the car and opened the trunk. Slamming it shut, he moved back to Luna.

"You going climbing, huh?" He slapped her in the face.

I let out a yell, but it only garnered me more pain in my upper extremities.

"Don't lie to me, bitch! You don't have no climbing gear in that car! You think we're just some stupid wetbacks don't know from nothing!"

He started to speak in Spanish to the man with the knife, but that man said, "She speaks Spanish." Both turned and looked at Luna.

I couldn't see the man holding me, but the one with the knife was young, no more than twenty. He wasn't particularly tall, shorter than me, maybe five-seven or eight, slender, and exceedingly handsome, almost femininely beautiful, with large dark eyes, thick hair, even features, beautiful skin, eyelashes to die for.

The third man was not beautiful. In fact, he was downright pug ugly. Shorter than the man with the knife, he wasn't much more than five-four, built like a fireplug, almost square in shape. Older than the other, maybe twenty-five, his face was pockmarked, his nose large and squashed against his face like it had been broken one too many times. His eyes were small and narrow, nothing more than slits in his face, and his teeth were stained, some missing. His hair was military short, exposing misshapen ears. Like I said, he was not beautiful.

The turkeys were getting louder by the minute, and my nose was not acclimating to the smell. Gnats swarmed in front of my face and I couldn't brush them away. One went down my throat and I coughed, choking.

"Take 'em in the storage room," Pug Ugly said.

"Naw, man, we gotta get rid of 'em!" Mr. Lovely said.

The one holding me spoke for the first time. "Come on, Jimmy. What you saying, man?"

Mr. Lovely looked our way. "Shut your mouth, Joe. You ain't got the stomach for this. You go on back to Mama, hear?"

Pug Ugly stepped between Jimmy the Beautiful and Luna. "Both of you shut up, okay? Nobody's killing nobody, got that? I gotta think this through, man. She's heat. We kill her, we gonna have seven kinds of hell breathing down our necks."

"Not if we hide the bodies, man," Jimmy said.

Pug Ugly rolled his eyes. "You been watching too much Rambo, swear to God, Jimmy. Now both of you take these bitches into the storage room and tie 'em up real good. And, Jimmy," Pug Ugly said, his pointing finger and his face very close to the lovelier one, "don't do nothing stupid. I mean it, man."

All of which just goes to prove the old maxim: Beauty is only skin deep.

Seventeen

When they threw us on the floor of the storage room in the turkey building, I finally got to see my captor, the one who'd been holding my arms behind my back. That he was Jimmy the Beautiful's brother was abundantly apparent—except he was the good-looking one. He was young—very young, no more than late teens.

Although he had been the one holding me and hurting me, he'd also been the one to balk at his brother's idea of killing Luna and me. I figured if we could ever get him alone, without his older brother around, we could work on that scant sensitivity.

Sensitivity he didn't show when he threw me on the floor and rolled me onto my stomach, grabbing my arms once again and trussing me like he would one of the turkeys in the yard.

He tied my hands together behind my back, then my

feet, then pulled my legs up to truss the hands and feet together. I felt like one of my daughters' roly-poly dolls.

Luna was getting the same treatment from Jimmy. After he'd finished with her, he said, "I still think a bullet in the brain would solve all our problems."

"Shut up about that," Joe the younger said. "Roberto told you to shut up about that."

Jimmy laughed. Out of the corner of my eye, I could see him poke his younger brother on the arm. "What'sa matter, baby, you getting all squeamish? Huh? Run home to Mama time?"

Joe slapped Jimmy's hand away. "Shut up, man. You're making me mad!"

"Oo," Jimmy said in a singsong voice, "Mr. Macho's getting mad, ladies. Best watch out!"

"I tol' you, man, shut your mouth!" In the blink of an eyelash, Joe had a knife in his hand and he swung it in a wide arch toward his brother.

Jimmy laughed and danced out of the way, like a matador with an ornery bull. "Oh boy. I'm gonna get it now, huh, little baby? You gonna cut me with your little knife?"

"I'm gonna gut you like a turkey, man!" Joe lunged and Jimmy jumped out of the way, swinging around and grabbing his younger brother in a neck hold with one arm, while with the other he twisted the knife out of Joe's hand.

"Hey, bro, you wanna cut somebody, you practice on the bitches, you hear me?" He shoved the boy into the wall of the storage room, the impact of which sent tools sliding to the floor, a hammer barely missing Luna's left shoulder.

The storage-room door opened and Roberto, Pug Ugly, came in.

"What the fuck you two doing in here, huh?" He slapped at Joe then at Jimmy. "I tol' you tie these bitches up and get outta here. Is that what I tol' you or what?"

Jimmy batted Roberto's hand away. "Yeah, yeah. We're just messing around a little, huh, Joe?"

"*Chingate,*" Joe said.

Jimmy laughed. "Little brother's just real sensitive, huh, little Joe? He don't like to hurt the pretty ladies, huh?"

Joe slapped at Jimmy one more time and walked out of the room. Roberto came over to where Luna and I were lying and checked out the ropes.

"These look pretty tight," he said.

"Tight enough, I guess," Jimmy said, "but a bullet from the bitch's own gun do a hell of a better job, man, than them ropes."

Roberto laughed. "I ain't killing no cop, Jimmy. Even thinking about it just shows how stupid you really are."

Jimmy lunged at Roberto, who grabbed one arm and twisted it behind Jimmy's back, throwing him against the wall of the storage room. More debris fell to the floor, barely missing Luna and me.

"You don't calm down, man, I gonna tell your daddy what you been up to, you understand me?" Roberto said.

"Yeah, you tell on me you telling on yourself, *puto.*"

"I tell your daddy I just happened to find out what you been doing, he gonna believe anything you say?"

He pulled Jimmy's arm up tighter. Jimmy let out a moan.

"I was just joking around, Roberto. Okay, man? Just joking—"

"See if your daddy likes them jokes, huh, man?"

"No, it's okay. I was just joking. I won't do it no more."

Roberto pushed Jimmy hard into the wall. Jimmy fell to the floor, nursing the injured arm. "Man, can't you tell when I'm just joking?" Jimmy said, trying hard at a grin.

"Get on out of here," Roberto said. "We got birds to move. Go help that stupid brother of yours."

Jimmy stood up. "Hey, man, don't be calling my brother stupid . . ."

Roberto shoved Jimmy out the door, then closed it after him. He came and squatted between Luna and me. "Ladies,

I know this isn't really comfortable, but it's the best I can do under the circumstances."

"Look," Luna said, turning her head as best she could to look at him. "We don't know what the hell's going on around here, okay? We have no idea. If you let us go, even if I break the promise I'm going to make you that I won't tell anybody, even if I were to do that, which I won't, whatever you got here you could move before anybody came looking. Then it would just be our word against yours."

Roberto sighed. "Yeah, and you're a cop. Even if you are a Chicana, they're gonna believe you before they believe me and the boys, right? I ain't that stupid, bitch." Roberto stood up. "Look, you two just try to stay calm awhile, okay? I'll let you go when I can."

Roberto left the room, flipping off the light switch as he went, sending Luna and me into total darkness.

I've always prided myself on my keen night vision, on my ability to move around in the dark while Willis bumped into chairs. I decided, lying there on the floor of the turkey farm supply room, that I'd just never been in total darkness before. I was experiencing something alien, and it felt heavy—like the dark was a living thing pressing down on me.

"Pugh?"

The last time I'd seen Luna, before Roberto had turned out the lights, she'd been lying right next to me. I knew she hadn't moved, yet her voice sounded far away. It may have been the rushing sound in my ears that made her voice sound that way.

"What?" I answered.

"You okay?"

"Dandy." I took as big a gulp of air as I could, lying like I was on my stomach, arms and legs tied behind me. "How about you? Did he hurt you?"

"I'm tougher than I look," she said. "I'm okay."

I wanted to touch her, to feel the warmth of another

human being, but that wasn't going to happen. I wondered if Willis was in the same situation. Was he hog-tied in another room of the turkey farm? In one of the upstairs rooms of the truck stop? Was he okay?

Was he still alive?

It seemed like days since he'd called, since I'd heard his voice for the first time in almost a week. But it had only been hours. I'd thought that first day he'd gone missing had been the longest day of my life. I was beginning to rethink that assumption.

How stupid was I coming after him this way? Was I going to leave my kids an orphan? What would that make Bessie? A double-orphan? How many times could one child lose her parents?

"We've got to get out of here," Luna said.

"Okay, great idea. You wanna lead or you want me to?"

"Cut the sarcasm. Can you roll over toward me?"

"How?"

"I don't know! Rock yourself. See if you can get by me."

"Why?"

"I need your help. Push me over toward the wall. All that crap that fell down when Roberto and Jimmy were fighting—surely there was something that fell that can help us!"

"Okay," I said, swinging my trussed arms and legs, trying to start up a rocking motion. I could barely feel my arms anymore; they'd gone numb. My toes were tingling. The rocking motion was mashing what some have called my massive breasts into the floor, causing more pain. I finally managed to roll on my side, kicking Luna in the process.

"Sorry—" I started.

"No! That's great. Now push me."

"Damnit, Luna, I can't move . . ." I kicked out as best I could with my legs, finding what felt like her legs, trussed in the same position. I pushed, using muscles I had neglected and forgotten about years ago.

She was rocking as I had been earlier. I felt her thighs come off the ground. I thrust my feet under them and pushed upward. Luna let out a yell and an *oomph* sound.

"You okay?" I whispered.

"Yeah, I'm in position, I think." I could hear her grunting as she moved around.

"Anything there?"

"No. Shit . . . wait. What's this? No . . . Oh . . . Ouch . . . What? Okay, this is good."

"What is it?"

"Hot-damn!" she said, too loud.

"Shhh! What is it?"

"A machete!"

"No kidding?"

"Yeah, now if I can just figure out . . . how . . . to . . ."

"Don't cut yourself!"

"I'm trying . . . not . . . to cut . . . ouch . . . no, it's okay, it's . . . coming . . . shit . . . ah-ha!"

"What?"

"I'm a genius!"

I could hear her fumbling around next to me. "Did you get it? Are you loose?"

"Shhh! We can't have them hear us now!"

I felt her hands on my arms, running down the length of them to where the ropes were. "Don't move, I don't want to accidentally cut you."

"I'd rather you didn't either," I whispered. "I won't move a muscle."

I lay as still as I could, the bindings tightening as Luna worked at them. Then, miraculously, my arms were hanging limply at my side, while Luna worked on my legs.

"Rub your arms! Get the circulation back," she said.

"Rub them with what?" I couldn't lift them. They were like dead weights attached to my shoulders. My feet were loose. I tried to sit up. Luna helped, pulling first my head, not being able to see what she was grabbing, then lowering her hold to my shoulders. Once I was in a sitting position, she grabbed an arm and began rubbing it. "Can you feel that?"

"Yes, and it's beginning to hurt like crazy!"

She grabbed my other arm, giving it the same treatment. Once the circulation was moving again—albeit sluggishly—through my arms, I started on my legs, rubbing them into submission. Then I felt a thumb in my nose.

"Hey!"

"Sorry," Luna said. "I can't see a damn thing. Come on."

"Where?"

"Hands and knees to the door. Keep ahold of my foot."

"Where's the door?"

"We find a wall, we get up and walk along it till we find the door, okay?"

"Sounds like a plan to me," I said, grabbing her foot with one hand and crawling behind her.

It was a long crawl, through dirt and debris scattered all over the floor of the storage room. At one point my knee landed on something sharp. I let out a cry, trying to muffle it with a hand. I could feel the warmth of blood traveling down my knee.

"What's wrong?" Luna whispered.

"I cut myself, I think."

"Bad?"

I shook my head. "I don't know. Just keep going."

Finally we made it to the wall. Gingerly we both stood up, clasping hands. I could feel the blood flowing down my leg.

"Okay," Luna said, "one hand on the wall, the other in mine. Can you walk?"

"Yeah," I said, gritting my teeth.

"Okay, slowly."

There was so much crap hanging on the walls of the

storage room that we (mostly Luna, who was leading) kept bumping into it, but finally we made it to the door.

Which was, of course, locked.

"The door's locked," Luna whispered.

"Can you find the light switch?" I breathed back.

"Maybe we shouldn't. They might see it!"

"At this point I don't care! Just turn on the damn light!"

The darkness was getting to me. I thought my eyes would adjust given time. But they hadn't. I figured the hall must be dark, too. No light seeped through the crack beneath the door. The dark was still absolute and total, like swimming through Jell-O. And my knee throbbed.

The overhead light sprung to life. I cringed, shielding my eyes from the glare, the wonderful, beautiful glare. Luna and I looked at each other and grinned.

"Yeah, this is better," she said.

"Oh, yeah," I agreed.

"Let's see your knee."

She knelt in front of me, widening the hole in my jeans caused by the object that cut my knee. "The bleeding seems to be stopping," Luna said. "Doesn't look like it needs stitches."

"Well, it hurts," I said, well aware of the petulant sound of my voice.

"Want me to kiss it?" Luna said, standing, which obviously meant she wasn't serious.

I ignored her and the two of us stood, looking at the door.

There was a push-button lock on our side, but that obviously wasn't what was stopping it from opening. This was the kind of lock that didn't need a key from the inside. I turned the knob and pulled. Nothing happened.

"I told you it was locked," Luna hissed.

"So, okay, you told me."

"Jesus."

Luna turned the knob and pulled. Still nothing happened.

"But it's always best to be absolutely sure," I said, sarcasm dripping ladylike from my tongue.

Luna began perusing the walls. Obviously finding what she was looking for, she walked to the wall opposite the door and took down what looked to be a professional-style jack.

"What? You're going to lift the room from around the door?"

"Something like that," she said, straining under the weight as she set it down and rolled it to the door. She worked the lever into the crack under the door, fumbled for a moment to find the locking apparatus, and then began to pump the jack handle.

Looking at me, she said, "Get that crowbar."

I limped to the wall and pulled the crowbar off.

"Now," she said, "stick it between the door and the jamb. While I pump, you pull."

"Why not?"

I did as she instructed, and within seconds we were both grunting with the unaccustomed effort. Nothing happened.

"Stick the crowbar on this side, by the hinges," Luna instructed.

I did as she told me. We repeated the process. This time it worked. The door fell on us, knocking us both to the floor and making a god-awful racket.

We scrambled up, Luna reaching quickly for the light switch and plunging us back into darkness. But this time the darkness was not total. As I had surmised, the hall was also unlit, but the hall led into the light, and that light shed enough for us to see each other's bare outlines.

Luna grabbed my hand and stepped gingerly with one foot on the broken door. It rocked slightly but didn't make a noise. She put both feet on and motioned for me to follow. We walked stealthily out into the hall. To the left was darkness and the dim outline of another door. To the right was the light and what might ultimately be freedom.

We crept along the hall, staying close to the wall until

we came to the opening. Beyond was row upon row of turkey cages and an open bay; a pickup truck backed up to it, its tailgate down.

We could hear raised male voices, speaking in Spanish. The voices sounded familiar enough to identify them as our captors. They were loading cages into the pickup's bed, but the cages' occupants looked to my untrained eye much more like chickens than turkeys.

''Damn,'' Luna whispered, ''cocks.''

''You don't have to be vulgar,'' I whispered back. ''But I agree.''

''No!'' she said, grabbing my arm. ''Roosters. Fighting cocks.''

Eighteen

I looked around at the rows of turkeys. Was there any other way out besides the bay? There was a door to our right, almost exactly opposite the bay. I nudged Luna and pointed at the door.

"They'll see us," she said. "And they've got my car keys."

"Then why'd we leave our cozy little room?" I breathed.

She poked me with her elbow and we backed up down the hall. Out of sight of the three men and the pickup truck, she said, "We don't even know if the door's unlocked. If we run to it and it is locked, then they'll catch us for sure."

"Then what?" I asked, my exasperation showing.

"We wait. They're loading up the cocks now. I'd bet they're getting ready to take them somewhere."

"And wouldn't it be natural to come check on us before they leave?"

Luna frowned and nodded her head.

You're always supposed to knock on wood when you make a statement like that. At least that's what my father always told me. I'd forgotten. The next thing we heard was Roberto's voice, getting closer.

"Gonna check on the bitches 'fore we take off. Be right back."

Luna grabbed me and we ran back into the room. "Lay down!" she ordered.

I gave her a look but she pushed me to the floor. "Possum!" she breathed, grabbing the crowbar I'd used earlier and throwing her body up against the wall next to what used to be the door.

I closed my eyes and tried to steady my breathing. It was only seconds before I heard Roberto's voice. "What the fuck—" Then I heard the Gallagher-watermelon-splatting sound of the crowbar and Roberto's head meeting it.

I jumped up as Luna knelt over Roberto. "Is he dead?" I breathed.

She felt the pulse at his neck. "No. Get the ropes."

I switched on the light and ran to our discarded bonds, grabbing one of the ropes and bringing it to Luna. We tied Roberto in a much gentler fashion than he had directed us to be tied earlier. I think it was just the head injury—nothing to do, really, with the supposed gentler and more nurturing nature of woman. I felt anything but gentle and nurturing at the moment.

And then, of course, it's always nice to remember that primitive tribes used to throw their captives to the women for disposal.

I knew in my heart that these three men had something to do with my husband's disappearance. Knowing that, I felt like a very primitive woman, indeed. I watched Luna pull her gun out of the waistband of Roberto's pants. She held it loosely in her hand.

There's something to be said for the combination of fear and acclimation. The stench of the turkeys had all but disappeared from my mind and my olfactory senses. Following Luna's lead, we crept down the hall again, stopping at the end to peer around. Jimmy and Joe were lounging against the side of the pickup, Jimmy sucking on a cigarette, Joe kicking dust up with the toe of his boot.

"The only weapons I saw them carrying were the knives. You?" Luna whispered.

"The only gun I saw was yours," I agreed.

"Okay. I'm going out there with this," she said, indicating the weapon in her hand. "You go the other direction. See if that other door's open. In case you need to run for it."

"Luna—"

"Do it!" she hissed, and stepped out into the open area, fully visible to the pickup beyond. I took off in the opposite direction, heading for the door as quietly as possible, but keeping one eye on Luna.

Joe saw her before Jimmy. He yelled something in Spanish and took off running. Luna jumped down the foot or so from the bay floor to the ground, grabbing Jimmy and throwing him hard against the truck, the muzzle of the gun shoved beneath his chin.

"Lock the door!" she yelled at me.

I ran to the door, fumbling around for the lock, found it and pressed it home, then ran back to the bay door.

"Now he's got only one way to get back in here," she said. Pushing Jimmy in front of her, she said, "Up! Get up the goddamn steps!"

Jimmy stumbled getting up, but Luna never let up the pressure of the gun. I grabbed his arm and pulled it up behind him, slamming him to the floor.

Luna said, "Go get the other rope."

I ran back to the room, picking up the discarded crowbar as I went. I didn't need it. Roberto was still out cold. I tried a trick Luna had taught me while we were watching a cop show on TV together one night. I kicked him in the butt, right at the junction of anus and genitalia. Someone playing possum will automatically clinch. It's almost impossible not to. If they don't clinch, it's a pretty sure bet they're unconscious. Roberto appeared to be in the latter category.

I grabbed the other rope and went back into the turkey room where Luna knelt with one knee pressed into Jimmy's back. I gleefully hog-tied him, then grabbed what appeared to be a clean handkerchief from his back pocket.

There was a water spigot by the turkey cages. I wet the handkerchief and cleaned up my knee. "What are we gonna do about Joe?" I asked Luna.

"Wait," she said.

Jimmy laughed. It was not a pleasant sound. "My little brother gonna come back here and gut you, hear?" He laughed until I stuck his now-dirty handkerchief in his mouth as a gag.

"Where are our purses?" Luna asked Jimmy, pulling the filthy gag out of his mouth.

"Not talking, bitch. Not a word," Jimmy said.

Luna kicked him in the testicles. I winced. Jimmy yelled. "I kill you, you whore! I'm gonna kill you bad!"

"Where are our purses?" Luna repeated.

Jimmy spat. Luna kicked him in the ribs. I pulled at her arm.

"Elena, don't—"

She pulled her arm away from me. "Get away!" She began stripping off Jimmy's shoes and socks. "I'm gonna start shooting off his toes!"

I wasn't sure, but I was certainly hoping we were playing "good cop/bad cop." Either that or my friend had gone totally over the edge.

"Elena, you don't want to shoot off his toes! Remember what happened the last time you did that? You got suspended for thirty days!"

"Yeah, but this time it would be worth it! Even sixty

days would be worth it! Look at his toes! They're truly ugly!''

Luna grabbed one of Jimmy's great toes and pressed the muzzle of the gun against it.

''Jesus! They're in the cab of the truck, for Christ's sake! Just look!'' Jimmy yelled.

I ran to the bay, looked both ways to make sure Joe wasn't around, and scrambled down to the driver's side of the truck. The purses were in there—as were the keys to the truck itself.

''Let's just take this and leave your car! It would be safer,'' I said.

''Okay, help me with twinkle toes here,'' Luna said, scraping Jimmy's stomach along the wood floor of the turkey room as she pulled him along.

''What about the game cocks?'' I asked.

''Leave 'em in there,'' Luna said. ''Evidence.''

We got Jimmy to the bay and tossed him none too gently into the bed of the pickup, in a small space not crammed with cages.

''You stay back here with him,'' Luna said. ''I'll drive.''

I wedged myself between Jimmy and a game cock, the tire iron in my hand in case Jimmy decided to try playing Superman.

The truck started right up. We rounded the side of the turkey farm building, heading for the main dirt road back to the truck stop. No Joe in sight. Luna hit the accelerator and we bounced over the potholes and mud puddles, Jimmy's head bouncing off the bed of the truck.

Nearing the back of the truck stop, Luna called back, ''There's Ray! The guy at the diner! He'll help us!''

She pulled the truck quickly to where Ray was standing, sliding to a stop.

Ray frowned at us. ''I thought you two left a long time ago,'' he said. He glanced in the back of the pickup then looked back at Luna and me. "Why you got my son trussed up like that?"

"Watch her, Daddy," Jimmy said, "she's got a gun."

Luna had been half out of the truck. Ray grabbed her arm, pulling her the rest of the way out. She had had her gun conveniently at her side on the seat of the cab. Now it was convenient for Ray. He picked it up and held it aimed at Luna.

"Untie my boy," he said to me, keeping his eyes on Luna.

"No," Luna said. "He tried to kill us. I don't think we can safely untie him."

Ray looked at his son in the back of the truck. "What's going on here, boy?"

"She's crazy, Daddy. They're both crazy bitches! They come in waving that gun and yelling at us. Joe, he ran away and left me, and they got me. I don't know what they gonna do with me if you didn't come along, Daddy, I swear to you."

"Boy, you'd swear night was day if you thought it would get you out of trouble," Ray said.

"Daddy, you just go look back there at the barn. They done something to Roberto, swear to God. I think they killed him."

"Roberto's not dead," Luna said. She smiled. It wasn't pleasant. "But I doubt if he's feeling great right about now."

Ray waved the gun at me. "Untie my boy."

I looked at Luna. She nodded her head and I began undoing the ropes that bound Jimmy. He sat up, rubbing his arms and legs; he hadn't been bound near as long as we'd been.

"What's this here in the truck?" Ray asked, looking at the cages. Seeing what was inside, he hauled his son roughly down from the bed of the truck. "Cock fighting? What kind of *desgrasiado* are you? You trying to bring disgrace to this family?'' The boy stood there, his head bowed, taking the verbal punishment his father dished out. Ray sighed. ''Go to the barn and check on Roberto. Now!''

''Okay, Daddy, sure thing.'' Jimmy glanced toward the barn and got an excited expression on his face, saying, ''Look! There's Joe now!''

Seeing us, Joe turned and started to run. Ray said loudly, ''Joseph! Come here!''

The boy stopped in midstride. Turning, his shoulders slumped, he walked toward us. Ray nodded to Jimmy. ''Go now. Go check on Roberto.''

Jimmy loped off toward the barn. Passing his brother, he hit his arm. Joe turned to retaliate. The three of us watched, and Ray said, ''Now, Joseph.''

Joe glanced back at Jimmy and picked up his pace getting to his father. Once at the truck, he wouldn't look at either Luna or me.

''Who are these women?'' Ray asked.

''I dunno,'' Joe answered.

''You ever seen these women before?''

Joe shrugged his shoulders. ''I dunno. Maybe.''

''Maybe where did you see them?'' Ray asked, his voice exceedingly calm.

''Maybe over at the barn,'' Joe answered, staring at the ground.

''Why were they at the barn?''

''I dunno.''

''What happened when they got to the barn?'' Ray asked.

Joe shrugged, not answering.

''I'm getting two stories here, Joseph. One from these women and one from your brother. Which one is true?''

''Jimmy's?'' Joe asked, looking up at his father with a hopeful expression.

''You don't know the two stories, why you know Jimmy's is the right one?''

Joe shrugged his shoulders again and looked back at the ground. Ray turned to Luna and me. "Ladies, I'm not sure what's been going on here, but I'd like to know."

Luna leaned against the side of the truck, crossing her arms in front of her. "You in on it with them, Ray?" she asked.

Ray frowned. "That trash?" he asked, pointing at the cocks in the back of the truck.

"All three of the boys seemed to be in on it," Luna said.

Ray turned and grabbed Joe by the shirt front, almost pulling his taller son's feet off the ground. "You messing with cocks? You and Jimmy such *desgrasiado* that you bet on the deaths of barn animals?"

Behind us, toward the barn, I could see Jimmy assisting a weak Roberto out of the barn and down the dirt road toward us. The September sun was beating down hard, baking the ground around us and heating up the bed of the truck.

Ray put down his youngest son and watched quietly as Roberto and Jimmy walked up to us. When they reached us, Ray said, "Roberto. I don't think for a moment you're not involved with this. My boys ain't smart enough to think this up without you. You got my boys messing with trash. I give you the most precious gift a man can give, his daughter, and you get my boys messing with trash."

"Ray—" Roberto started, but Ray held up his hand for quiet.

"Shut up. I don't want to hear what you got to say."

Roberto, still reeling from the possible concussion from being hit with the tire iron, tried to straighten up. "She's a cop, Ray. The Chicana's a cop. Whatever you think 'bout what we been doing, and I'll take what blame you wanna give me, it don't mean a thing 'cause she's a cop, Ray. And cock fightin's against the law in this state. Won't be just me going down."

Ray turned to Luna. "This true? You a cop?"

Luna nodded her head once.

Ray sighed. Turning to Jimmy, he said, "Get Roberto in the bed of the truck. You ladies in the front please. What's your name?" he asked Luna.

"Elena Luna," she said. "This is my friend E. J. Pugh."

Ray nodded politely at me. "Miss Luna, please drive. Miss Pugh, you sit in the middle. Joe, get in the back."

We did as he said. Luna started the truck and followed Ray's instructions, pulling the vehicle up to a side door of the pre-fab building I knew housed the Taj Mahal Lounge. Once there, he got us all out of the truck and, using a key from a large key ring at his waist, unlocked the door, letting the boys in first, then me, Luna following with the gun at her back and Ray's hand on her arm.

The side door led into the storage room with the staircase. He pointed everybody up the stairs with admonitions for quiet. We trooped up, Jimmy and Joe both helping to support Roberto up the stairs.

Once on the upper hall, he pointed us toward the door at the other end of the hall. We started walking.

As we passed the stairway opening to the diner, Ray stopped, bending down. "What's this?" he said.

He held it out to me. It was the broken half of my charge card.

Nineteen

"What's this?" Ray repeated, his voice low, not much above a whisper. He held the broken credit card in my face.

I didn't say anything. Ray grabbed my shoulder, pulling my face even closer to his. "You were up here snooping, weren't you? What were you doing up here?"

Not getting an answer from me, he pushed me and Luna farther down the hall, pulling a key off his large key chain and inserting it into the door. The three younger men preceded us inside, then, even though we were moving, Ray pushed us the rest of the way.

I landed on my knees on the floor. "Get up!" Ray hissed. "Now you tell me! What you doing up here snooping around?"

"Tell him," Luna said.

I sighed. "I'm looking for Willis Pugh," I said.

Ray just looked at me. Finally he said, "So? Who's Willis Pugh?"

"My husband."

Ray shrugged, his face a mask of total confusion. "So why you looking for him up here?"

"Because he's been missing since Sunday, and I got a call from him from a number here last night."

"I don't know nobody named that!" Ray said. "Lady, you're lying to me!"

I pointed at my purse, clutched under Ray's arm. "Hand me my purse. I have a picture of him."

"Yeah and a gun like your friend here?"

I sighed. This was really getting ridiculous. "Look inside yourself. In my wallet."

"Joseph, come here. Find it for me." He handed my purse to his youngest son, keeping the gun aimed at Luna and me.

Joe was fiddling with my wallet, flipping through the pictures of my kids. "There," I said. "That one."

Ray looked at the picture and back at me, a frown deepening lines in his forehead and around his eyes. "Lady, that's Tater's cousin Marvin from the Valley."

"Daddy, what's going on?" Jimmy asked.

"Shut up," Ray said. "I gotta think."

"My husband's here, isn't he?" I said, starting to stand up. Ray pushed me back down.

"Tie 'em both up. Real good," he said. "I gotta think."

I stood up again. "Uh-uh," I said emphatically. "I'm not going to be tied up again!"

Ray pointed the gun at my nose. "Okay, then I just kill you."

I sat back down and placed my arms behind my back.

"Daddy," Joe whined. "What are we gonna do?"

"Shut up! All of you just shut up!" Ray said.

Luna and I sat on the floor, our arms tied behind us and our feet tied in front of us. I was hoping when this was all over I could get the name of a good chiropractor.

"I want to see my husband," I said.

"Did I say shut up or what?" Ray said. His face was getting red, a vein was pulsing in his forehead. In a very unchristianlike way, I prayed for a minor, yet debilitating, stroke.

Luna nudged me with her shoulder. I wasn't sure if it was a nudge of encouragement or a warning nudge for me to shut my mouth. I decided it was the former.

"I think I have the right to see my husband," I insisted. "And I would also like an explanation of what in the world is going on around here. Ray, you're going to get in a lot of trouble—"

He drew his hand back as if to hit me. I flinched, leaning against Luna. The man in front of me was losing it. In a very serious way.

I was leaning against Luna, both of us watching the man who was holding us captive as he slowly but steadily lost control. Ray was pacing the room, making me dizzy if I watched. I closed my eyes, which didn't seem to help.

"Daddy—" Joe started.

"Shut up! I'm thinking!"

Finally Ray stopped by the door of the room. "I gotta get back downstairs and work. It's my shift and Rogene's probably already missing me. You keep these ladies in here. If they make a noise gag 'em, but y'all be nice, okay? No rough stuff?"

"Sure, Daddy," Jimmy said, giving us both a look.

I wasn't sure what I was more afraid of: Jimmy's obvious pleasure in causing us pain, or Ray's erratic behavior. That the cook was losing it was obvious. I just wasn't sure exactly why.

"You bitches think you're hot stuff, huh?" Jimmy said, moving close to us. "I owe you big-time!" He had his knife out, the blade only inches from Luna's face. "You ain't all that pretty, bitch, but I'm gonna make you real ugly!"

Jimmy was on his knees, leaning in close to Luna. I was next to her, my shoulder leaning against hers, when Roberto stood up and carelessly kicked Jimmy in the head, sending the knife flying and Jimmy sprawling.

"Try to act like a grown-up, *puto!*" he said, sitting back down in the only chair in the room. "Goddamn, what I gotta put up with."

Thursday
Willis's story

I woke up and tried to stretch, but the rottweiler lying beside me in the single bed didn't give me a lot of room for maneuvering. I sat up and Dumplin's eyes popped open. "I have to pee," I told her. She growled. "Tater!" I yelled. "I have to pee!"

"God a'mighty," Tater said a few minutes later, wandering in the room munching on an apple. "Now the whole world knows Cousin Marvin from the Valley needs to pee."

At the top of my voice I shouted, "My name is Willis Pugh! Area code 512/555-9377! Call my wife—" Tater shoved the apple in my mouth.

"You are a piece of work, boy, you really are. Go pee and be quick about it. We got things to do."

After my morning toilet, I meandered into the living room. Tater was letting Dumplin' out the front door for her morning constitutional. "Over easy or scrambled?" Rogene asked from the kitchen island.

"Whatever's easiest," I said.

"Easiest would be if you left," she shot back.

"Fine by me," I said, sinking down in the baby blue Early-American rocking recliner. "In case anybody needs reminding, it has *never* been my idea to be here in the first place!"

"Boy, you are wearing my patience thin!" Tater said

from the couch. "One more word out of you and I'm gonna knock you upside the head!"

I leaned forward in the chair, my temper winning out. "Tell you what, Tater, my man, you get rid of that fucking dog and then you just try me!"

"I don't need Dumplin' to keep you in line, boy! You may be bigger than me, but I'll wipe up the floor with you—"

"Now y'all stop it! I never did hear two grown men go on the way you two are doing!" Rogene said. "Jest quit!"

Tater and I glared at each other but neither said a word.

We sat down to breakfast and Tater said, through a mouthful of scrambled eggs, "We'll go check out Claudia soon's we get through here."

"Um," I said back, stuffing my mouth. I didn't want to think of the stomach crunches I was going to have to do once I got back home.

We finished up and headed for Rogene's Buick, leaving her to wash the dishes.

E.J. and I have this system—since we both work. We take turns cooking: me on the weekends, her during the week. If one cooks, the other does the dishes. Not having to do the dishes once during my captivity had been the highlight of my week.

Tater started the Buick and we headed toward the Rock, on our way to Fredericksburg. I stared at Enchanted Rock out the window, wondering if being this close the feelings would come. They didn't.

Claudia lived about eight miles our side of Fredericksburg in a single-wide trailer on a piece of land with a breathtaking view and about a dozen Angora goats. A dilapidated Datsun sat in the yard, close to the front door. A rusted washing machine resided under a tattered green awning next to the backseat of a fifties vintage auto. A little girl of about three sat on the car seat, a naked Barbie doll in her hands, walking the doll across her legs.

"Hey, Tey," the child said.

"Hey your own self, Rachel darlin'. Your mama in the house?"

"She sleepin'. You wanna play wid me?"

"Later sweetheart, okay? I gotta talk to your mama about grown-up stuff."

"Okay." She bent her head back to her naked Barbie-doll play.

I had no idea what color Claudia's natural hair might be, but the child's hair was the same pale whitish blond as Calvin's.

Tater hammered on the front door.

A querulous "What?" sounded from within.

"Hey, Claudia, it's me, Tater Bascomb. Need to talk at you!"

"Tater, goddamnit!" she yelled through the trailer. "I didn't get to bed till near four o'clock! Have mercy, you old rascal."

The voice had progressively sounded closer, and on the "old rascal," the door opened and she peered down at us from the three steps up to the door of the trailer. Her makeup, which she obviously hadn't washed off from the night before, was smeared on her face and her hair was sticking up in dirty clumps on her head. When she saw me, she attempted to brush the hair back and smiled.

"Well, hey," she said, "you brought your cousin."

"Yes'm, and we need to come in and talk to you a minute."

"Well, Tater, I'm practically in my all-together! Just give me a minute." She started to shut the door, then opened it and asked, "Is Rachel out there?"

Tater pointed to where the little girl was.

"Honey," she called, "Beth Ann be by in a minute to pick you up. You eat anything?"

Rachel nodded her head and said, "Cocoa Puffs."

"Good girl," Claudia said, and closed the door in our faces.

"Who's Beth Ann?" I asked Tater.

"Claudia's daughter from her first marriage. Or maybe her second. I dunno. She lives up yonder a ways," he said, pointing toward Fredericksburg, "and she keeps Rachel with her own kids while Claudia's working."

Finally the door opened and Claudia let us in. She was wearing rose-colored, skin-hugging leggings and a large white top with the picture of a giant rose on the chest. The hair had been combed and fresh makeup smeared over the remainder of last night's.

"What brings you fellas way out this way?" she said, indicating we sit. The trailer smelled of sour milk and pee. I perched on a black Naugahyde sofa while Tater took a soiled-looking yellow cloth-covered recliner. Claudia came and sat next to me on the sofa.

She'd put on cologne along with the fresh makeup, but it couldn't cover the musty smell of dirty hair and the need for a bath.

All of a sudden a longing for my wife welled up inside me so hard I thought it might bring tears to my eyes. I tried to push it back down and concentrate on the business at hand.

Tater started. "You seen Calvin?" he asked.

"Calvin?" She snorted. "No, and I'd just as soon never lay eyes on that pig!"

She looked from me to Tater.

"Why?" she asked.

"Well, he took off and we're trying to find him for Rogene and the young'uns," Tater said.

Claudia leaned back against the sofa and crossed her arms over her chest, frowning at Tater.

"Why would you come looking here? I ain't had no truck with that scum in three wonderful years!"

"Claudia, can I ask you a real personal question?" Tater asked.

"Well, you can ask, Tater Bascomb, but that don't mean I gotta answer." She laughed at her own wit.

"Fair enough. Is Rachel Calvin Hardy's child?"

Claudia leaned up. ''Well, goddamn!'' She stood. ''That ain't none of your business!'' She walked to the door and held it open. ''How dare you come in here and ask me something like that! I'm gonna tell Rogene you asked me that!''

''I couldn't help but notice she's got Calvin's hair,'' I said.

Claudia glared at me. ''You know, I thought you were kinda cute, but I think I done changed my mind!''

''Did Calvin ever pay you any child support?'' I asked.

''Calvin Hardy wouldn't pay to have his mama put out if she was on fire,'' Claudia said. Her anger dissipated. ''Y'all, look. Junior's paying me a little something for Rachel ever month, and if he thought for a minute that baby wasn't his, he'd probably sue me for everything he's paid in the last three years. Now I need that money. I can't have no rumor going around that Rachel ain't his kid.'' She looked at both of us, her eyes pleading. ''Please.''

''Did Calvin threaten to tell Junior that Rachel was his?'' I asked.

She snorted. ''And own up to it? No way Calvin Hardy'd do a damn fool thing like that.''

''Why don't you have a paternity test? Prove the child's his and make him pay support,'' I said.

Claudia's arms went around her body. ''Because I enjoy breathing a little too much for that, Mister. Y'all just go on now.''

She shoved us out the door and we walked back to the Buick. Rachel waved at us from her car seat and we waved back.

Once in the car, I said, ''I wish we could have just come out and asked her why she killed Calvin. You know, a sneak attack.''

''Yeah, I know. But we even breathe a word about that, the cops'll be all over the place.''

''So? The body's gone.''

''Gone, yeah,'' Tater said, starting the Buick and backing out to the road, ''but where?''

Thursday
E.J.'s story

Ray came back in the room, wiping his face with his handkerchief. He was sweating profusely, and I doubt if all of it had to do with the heat of the kitchen. Luna and I, and Ray's sons, had brought an entirely different kind of heat on him.

Jimmy had been sitting on the floor, leaning against the far wall, when his father walked in. He jumped up and said, ''Daddy, Roberto kicked me in the head! Look!''

He leaned his head toward his father, pointing at the swelling near his left temple.

Ray looked at Roberto, who calmly sat in the chair by the door. ''He was trying to take a knife to the cop's face,'' he said.

Ray shoved Jimmy to the floor. ''Shut up 'fore I kick you myself!''

''Where's my husband?'' I asked again.

''I don't know where your husband is and I don't give a good goddamn!'' Ray shouted. ''Okay? Are we straight on this?''

I shrugged.

''He's probably over to the double-wide,'' Joe said from his perch in the corner of the room. ''I seen him over there.''

Twenty

Thursday
Willis's story

We spent the rest of the afternoon searching the woods behind the truck stop, toward the rock, looking for Calvin. He certainly wasn't propped up against any of the trees, nor did we find any freshly dug up ground. We headed back to the double-wide around five-thirty, feet dragging and supper on our minds. As we entered the double-wide, Tater took a strong grip on my arm and sent Dumplin' off for a run. She went with carefree abandon, tongue lolling and a wide grin on her face.

"Anything?" Rogene asked when we came in.

We both shook our heads, collapsing on furniture.

Rogene came in from the kitchen and sat down on the couch next to Tater, taking his feet up to her lap and rubbing the toes. I looked on enviously, thinking how E.J. sometimes did that, when I'd had a rough day and needed the TLC.

"I been thinking," Rogene said. "The way I see it, we don't got to worry about anything now, right?"

Tater and I both looked at her, then at each other, rolling our eyes.

"Now, listen!" Rogene said, swatting Tater's leg. "The body's gone. Far as we know, Calvin took off on one of his usual binges. We don't know where he is or what he's up to. If they find his body someplace, we don't know nothing!"

I nodded my head. As far as I was concerned, it was the best plan I'd heard all week.

"What about him?" Tater said, nodding his head toward me.

"What about me?" I said, leaning my head back against the blue of the rocking recliner. "At this point, if I try to tell what I know they'd throw me in jail right along with the two of you for obstructing justice. How many people have seen me coming and going around the truck stop? No way to prove I've been held hostage here."

"He's right about that," Rogene said.

"I dunno—" Tater started.

But then the front door of the trailer banged open and my wife fell in, followed by my next-door neighbor, Elena Luna. I stood up.

"Jesus! Honey, you found me!"

My grin faded when Ray Maladondo came in behind the two women, a gun in his hand, pointed at my wife's prone body. Ray almost lost his balance when three more men barged through the door of the trailer, shoving Ray up against the wall. One of the men was the husband of the beautiful Trudy. The other two were obviously her brothers.

Ray shoved the boys back. "For God's sake! Act like you got sense!"

"Ray," Rogene said, "what's going on here?"

"Tie 'em all up," Ray said to the boys. He shoved at the three. "Now!"

I hit my head like I coulda had a V8. "Damn!" I said. "Trudy had a girl! Purvis said that about shooting girl bullets right after Trudy had her baby! Tater, he was talking about Trudy, too! Calvin was the father of Trudy's baby, just like Claudia's!"

All eyes turned to Ray.

After a long silence, I said, "Is that why you killed Calvin?"

"Daddy?" Jimmy said, his eyes wide. "Did you? Wow!"

"That baby's mine!" the jug-eared husband said.

"Don't lie, Roberto," Ray said. "It's too late for that. Trudy told me. She don' wanna be married to you no more, so she told me about her and Calvin."

"She's my wife!"

"When'd she tell you?" I asked. "Last Sunday?"

Ray snorted. "She says she loves him. Wants to marry him. Gonna have his baby, not Roberto's. So I come over here. I'm mad. Madder than I ever been. But I just wanted to talk, ya know? Just wanted to tell him what I think of him! I come in here and he's pounding on Rogene. I push him off and Rogene falls. He's so mad he's pounding on me. Then when he realizes it's me, he starts to laugh. I tell him I know about him and Trudy, and he's gotta marry my Trudy soon's the baby comes and she can divorce Roberto. And he says . . ."

Ray stopped, sobbing in a breath. "He calls my beautiful daughter bad names. Ugly names! Says she's nothing to him. His wife's laying in a bloody heap on the floor, and he's calling my Trudy ugly names!"

The gun was shaking in his hand. I looked at Tater, who was watching Ray hard.

"So that's when you grabbed the knife in the kitchen?" I said, trying to distract him.

Ray shrugged. "Didn't even know I'd done it till it was over. He was dead. I thought maybe Rogene was dead, too. I just left."

Tater came in from Ray's left side, grabbing the gun hand. The sound of the gun going off inside the double-wide trailer was deafening. Ray backed up as Tater slowly crumbled to the floor.

"Tater!" Rogene screamed, running to the still form on the floor.

Ray stared at Tater then looked at me. Turning to his sons, he said, "Tie 'em all up. Now!"

He shoved the boys forward and the two of them grabbed me and began tying my arms behind my back with ropes from their back pockets.

Rogene looked at me. "Marvin, he's alive! We gotta call an ambulance!"

Ray grabbed Rogene by the hair and pulled her up. "Nobody's calling nobody!" He shoved her toward the couch. "Tie her up! Find something and tie everybody up!"

Ray went to the area by the door and hauled E.J. and Luna to their feet. "Get over there with the rest of them! On the couch!"

"No," E.J. said. "I want to sit next to Marvin."

He shoved her down next to me on the floor by the baby blue rocker-recliner and I kissed her. "Hi, babe," I said.

"I don't think we should get mixed up in this sort of thing anymore," she said, kissing me back.

"Okay by me."

Ray shoved Luna on the couch next to Rogene. Rogene was crying. She looked up at Ray. "Ray, we been friends a long time, and I don't begrudge you killing my husband. If ever a man deserved killing, it was Calvin Hardy. But Ray, you and Tater been friends long as me and you been, and you gotta see that he's bleeding to death over there!"

Ray looked at Roberto, who stood like a statue by the

front door. "Roberto," Ray said, "see if you can staunch that bleeding."

Rogene worked at a smile. "Thank you, Ray. I 'preciate it."

Roberto went into the bathroom and brought out some towels, kneeling down by Tater. I heard Tater groan. It was music to my ears.

After the two boys had tied everyone up, the older one turned to Ray. "Daddy, what we gonna do? This is getting real messy, Daddy. I think the best thing to do, so nobody ever knows what's been going on, is we just kill 'em all."

Ray looked at his son. "God will strike you dead one of these days, Jimmy. And maybe me for raising you. If your mother was alive—"

"Well, Daddy, she ain't! And Trudy and that baby are gonna need us around to take care of her! These people get out, Daddy, me and Joe and Roberto are all going to jail for cockfighting and you're gonna get the needle!"

"Shut up, boy. Just shut up."

"Daddy, he's right," Joe said. "He wanted to kill them bitches earlier but I said no. I tried to do the right thing, Daddy, but this is just getting out of hand."

"We got no other choice, Ray," Roberto said from where he knelt by Tater. "Tater's always been real good to me, but this is survival, Ray."

Ray sighed. "You boys just shut up. I gotta think." He sighed. "Check all the rooms for telephones, and that CB over there," he said, pointing to the contraption on the desk by the window. "Disconnect everything, smash 'em up if you have to. Just make sure nothing works."

In a minute we heard the gleeful sounds of the boys destroying the three phones and the CB.

The doorknob of the double-wide's front door rattled. Since Ray had locked it, it didn't open. A knock sounded instead. Ray went to the door and opened it a crack.

Bubba's voice could be heard from outside. "Hey, Ray, whatja doing here? I need to talk to my mama."

"She's got roaches," Ray said, "and I'm fumigating. She and Tater and his cousin Marvin went into Fredericksburg. They want you to watch the diner."

"Oh, well. Okay, then. Don't let them fumes get to you, Ray!" Bubba said, laughing, and left.

Like anybody actually thought Bubba would come to the rescue.

The trailer was quiet for a long time. I sat next to E.J., breathing in her sweet scent. My mind was numb. I had to think of something to do. I had three kids about to become orphans. Nine, if you counted Rogene's.

"Daddy, we gotta do something!" Jimmy said. "We can't just sit in here all day!"

"You want me to traipse these people out in practically broad daylight? Or start shooting 'em now, where everybody and their brother can hear? We're damn lucky nobody heard that shot earlier. Be smart, son!" he said, tapping the side of his head with his index finger.

My arms were going numb. I twisted around, trying to get some play in the rope, but there was none.

"Stop fidgeting!" Ray said.

Jimmy brought a knife out of his pocket. "Shooting's not the only way of getting the job done, Daddy."

Ray walked up to his son and stared down at him, then wrenched the knife out of his hand. "You ever stick somebody with a knife till they dead, boy? Huh? You ever do that?"

Jimmy shook his head.

"I did. I did that to Calvin. I ain't doing it again and I ain't letting you boys do it. Now, all of you get out of here. I'll come get you when we need to move the bodies."

The three younger men left.

"Where's Calvin's body, Ray?" I asked.

He glared at me. "You ain't Tater's cousin Marvin from the Valley, are you?"

"No, I'm not. I'm Willis Pugh, husband of this lady

right here, and we're from Codderville, Texas. And we would like very much to go home, if you don't mind."

"Well, I do mind!"

"Where's Calvin?" I asked again.

"Where he ain't never gonna be found, *sangron.*"

"You think you can make five more bodies disappear, Ray?" I shook my head. "That's not the man you are. Ray, this will eat you alive, what you're talking about doing."

"Shut up!" he said, waving the gun at me. He looked toward the kitchen, where preparations for dinner had been interrupted by the intrusion of Ray and his sons. He turned to the couch where Rogene and Luna sat.

"Rogene, fix something to eat," he said.

Rogene just looked at him. "Ray, my hands is tied!"

Taking his son's knife, Ray went to Rogene and began cutting the ropes that bound her hands. He was bending over her, his back to Tater where he lay bleeding to death on the floor. Tater moved. Quietly he got to his feet, leaning heavily against the wall. I held my breath, trying not to look at him. He picked up a floor lamp with one hand and hit Ray across the back of the head. Ray landed in Rogene's lap, Tater on top of him, all his energy spent in that last attempt to save the woman he loved.

We got Tater laid out on the couch, clean towels pressed against the wound to stop the round of fresh blood.

E.J. and I have always been big on recycling. We used our ropes to tie Ray.

"Okay," I said, rubbing my wife's beautiful, wonderful arms, "the boys aren't supposed to come back until Ray goes and gets them, but as anxious as they are to see us dead, they might come back at any time. We've got to get out of here."

I could see E.J. looking at me. All I wanted to do was look back, hold her in my arms for a year or two, but if I ever wanted to hold her again, I had to get us all out of the mess we were in, and all hopefully alive.

Tater lay on the couch with his head in Rogene's lap. She was stroking his brow. His face was pale; a weak but wistful smile played across his lips.

"We've got to get Tater to the hospital," Rogene said, kissing him on the forehead.

"Where do you think the boys are?" I asked.

"Probably in the diner," Rogene said. "Where'd y'all park the Buick?"

I sighed. "In the front."

"Damn," Rogene said. "Check the phones?"

I went into the master bedroom. The phone was disconnected, but that would have been easy to fix—if the instrument itself hadn't been smashed to bits. Checking out the other phones, I found the same thing.

"No good," I said, coming back into the living room.

"Okay, look, everybody," Luna said, speaking up for the first time since entering the trailer. "I'm the professional here, okay?"

"And who would you be, honey?" Rogene asked syrupy sweet from the couch.

"I'm Detective Elena Luna, Codderville P.D."

"And where's your gun, honey?" Rogene asked.

Luna glared at her, blushed, and went to retrieve the gun from the floor, where it had fallen from Ray's hand.

"And just how well do you know this area, Miz Detective Elena Luna?"

Luna sat down. "What do you suggest?" she said to Rogene, imitating her syrupy-sweet voice.

"Well, honey, I suggest we get the hell out of here and find some more cops to go with the one we got," Rogene said.

Luna smiled for real. "My thoughts exactly."

I peeked out the front window next to the door of the double-wide. Roberto was leaning against the back door of the truck stop, smoking a cigarette.

I went back to the living room. "Is there a back way out of the trailer?"

"On the other side of the master bedroom's the utility room. That's got a back door," Rogene said.

I went to the utility room and peeked out the glass window of the back door. Nothing in sight between us and the turkey farm. But how far could we get before we were in the line of sight for Roberto standing by the back door of the truck stop?

I glanced at my watch. It was seven-thirty. Maybe another hour before it got dark. But did we have an hour? Would the boys wait that long before they came barging in, demanding to see our bodies?

Maybe the best defense was an offense. Just charge Roberto. Luna and I could do it together, take him off guard. He didn't have a weapon as far as I knew. As far as I knew.

I went back in the living room and sat down next to my wife on the arm of the rocking recliner. I leaned down and kissed her.

God, it felt good.

"What weapons did you see when you were at the turkey farm?" I asked her.

"Both the boys, Jimmy and Joe, have knives."

I nodded my head. "Ray took Jimmy's. What about Roberto?"

"He had my gun the whole time," Luna said. "I didn't see him with another weapon."

"Which means we don't know if he has one or not," I said.

"I doubt if he has a gun," Luna said, "or he would have used it instead of mine. He would have given my gun to one of the boys. He didn't do that."

E.J. laughed without humor. "I didn't get the idea Roberto was too impressed with his partners' abilities. He might not have trusted them with a gun."

"That's a point," Luna said.

"Well, are y'all gonna go on like this all night or are we gonna get my Tater to a hospital?" Rogene asked.

"Let me look at his wound," Luna said.

She moved to the couch, kneeling on the floor and gingerly pulled the bloodied towel away from Tater's wound.

"The bleeding's stopped," she said. She turned to me. "But it doesn't look good. He could lose this arm if we don't get him some help. Or bleed to death."

"Here's the thing," I said, standing up and addressing the room. "Roberto's right outside the front door. I don't know where the other two are. Our options are this: out the back door and head to the turkey farm—is there a phone there?"

"Yeah," said Tater, his voice weak. "There's a phone."

"Okay, but I don't know how far we'd get before Roberto saw us. Our other option is for Luna and I to go barreling out the front door and attack Roberto. Even if he's armed, so are we."

"You don't got any bullets," came a voice from the floor.

We all looked down at Ray, trying to work his way to sitting position. Luna pulled the magazine out of the butt of the automatic. The clip was empty.

"What the hell?" she said, looking at Ray.

"I was worried about the boys taking the gun away and shooting somebody. I threw the bullets away while y'all was upstairs with 'em."

"Then how in the world did you figure on killing all of us?" Rogene asked, a legitimate question I felt.

Ray's eyes teared. "I don't wanna kill nobody, okay? This thing . . . this thing just got, well, you know, out of hand."

"Oh, yeah, you could say that," E.J. said.

"Does Roberto have a gun?" I asked Ray.

He shook his head. "I dunno. He's got guns at the

house. I know he's got a revolver. He showed it to me when he bought it, but I don't know if he's got it on him."

"What about your sons?" Luna asked.

Again he shook his head, wincing at the pain. "They're not supposed to. But they're both practically grown. They live with me, but I don't know what they keep out at the turkey farm—or in their trucks. "

I peeked out the front window again. Roberto was nowhere in sight.

"He's gone," I reported to the group. We all looked at each other. "Gag Ray," I said to Luna.

She got a kitchen towel and headed for Ray. "Go ahead," he said, "but you don't gotta. I'm just gonna sit here quietlike until the cops come and get me."

Luna looked at me, then back at Ray. "Under the circumstances," she said, and shrugged her shoulders. She went to Ray and stuffed the kitchen towel in his mouth, using masking tape Rogene supplied to keep it in place. "Sorry," she said when she finished. Ray just nodded his head.

"Now lookee here," Tater said from the couch, his voice weak, his face pale. "I know what you wanna do is just go barging into the diner and head for a phone. That's what I wanna do, too. But Bubba's in there. And a lot of innocent truckers. We don't know what kinda fire power those boys have got. Marvin, you done proved that. Now I think heading for the turkey farm's the best idea."

We all looked out the windows at the back of the doublewide, which looked toward the turkey farm. It was only about a hundred yards away. But sometimes a hundred yards can be a very long way.

"Let's do it," I said.

The sky was darkening. Less than a mile to the west, the sun was setting behind Enchanted Rock. It was a beautiful sight, but one I didn't think was politic to ponder at the moment.

Rogene gathered up flashlights. She had two. "Got another in the Buick . . ." She looked at me and shrugged.

"You wouldn't have any bullets for a .38 Special, would you?" Luna asked Rogene.

"No. Calvin kept all that stuff in his office above the diner. He didn't keep no guns around here. And rightly so. Given half a chance, I'da killed him my ownself."

"Keep the gun," I told Luna. "The boys don't know it's not loaded."

We headed for the back door. "I'll take Tater," I said. "Luna, you lead. Rogene after her . . ."

Luna gave me a look.

"Okay, Miz Detective," I said, "what do you suggest?"

She sighed. "I'll take the lead, Rogene after me with one flashlight, then you and Tater. E.J., you take up the rear with the other flashlight."

"No," I said. "I want E.J. in front of me."

"You've got Tater. She'll be behind you to help you if you need it."

"She's right, honey," E.J. said. "Don't be macho now, okay?"

I nodded my head. Once in the utility room at the back door, Luna tentatively stuck her head out, scoping the lay of the land.

"Don't turn on your flashes until we're at the turkey farm, okay?" she said, her voice barely above a whisper.

She stepped down the aluminum back steps, holding out her hand for Rogene. Quietly we all trailed out. We headed in a straight line from the trailer to the turkey farm. There was a fence between us, but we'd follow that to the gate. The terrain was rough—rocky and full of grass clumps and weeds. My ankles began to sting from chigger bites before we'd gotten a hundred feet.

And that's when Dumplin' found us. She came from the east, her head held high over the tall grasses, tongue lolling as she ran in ecstasy toward her master. And as she neared she began to bark.

Loud barks. Real loud barks.

Rogene, Tater, and I all made shushing sounds at the giant rottweiler as she lumbered toward us. Thinking it was a game, the barking only got louder.

That's when Roberto came running out the back door of the truck stop, shouting at us.

And that's when Jimmy came out of the turkey farm ahead of us. He fell to one knee, held his two arms in front of him. In the semi-dark it was hard to see. But the muzzle flash of the rifle in his hands was easy to see.

"The rock!" Tater shouted. "Head for the rock! They got rangers there! Go!"

Twenty-one

Thursday
E.J.'s story

Luna and Rogene were running toward the rock. Willis, with his burden, stumbled and almost fell. I grabbed Tater's injured arm and, trying not to touch the wound, got it around my neck. Willis and I are both tall; when we straightened up, Tater's feet dangled in thin air. The wound must have opened up again—I could feel the warmth of Tater's fresh blood oozing down his arm to my neck.

As we began to move faster, I looked behind me. Jimmy was still on one knee, although turned in our new direction. The giant dog must have stopped following us when she heard the shot. She was turned now, facing Jimmy, in what looked like an attack stance. As he brought the gun to his shoulder again, the dog leaped forward, snarling.

Jimmy had barely enough time, but he managed it. He swung the gun and fired; a bullet caught the dog in midflight. The rottweiler fell to the ground with a thud.

Tater turned his head when he heard the dog's attack, and saw her fall. He tried to pull away from Willis and me. "I'm gonna kill him! The son-of-a-bitch killed my dog!"

"Keep going!" Willis said.

I grabbed harder at Tater's arm around my neck, feeling the little man wince beside me, and rushed after the two women ahead of us. A sprig of grass flew up in front of us, and I heard the retort of a gun.

Was it Jimmy's rifle, or was Roberto firing from the other side? Keep running, I told myself. Keep running.

We reached a small clump of trees—shelter, in that it was harder to see us in the darkness.

"Come on," Rogene said. "I know the way. Hurry!"

We followed her serpentine-style through the trees to a barbed wire, four-foot-high cattle fence.

"This is it," Rogene said. "There's the park."

Ahead of us was darkness. From our camping trip I remembered there were no lights in the park at night. This was a wilderness, and the parks department liked to keep it that way—even if there was a nightly population of a couple of hundred.

"Which way's the ranger's station?" Willis asked. "I'm losing my bearings here."

"That way," Rogene said, pointing left, vaguely southwest.

Those of us who could climbed over or through the barbed wire. It was harder getting Tater through, but we managed. Behind us I could hear that the boys had teamed up. They were tramping through the small wooded section getting closer.

"Hurry!" I hissed at Willis, pulling on Tater's good arm to get him through the barbed wire.

"Shit!" Tater hissed. "I done tore my good jeans!"

"Shut up!" Willis whispered back.

"Come on!" Rogene was ahead of us, waving us forward, her light a beacon—but not just to us.

"There they are!" came from behind us.

I saw Luna's hand shoot out and knock the flashlight from Rogene's hand. I heard the tinkle of glass and realized I had the only light left. I grabbed my side of Tater and hurried with my husband to catch up.

"This way!" Rogene said. "The ranger station's at the front of the park."

We went through another small stand of trees, down the dry creek bed, now running ankle-deep with fall rain. The rock was behind us at the back of the park as we ran toward the front, toward the ranger station. I tripped over a boulder in the creek, hitting my cut knee so hard it brought tears to my eyes, and almost losing my grip on Tater.

"Let me go, girl," he said, his voice weaker than it had been before. "Y'all just leave me here. They won't see me more'n likely. I'll hide here in the crick—"

"Shut up, old man," Willis said, his voice gruff. "Nobody's staying behind."

We stumbled getting up the bank of the creek. Luna came back, helping us up. "E.J., I've got him," she said. "Go with Rogene—"

"No—"

Willis shoved at me. "Go!"

I ran ahead, looking behind me to see if I could distinguish our pursuers in the dark. Nothing. I moved as fast as I could toward Rogene, my soggy socks and wet shoes from the creek, my cut knee, slowing me down. Luna and Willis came up fast behind me.

"There's the station!" Rogene hissed, pointed ahead of her.

I could see it, a faint light penetrating the darkness. We ran forward, stumbling up the step to the front door. Rogene grabbed the handle and pulled.

The door was locked.

"Where's the ranger?" Willis demanded, setting Tater down on the porch.

Rogene was literally wringing her hands. "Must be on his rounds. They usually only got one on duty at night when it ain't summer. Budget cutbacks and all."

"Fuck this!" Willis said, and grabbed a rock out of the flower bed, drawing his arm back at a window of the ranger station.

That's when the headlights caught us square on as a pickup truck rammed through the flimsy gate at the front of the park.

Thursday
Willis's story

The pickup barreled straight at us. Luna and I grabbed Tater, dragging him off the porch as the others fled. The truck hit the wood post holding up the porch of the ranger station.

"The rock!" Tater breathed. "Get to the rock. The caves . . ."

I could feel it—the pulse of the giant engine, the big machine—the rock. I could feel it all around me, pulsing, throbbing. I moved Tater to my back, piggyback fashion, and started running, shouting at the others, "The rock! Go up the rock!"

I knew Tater was mine now. If he was going to live, it would be because of the strength I could gain from the rock. If he died, it would be my failure.

There was no moon, only stars to guide me. Before me I could see the dome-shaped outline hiding the stars—the rock.

I hit the creek, running, water splashing up around me, and struggled up the other side. I could hear the others behind me, doing the same. Down the hill to the wash, then up the steep climb on the walking side of the rock.

I could only hope that they wouldn't shoot now—not in the park. The rangers would clearly hear that in the still night. No guns or hunting allowed in state parks.

''Get to the top,'' Tater croaked behind me. ''Then head northwest. There's an arrow to the caves.''

I could feel someone behind me, hands on my butt, pushing. I knew those hands. E.J. was behind me, pushing me up the rock. Keeping me from falling backward with the burden on my back. I trudged on, my legs burning from the pain. No pain, no gain said Jane. My lungs were burning, my thighs on fire, my feet numb. But the hands on my butt pushed me upward, ever upward.

We reached the summit and hands came forward to help. E.J., Rogene, Luna, all pulled us to the top. I looked behind me. No one was there. Whose hands—

''Northwest corner,'' Tater whispered. ''Go!''

We ran along the slippery summit, clearly visible to anyone watching from below. Where were they? Had they given up?

Facing northwest, there was an upgrade and then a hump in the dark, and on the side of the hump was an arrow and the entrance to the cave—a hole about four feet in diameter. A very small hole.

''We go down in there, we're going to be sitting ducks, Willis!'' Luna said.

Tater shook his head. ''I been coming here since it was private land and I was knee-high to a snake. I know these caves like I know my truck. There's a route that's not marked. It don't have an exit, but it's got lots of twists and turns and hidy-holes. Them boys won't find us in there.''

Luna looked at the hole again. ''I can't do it,'' she said with finality.

Then we heard the voices—three male voices arguing—definitely the boys.

''We gotta do it now,'' I said. ''Somebody needs to go in first and help Tater.''

''I'll go,'' Rogene said. ''I ain't been in there since I

was a little girl, 'member, Tater?" They smiled at each other. "But I'm game."

She went to the hole and slid in feet first, squirming her body down and through the hole. After a few minutes, we heard her hit bottom with a squashing sound.

"It's nasty down here!" she called up.

"Hush!" we all said at once.

I helped Tater position himself in the hole and pushed him forward. His grunts and groans as his bad arm hit against the rocks were heart-wrenching.

Luna handed me the gun. "Fat lot of good it's going to do you, but here it is, anyway," she said.

"What are you going to do?" I asked her.

She pointed toward the saddle between Enchanted Rock and Little Rock. "I'm going to head that way. Maybe they'll see me and I'll head them off—maybe I'll find the ranger. All I know is I can't go down there, Willis."

E.J. looked at her friend. I knew what she was thinking, as if I could hear her thoughts. Our daughter Bessie's birth mother had been E.J.'s best friend for a very long time. After her death, E.J. had been slowly replacing her feelings for Terry with her feelings for Elena Luna. These two no-nonsense women hugged awkwardly.

"We'll regroup at dawn," Luna said and smiled.

We smiled back and she was gone in the darkness. I pushed E.J. toward the hole.

"Maybe I should go with Luna," she said.

"Baby, just get in there!" I said, grabbing her in my arms and thrusting her feet through the hole.

"I swear to God, Willis, if I get stuck in here I will be terribly embarrassed. And you *know* how pissed I get when I'm embarrassed!"

I could hear the voices coming nearer—all three of them still arguing, looking for us.

I shoved myself feet first into the hole, pushing myself forward. The hole got smaller as I pushed through and I could feel my chest and back both touching rock. Then my body stopped moving. I was stuck.

The panic began rising from my gut—then I felt the hand on my head. A strong hand pushing me through. My time for asking why was over. I took the guidance given me, from whatever source. I wiggled my way down the tunnel, stretching my body, helping the hand. In seconds I was dropping off into a slick, wet mess.

"E.J.?" I called out into the pitch blackness.

A light shown in my face and I shielded my eyes. "What is that awful smell?" my wife asked.

"Bat guano," Tater said. "Y'all come on. Miz Marvin, you give me your light and I'll lead."

The cave was about shoulder-width as we began, not quite tall enough for me to stand up straight. The others were okay, but I'm six-four and sometimes that's a problem—like right that minute. As we progressed through the cave—which seemed more like a tunnel to my way of thinking—the ceiling dipped down. With the light way up front with Tater, I found myself banging my face into rock. I held my hands out in front of me to shield myself. Finally I was on my hands and knees, crawling through the muck and mire on the bottom of the cave, feeling my nose going numb from the fumes of bat droppings.

Then the shots began to ring out. I turned to look behind me. I couldn't see any light from a flashlight, but sparks flew as bullets hit rock. The boys were shooting wildly down the entrance hole. Rock began to fly and bullets ricocheted off the walls. I slithered quickly through the mess, crawling over humps of rock. At one point I lost the light in front of me and found myself totally disoriented and in total darkness.

"E.J.," I whispered.

"Come on, honey. Hurry," she said.

I crawled toward her voice and found my face up close and personal with her butt. I patted it affectionately. "Where's the light?"

"I dunno. I think I've lost them," she whispered back.

"Great."

"Over here!" The flash blinked once from our right. There was a tunnel moving off in that direction. We turned awkwardly and pushed ourselves into the tunnel with Tater and Rogene.

"We got company," Tater said.

"What?" I whispered.

He flashed the light briefly, illuminating the remains of Calvin Hardy, still stiff from his captivity in the truck-stop freezer. E.J. grabbed my arm and turned her head away.

We moved back about fifty feet from the entrance, finding a dry bit of uplifted rock on which to perch. It was better than sitting in the damp bat shit, but still far enough away from the body of the late Calvin Hardy.

Shots sounded again, and then the repeated ricocheting of the bullets and flying rock.

"Are they going to cave us in?" E.J. asked.

"No way," Tater said, his voice weak from the pain and loss of blood. "This thing's solid granite. Take plastique to do any harm in here."

"Uh-huh," E.J. said, her voice disbelieving.

"Hey, Tater!" came a shout from the mouth of the cave. "Tater, you in there? Yo, Marvin!"

We were quiet.

"We know y'all are in there, man, and we're gonna getja. You can't get out! Joe's at the back entrance. You let the women go, we won't hurt them none, okay? And Tater's dying, anyway. Right, Marvin? So we work out a deal, okay? You come on out, send your women first. We won't hurt nobody. That Rogene's been like a second mama to me. Huh, Rogene?"

"The little shit," Rogene said under her breath. "Never did like that Jimmy. Marvin, first thing he's gonna do is kill me and your wife, you know that, don't you?"

"Yes, ma'am, I know that," I said. I was beginning to wonder at the wisdom of the moves we'd taken.

Where was Luna? Had she made it? Had she found the ranger?

Would it have been better if we'd split up—going four or five different directions? But somehow I wasn't as worried as I probably should have been.

The soothing beat of the rock calmed me—uncanny for a man who'd been known to scream like a thirteen-year-old girl at a rock concert when once stuck in an elevator for two very long minutes.

But instead of feeling claustrophobic, I felt nurtured, back in my mother's womb. The throbbing of the rock and the beat of my heart were in sync, in a rhythm remembered from whispered lullabies.

The gunshots came again. I shielded E.J. with my body. But there was no ricocheting this time. No flying rock. They were shooting at something else. Had they found Luna?

I heard the thump as a body landed inside the cave.

Twenty-two

I could see E.J. in front of me, shivering from the cold. I slid my arm around her shoulders and pulled her against me. Was this going to be it? I couldn't help thinking what a stupid way to go—knee-deep in bat guano.

With the sound of someone landing inside the cave, I felt Rogene pulling on my shirt. Holding on to E.J., I started butt-scooching backwards away from the entrance to the main cave. All they would have to do would be shoot in this direction and at least one, if not all, of us would be hit. Enough shots and we'd all be dead.

I felt rock against my back; I turned toward Rogene, trying to get my bearings. She wasn't there. I couldn't feel her and there was no way I could see her. I held E.J. tight against my chest. A light shown into our tunnel.

This was it. The light showed me my wife's face. I took it in my hands and kissed her.

"Hey, Cousin Marvin, is that you?"

I almost laughed out loud. "Bubba?" I called.

"Hey, that *is* you! Who's the lady?"

I started laughing and couldn't stop. "That's no lady, Bubba, that's my wife."

"Is my mama in there with you? Where's Tater?"

I heard Rogene's voice behind us, and my relieved laughter stopped.

"I'm here, honey," she said. "But I'm afraid Tater's gone."

I shoved E.J. out of the way, heading to the back of the tunnel. "Move!" I shouted at Rogene.

She backed out of my way. I heard E.J. say, "Bubba, bring that light."

I found the flashlight that Tater had taken from E.J., and shone it on Tater's body.

"You remember your CPR?" I asked my wife.

She nodded her head. As any parent of three children should, we'd taken a CPR course at the county health department six months before. I'd never used it. Did I remember any of it? I wasn't sure. Could I use it? I didn't know.

I moved into position, straddling Tater's small frame, my hands at his chest. E.J. cleared the airway and began to breathe. At her break, I pushed.

I was vaguely aware of more light entering the cave, more voices. Bubba and his light moved away, replaced by a more powerful light and a bigger body. "Whatja got?" a man asked.

"Three, four, gunshot, one, two—"

"How long's he been out?"

"Three, I don't, four, know, one, two—"

"Paramedics on the way up the rock now."

I nodded my head in rhythm to my hands.

There were more voices at the juncture of the two tunnels, and the big body moved backward, leaving the light in place.

"Paramedics, sir," came a female voice.

I was pushing, thrusting the heels of my hands into Tater's chest cavity. E.J. put her fingers to Tater's carotid artery.

"We've got it! A pulse—"

"Out of the way, sir," the paramedic said. Then her voice rang out, "We got two bodies in here, deputy!"

I let her pass me and began backing my way out of the tunnel, E.J. in front of me. At the juncture, arms took mine and led both of us back to the mouth of the cave. It was still dark in the tunnel, all the lights were being used to save Tater, as it should have been. With the help of people in the tunnel and people on the summit, we worked our way back up the hole to the starry night and clean air. And it was a rebirth. The rock had pushed me from its womb much as my mother had done forty years before. But this time I didn't need a slap on the butt to get going.

Friday

There was a crowd in Tater's room at the hospital—E.J. and I, Rogene, Bubba, Luna, and Delbert McKay, deputy in charge of that area of the county.

"He's done gone, Tater," McKay was saying. "And the girl and her baby, too."

We'd found out from Bubba that he'd been the one to sound the alarm. Okay, so I'd been wrong. Bubba had saved us. On hearing all the shooting going on outside the truck stop, he hadn't stopped to look, just called the law. Finding Ray Maladondo's trussed-up body in the double-wide trailer, they'd naturally untied him, to learn about the seventeen armed terrorists, Middle Eastern, he was pretty sure, who'd tied him up and kidnapped everybody else.

The authorities followed the rather noisy chase of the

boys following us through the woods, then, once in the park, followed the sounds of the shots. By that time, Luna had found the park ranger, who'd already radioed for more help when he heard the shots. With the theory that Middle Eastern terrorists were taking over Enchanted Rock State Natural Area, law enforcement agencies from as far away as San Antonio and Austin had shown up to help—not to mention two Texas Rangers and an FBI unit in Austin on alert.

During all this, it seems, Ray Maladondo quietly left the double-wide, got in his car, apparently drove to the very hospital we were now in, retrieved his daughter and newborn granddaughter, and headed for parts unknown.

''We got them boys, though,'' Delbert McKay said. ''So far they're being charged with attempted murder, assault, destruction of state property, discharging a firearm in a state park, attempted kidnapping, you name it—''

''And don't forget cock fighting,'' Luna and E.J. said, almost in unison.

Delbert scratched his head. ''Cock fighting? Don't know nothing about that.''

Luna put her arm around the deputy and walked him toward the door of Tater's room. ''I'll be happy to fill you in,'' she said, closing the door behind them.

''Probably gone to Mexico,'' Rogene said.

''Jimmy and Joe swear they have no relatives in Mexico,'' I said, ''according to the deputy.''

''He'll turn up,'' Tater said from his bed, his skin pale but his life no longer threatened. ''Knowing Ray like I do, he'll send papers to Roberto in prison so's Trudy can get a proper divorce. They'll find him.''

The way he said it sounded as if he really didn't want them to, and in a way, I agreed. It wasn't something I'd be able to explain to E.J., but in that one horrible act, Ray may have changed several lives for the better.

''They found Calvin's body?'' Tater asked.

''Pulled him out right after you,'' I told him—then

grinned. ''They can't seem to figure out how he got frozen.''

''Now, Tater,'' Rogene said, sitting down in the chair next to the hospital bed. ''We got some good news and some bad news.''

Tater raised an eyebrow. Rogene smiled. ''The good news is Dumplin's gonna live.''

The old man's face lit up, and a tear came to his eye. ''Praise Jesus,'' he said.

''She lost a leg, but she's gonna live,'' Rogene said.

''Hell, ain't had me a three-legged dog since I was a kid,'' Tater said. ''Don't mean I'm gonna love her any less. Is that the bad news?''

Rogene looked at me. ''Marvin, you wanna do the honors?''

I cleared my throat, not sure how Tater was going to take this news. ''Ah, seems they had this bassett hound in the clinic for an emergency neutering. Seems he was mounting anything that moved. Well . . .''

Tater sat up in bed. ''Don't tell me . . .''

Willis nodded his head.

''Almost like to've seen that,'' Tater said, lying back and shaking his head in wonderment.

''May we have pick of the litter?'' E.J. asked.

I just shook my head. Three damned cats and now a dog. Megan would be thrilled.

Epilogue

Saturday
Willis's story

"I can't believe after all I've been through Mama still wants me to come over and clear her gutters," I said, driving E.J.'s wagon toward Codderville.

"Honey, her gutters are in really bad shape," my wife said sweetly.

One thing I can say about the way things used to be, before E.J. and my mom started getting along. At least then, at a time like this, E.J. would have been on my side.

Coming home the night before, I'd beheld something wonderful—my home. My home, my kids, my cats.

My life.

I guess you don't really miss something until it's almost taken from you. The spots on the rug from spilled Kool-

Aid were more beautiful than a Picasso. The crayon markings on the wall of the utility room could be framed exactly the way they were. *Things* can be fixed. *Things* can be replaced.

The girls were all over me—hugging and kissing me; but E.J. told me on the ride home that as far as they knew, I'd been away on business.

Graham had known the truth.

He sat in the living room, watching his sisters shower me with affection, telling me the minute-by-minute events of their lives for the past week. He didn't say a word—just watched. When they were finally coerced upstairs for bath time, my son walked over to me and held out his hand.

I shook it. Our first.

He said, "Glad you're okay."

"Thanks, son."

"See ya," he said, and headed upstairs.

"I'm sorry I worried you," I said to his retreating back.

He shrugged but said nothing.

The next day was my birthday, but nobody seemed to notice. My mother had gutters to clean. We parked the car in her driveway and the kids jumped out, heading for the porch and grandma. My mother put her arms around me and hugged me.

"'Bout time you got your butt home, boy!" she said.

"Mama, I told you, this wasn't my doing—"

"Uh-huh," she said. "Come on in and have a glass of tea before we get started."

"Mom, I'd just as soon get this over with—"

"Come in the house," my mother said sternly.

I followed behind E.J.

The living room was awash in banners proclaiming me OVER THE HILL and swearing that LIFE BEGINS AT 40. And with people. Old friends from high school, from church, from our neighborhood. My old college roommate and the biggest pot dealer at U.T. in 1972. People I see every day and people I hadn't seen in years. And more than half those people E.J. said had been in on the search-and-rescue for me.

There was enough food filled with enough fat to rival anything Rogene Scoggins Hardy soon-to-be Bascomb had fed me during my ordeal.

My daughters were jumping up and down with the joy of having kept a secret from Daddy.

''We have a present for you!'' Bessie said, coming up and crawling in my lap. I hugged her to me. Megan grabbed the other knee, and I pulled them both in close.

''Let's see,'' I said, taking the obviously child-wrapped box from Bessie's hand.

I unwrapped it and opened the jeweler's box. Inside was a pocket watch with the face of the Lion King.

''Wow,'' I said. ''This is the most beautiful watch I've ever seen.'' I kissed them both. ''You two bought this yourselves?''

''Yeah, we saved up!'' Megan said.

''Mommy helped a little,'' Bessie said. ''You like it, Daddy?''

I almost dropped her. Daddy. She'd called me Daddy. Not Willis, or Uncle Willis, or even Daddy Willis. Just Daddy.

A new milestone.

One of many more to come with my three kids. I looked around the room at family and friends and wondered how I'd ever come to think of it as a burden.

Graham came up behind me. ''Dad?'' he asked.

The girls jumped down and ran to the back door, eager to play with grandma's dogs. E.J. and I were trying to keep secret the new dog we had coming from Dumplin's litter.

I turned to my son and ruffled his hair. ''Hey, Graham. What's up?''

''I made you something,'' he said, handing me a package tied up in Sunday's comics.

I unwrapped the present. Inside was a scrapbook. Graham opened the book and began to riffle pages.

"See, here's the crossword puzzle from every paper you missed while you were away. And I cut out articles you wouldn't want to miss. See, here's one about that new sewer plant they want to put in on the river. I knew how mad that'd make you."

He beamed at me. I pulled him to me and hugged him hard.

"Dad! Geez!" He pulled away. "How embarrassing."

I grinned at him. "I don't care. I love you."

"Ah, gawd, Dad."

He turned red and walked away.

We stuffed our faces with cake and ice cream, potato chips and dips. Everyone sang the happy-birthday song, and I talked for hours with old friends and new, all the time watching my wife—watching her move among our friends: in the kitchen, laughing with my mother, bending down to tie a shoelace. And got a woody you wouldn't believe.

Saturday
E.J.'s story

"You think Mama will keep the kids tonight?" Willis asked me, nuzzling my ear.

"Don't you think she's kept them enough lately?" I was clearing off the coffee table. Half the crowd had gone—but that only meant half of them were still there. We might have to go out for more food.

"But it's my birthday," Willis whispered.

"You ask," I said. "I'm not going to."

He left me, heading for the kitchen. I used my fingernail to scrape embedded frosting off my mother-in-law's Irish-lace tablecloth. I turned and looked into the kitchen, Willis with his arm resting lightly on his mother's head, in that way he had of happily infuriating her. He looked a little heavier around the middle, I thought. Maybe not enough exercise while he was in captivity. But he still looked good. I smiled and quietly thanked all the powers that be that I had him back.

Willis turned from his mother and came back to me, grabbing my hand. "Come on," he said.

"Where are we going?" I asked as he pulled me toward the front door.

"We're slipping out for a moment," he said.

We got in the car and he started the engine. "I forgot my purse—"

"You don't need it."

"Did you enjoy the party?"

He looked at me, took my hand and kissed it. "Best party I've ever had."

I grinned at him. "You don't look half bad for forty."

"You're only two years behind me, you know."

"Yeah, but those are a long two years."

I noticed we'd driven out of Codderville, not headed in the direction of home. "Where are we going?" I asked.

"Someplace special," he said.

An hour later it dawned on me we might be heading for that blasted rock.

Saturday
Willis's story

The gate was closed when we got there, so I parked the car on the side of the road, took a blanket out of the cargo area, and walked my wife hand in hand into the park.

The air was crisp and cool, the stars bright above us. A quarter moon shown, its light reflecting off the dome of the rock.

I could feel the rock as we approached—the swelling in my head, the pressure; the wonderful, miracle pressure. Without a word, we began to climb the walking side. In twenty minutes we were at the summit. I spread out the blanket on the top of the rock and laid my wife down. E.J. put her arms around my neck.

"You are a romantic fool for an old fart," she said, her voice husky.

"You don't know the half of it," I said, and kissed her for a very long time, barely thinking about the breakfast I planned for the morning at Scoggins Truck Stop & Turkey Farm.